The Dream Keeper
Ané Lombaard

Published by

MELROSE
BOOKS

An Imprint of Melrose Press Limited
St Thomas Place, Ely
Cambridgeshire
CB7 4GG, UK
www.melrosebooks.com

FIRST EDITION

Cover designed by Catherine McIntyre

ISBN 978 1 907732 48 5

Printed and bound in Great Britain by:
Mimeo Ltd, Huntingdon, Cambridgeshire

FSC
www.fsc.org
MIX
From responsible
sources
FSC® C019549

Contents

Acknowledgements

There are so many people I have to thank for this book, without whom it would have never been possible.

First of all, thank you to my parents without whose emotional and financial support this dream would not have been realised. And thank you to my sister Renée who read the earlier proofs and gave me so much praise. Thanks to my whole family for having so much faith in me and for all the encouragement. Thanks also to my cousin Sané for the enthusiasm and tips after reading an early draft.

Thanks to all my friends, who are spread far and wide, for all your support and help. Even though we are even more scattered than before, I know we'll stay friends for a long time to come. I hope you all enjoy this book.

A special thank you to my first two high school English teachers, Mrs Glenda Birchfield and Mrs Tanith von Myer, for being such wonderful people and for all the things I learned in the short time I had with you.

Finally, an enormous thank you to everyone at Melrose Books; first, for accepting my book and second, for all the care to make it as perfect as possible. Thank you for the praise you gave my story even though it is the wild imaginings of a teenager. Without you none of this would be possible!

Chapter 1:
A Snake in the Grass

"The Shifters are creatures of shadow and the night. They feed upon the blood of their helpless victims and once they have done so, can change into anything they drank from. You never know if someone is your neighbour or a Shifter—until it's too late!"

Jason listened wide-eyed, his blanket pulled under his chin and his legs drawn to his chest. Caleb was seated on the opposite end of the bed, holding a spark lantern in his lap. The white light was dimmed and reached only a few centimetres away before failing in the gloom. Bastian was hanging upside down from the top bunk, eager to hear more. Caleb grinned wickedly before continuing his narration.

"Because the Shifters are made of shadow, they hate light. They don't come out when it's day because the sun is too bright. Only at night do they emerge from their lairs to feed."

Jason released his breath with a sigh. Caleb's eyes flickered to him. "Don't think you are safe though," the little boy stiffened. "The Shifters have hounds larger than bears that can go out in the daylight because they are made of more solid stuff than the Shifters. The hounds don't like the light though, so they are angry and vicious and they can smell you from kilometres away. Watch every shadow and don't trust anyone! Because one night you just might feel—"

Just then Bastian decided to swoop down and jump on top of Jason. The eight-year-old released a high-pitched scream and the spark lantern was thrown on the floor where the glass cracked and the spark's light went out.

"Bastian!" Caleb scolded. "You're going to get us in trouble!"

Jason had crawled to the corner of his bed with his blanket over his head, shaking uncontrollably. Bastian was curled up in a fit of giggling while Caleb glared at him. A footstep sounded outside their door and Bastian abruptly fell silent. With eyes the sizes of coins they watched the handle turn and the door swing open. A tall figure stepped into the room. Suddenly Jason screamed again and the other two boys jumped. The figure turned on the lamp hanging from the ceiling and the room was illuminated by a cheerful white glow.

"Why aren't you three in bed?" Dad demanded.

"But I am in my bed," Jason replied quietly.

Dad's eyes roved from one boy's face to another, resting on Jason who was still cowering under his blanket. "You boys should know better than to frighten your brother like that!" he scolded. "He's only eight years old, you'll give him nightmares and he'll be having us up 'til dawn for weeks!"

"Sorry, Dad," Caleb mumbled, staring at the floor. Bastian was also avoiding Dad's gaze.

"Come on," Dad grunted. "Bed, all of you."

A young girl emerged in the doorway. Her fair hair was tangled and her expression murderous. "I am trying to sleep!" she hissed.

Bastian stuck his tongue out at her while he clambered up to his bunk. She returned the gesture.

"Catherine, go to bed," Dad said over his shoulder while he tucked Jason in. Caleb followed her out to his room.

When Dad turned to leave, Jason reached out and grabbed his hand. “No wait,” Dad leaned in close to hear what his youngest was whispering. “What if the Shifters come and drink my blood?”

Dad smiled and ruffled his hair. “Don’t you worry about the Shifters Jason, they won’t bother you.”

“But Caleb said—”

“It was only a story Jason. Now go to sleep.” Dad kissed him on the brow then he straightened up. After turning off the light, he left and closed the door behind him.

After some silence Jason called out softly, “Bastian?”

“Hmm?”

“Can I sleep with you tonight?”

“Fine.”

Quick as a little squirrel, Jason had clambered up and was snuggling up to his brother. “Thanks,” he whispered.

“Go to sleep,” Bastian growled.

“All right. Good night!”

“You’re not sleeping.”

“Oops, sorry.”

Eventually they drifted off into quiet slumber, their dreams untouched by shadows and monsters.

Six years later

Bastian was grumbling and gnashing his teeth nonstop, an empty page before him on the kitchen table and a battered textbook beside him. His pen lay untouched next to the little inkwell. Jason sat opposite him, eating lunch while he watched his brother suffer.

He chewed thoughtfully while reading the page that was causing his brother so much grief upside down. After swallowing, he took another bite of his pasty and read through the paragraph on gremlin society. A detailed sketch was provided of a spark cylinder and the next paragraph listed its uses in human society.

"I don't understand," Jason said after he swallowed again.

Bastian glared at him. "Understand what?"

"What are you finding so difficult about this chapter?"

"I have to write an essay on the history of gremlin creations used by humans."

"So—?"

"It's hard, all right!"

"Why don't you start with a heading?" Jason offered.

Bastian slammed the book shut and packed the things into his satchel. He got to his feet and said, "I'll do it later, I'm going to play ball with the others."

"Can I come?"

"All right."

Together they made their way down the cobbled street toward the empty field just outside of Brim. A dozen or so boys were kicking a leather ball around. They were all wearing shoes, an occurrence rarer than chicken teeth, but forced by the drop in temperature. Jason and Bastian's arrival was greeted with enthusiasm and they were sorted into opposing teams. A few minutes into the game Jason caught the ball and he tore down the field toward the goal post with a handful of boys charging after him. He nimbly dodged a tackle and slipped through a small gap when three of the opposing team's players barred his way. Boys cheered and roared as he flew toward victory. Bastian's feet thumped heavily close behind Jason and he could almost feel Bastian's breath tickle his neck. Suddenly he increased his tempo and left the others far behind as he buried the ball beneath the goal post. Gasping for breath, the others finally arrived. Teammates patted him on the back and praised his amazing score, while the opposing team glared at him.

"How in the world did you do that?" Bastian demanded. Jason grinned and shrugged. "I was this close," Bastian held his hands an inch apart, "this close to touching you."

"You ran like the wind, Thorn!" a boy gripped Jason's shoulder.

The game continued, but the opposing team made sure that Jason never came near the ball again. He spent the rest of the game jogging up and down the field watching his teammates score or defend their goal post. Eventually he just gave up and went to stand on the side lines. Bastian was the hero on the field, as usual. His tall, broad frame was perfect for any activity that required physical prowess. All Jason could do was run faster than everyone else, which was rarely a celebrated talent. He watched Bastian tackle another boy just before he could pass the ball to safety. Another of his teammates salvaged it and ran into the opposite direction. Sighing, he watched with a dull hollow feeling in his chest. After some deliberation, he turned and went back down the street.

A horse-drawn carriage clip-clopped past him on its way toward Lothair, a city in the distance. King James' castle could just be seen from Brim with its high towers and billowing green banners. Jason walked with his hands in his pockets past shops and street lamps with faded posters and advertisements stuck to them. Occasionally he had to sidestep a smelly pile left by some animal. He passed an Ard-man along the way, his figure towering over Jason and throwing a long shadow across the street. The

Ard-man's skin was pale green like the most of his race and he had stoney bumps that encircled his bald head and grew down along his jaw.

Jason paused as he saw a new poster up. It was bright and colourful and he hated it. The poster depicted a young man in the regulation uniform of the border guard. He was smiling proudly with one hand on the hilt of a sword and the other saluting informally. In his belt he carried a pistol. The bold lettering read:

**SERVE YOUR COUNTRY!
YOUNG MEN ARE NEEDED TO PROTECT THE
BORDER AND KEEP OUR HOMES SAFE!
ANYONE NINETEEN YEARS OF AGE MUST
REGISTER.
ONLY YOU CAN MAKE
A DIFFERENCE!**

The new law was instated at the beginning of summer. Unexpectedly young men were forced to enter the border guard for three years of 'patriotic service' to their kingdom. Even though there was no unrest currently in West Balisme, incidents did occur where young men died. Jason had five years ahead of him before he had to join, but just the idea made his blood boil. Caleb had to leave next summer and would only return once a year at Christmas. He longed to rip the poster from the wall, but the street was full of witnesses and there was an officer in his forest green uniform across the street.

Returning home, Jason found Mum preparing supper in the

kitchen. He kissed her cheek and wandered through the house in search of something to do. Caleb was in his room tinkering away at an old radio. Parts were strewn across the floor, bed and desk space, cluttered with various inventions or old and broken appliances. His fair hair was drawn back into a short ponytail and a two-day-old beard was growing along his jaw. Jason cleared a space on the bed and sat down. Caleb barely acknowledged his presence, too absorbed in examining an old spark cylinder under his magnifying glass. Jason often spent hours watching his brother work; they rarely exchanged words. It fascinated him how Caleb's clever fingers could make the seemingly dead and inanimate objects come to life. He had tried before, but technology just never could work as effortlessly for him as for Caleb.

In some ways Jason and Caleb were the most alike of the four Thorn children. They both inherited their father's quiet, curious nature, while Catherine and Bastian were fiery and determined like their mother. The only differences were their appearances, age and the direction of their curiosity. Jason was fascinated by all things living, while Caleb could spend hours investigating a broken tool.

Jason combed some brown locks out of his eyes with his fingers. Of the four Thorn children he was the youngest. People often argued who he resembled the most, his mother or his father. He had a healthy and equal combination of both in his appearance: his father's brown hair, his mother's gentle hazel eyes, a nose here, a mouth there. Catherine, fair and pretty, resembled their mother, and Caleb and Bastian looked like their father (with the exception that Caleb also had fair hair).

"So," Caleb said while unscrewing one of the metal caps from the spark cylinder. "How is the apprenticeship going?"

"All right I suppose. Dad's making me study poisons next."

"Great," Caleb grinned. "Maybe we can cure ourselves of Bastian now."

Jason chuckled along. They fell into silence again; the only sounds were that of Caleb's tinkering and the ticking of some mysterious object in the room. He remembered the poster he saw in the street and an empty feeling stole through his stomach. In less than two seasons this room would be empty and cold, its occupant far away on the border to protect the kingdom against imagined enemies. His hands clenched into tight fists and he felt a heavy sigh build in his chest, which he released loudly.

"What's wrong?" Caleb put the spark cylinder down, a luminescent, white, misty substance pouring out of the opened end due to his absent mindedness. Glowing blue tendrils crept from the mouth of the tube and spilled out along with the vapour.

"I hate that you have to leave. I hate the new law."

"Don't worry about it, and don't try to oppose it because it won't bring you anywhere but prison. Just accept that things are how they are."

"But it's wrong."

"Maybe, maybe not. Remember it's just your opinion. Bastian, for example, would murder someone if he wasn't allowed to go."

"Yes, but Bastian is Bastian."

Caleb chuckled. "I know. And you're you. Maybe it will be good for me to get some fresh air. They can toughen me up a little, eh?"

"I don't want you to go. Who will I talk to?"

"Your friends?"

"Yeah—but still, none of them know me like you do."

"Don't give up. One day you'll make great friends, they might just be in unlikely places."

Later when Jason entered his room, Bastian was sprawled across the bottom bunk, reading an old magazine of his. He glanced over his shoulder and mumbled something before continuing with his reading. Jason hardly noticed the pictures of the latest guns and posters of heroes on the walls anymore, though they irritated him when Bastian first put them up. Peering over his brother's shoulder he saw it was an article on the latest pistols used by infantry in the army. Bastian scooted a little way to make space for him and Jason joined him on the bed. The right page had small drawn pictures of pistols used in the army with short descriptions written underneath and the left page was dedicated to written content.

"Why do you like the army so much?" Jason asked.

"Because," Bastian shrugged. "It's exciting and you can do real heroic things like in the stories. Look at this," he turned a few pages until he found the article he was looking for. It was about King James' knights. Bastian pointed at one of the armoured men in the picture, a unique coat of arms embroidered on his tunic. "This is Sir Nathan de Luc; he fought off dozens of goblins single-handedly. This is Sir Thomas Green who saved the king's life at the Battle of the Pass. These are all heroes; people remember their names because they did something great. I want to be one of them one day," he rolled onto his back, the magazine on his stomach. Staring at the bottom of the bunk above he said dreamily, "Imagine I'm the one marching along with the king someday, with my own coat of arms and a squire and the name Bastian Thorn written into history books. And if I get injured, I could always visit Jason Thorn, the most famous healer in the entire kingdom!"

"I'm not so sure about becoming a healer anymore," Jason mused.

"But that's what you've wanted all your life."

"I know, but recently I've just had this feeling that maybe I could be more than just that. I feel like the world is such a big place and I want to see it. There is so much out there. Maybe I'll be an explorer like Damian Salt and I'll sail across the ocean to find uncharted lands."

"You actually sounded brave there Jason," Bastian joked.

"Ha, ha, laugh all you want."

"Jason Thorn," Bastian said in a deep voice. "Fearless explorer, adventurer extraordinaire! Where won't he go?"

Jason playfully kicked Bastian. "What about you *Sir* Bastian?" in a falsetto voice he said, "Oh please Sir Bastian! Save this fair maiden from the evil sorcerer!"

The boys clutched their stomachs as they chuckled and wiped tears of merriment from their eyes. Regaining some control, Jason said, "I thought it's against the knights' code of valour to used ranged weaponry."

"It is," Bastian replied breathlessly.

"So, no gun for Bastian."

"Oh—" Bastian said looking slightly crestfallen.

"At least you get a gigantic sword."

They returned to their fits of laughter, joking about possible futures and inventing wild adventures like they did when they were smaller.

The following morning, Bastian was in the same position as the afternoon before; with his history textbook and a blank page. This time Jason was working in the surgery; he had a healer's apprenticeship with Dad. Bastian's brows were heavily furrowed as he glared at the blank page. *Stupid school*, he thought. *Why would I ever have to know when gremlins started trading with humans?*

A knock on the door interrupted his thoughts. He rose to open the door and what he saw made his jaw drop. A tall, armoured figure with a coat of arms of a rearing white horse on a red background stood before Bastian.

"S-sir Nathan," Bastian managed to whisper.

"Good morning," the knight greeted. "I hear there is an excellent healer here, are you his assistant?"

Bastian dumbly shook his head.

"Do you know where I can find the healer?"

It took a few seconds for Bastian to register what the knight said before he nodded eagerly. "This way S-sir."

He led Sir Nathan through the kitchen toward the surgery. Jason was frowning over a heavy book while Dad was inspecting a crystal vial with clear violet liquid inside. Both of them looked up as Bastian and the knight entered. Jason's brow lifted in slight surprise, but Dad seemed unfazed.

"Good morning Sir, what may I do for you?" Dad said as he returned the vial to its shelf.

"I came to see you about an old war injury of mine that's giving me some trouble. The court physician has tried everything but to no avail, so now I come to you."

Bastian made a queer squeaking sound that drew everyone's attention momentarily to him.

"I'll see what I can do," Dad smiled. "Bastian you are excused."

"Can't I stay? I promise I'll be good!"

"No, you'll only be in the way. I'm sorry."

"What about Jason?" he persisted.

"Jason is my apprentice, he may stay."

Shooting Jason a vicious glare Bastian left. He grumbled all the way to the kitchen and had completely forgotten about his homework. All he could think of was that one of his greatest heroes was sitting literally metres away and he was not allowed to see him. The very idea almost drove him mad and that Jason could be there in his presence the whole time was unbearable. After what seemed like hours, Dad, Sir Nathan and Jason entered the kitchen. Bastian jumped to his feet, bumping his knee against the table edge and knocking his chair over in the process.

"Thank you very much, Gordon. I will be sure to send my friends when they need anything." Sir Nathan shook Dad's hand warmly.

"It is my pleasure to serve." Dad smiled.

Sir Nathan waved at Jason and then Bastian before finally exiting. Bastian was upon Jason like a cat on its prey. "What was he like? Did you see his sword? What did he say?"

Jason took a few steps back before replying, "He was— knightly."

Bastian pulled a face. "Knightly?"

"Yes," Jason shrugged. "He was chivalrous and he talked a lot about the battle where he got his injury—a lot."

"You are so lucky," Bastian fumed.

Jason rolled his eyes and returned to his studying of poisonous mushrooms, while Bastian dreamed of his own coat of arms one day.

A while after noon, Caleb stormed into the surgery with his

cheeks slightly flushed. Jason jumped and cut his finger on the edge of the page. He sucked on the microscopic thin cut while staring accusingly at Caleb.

"You have to see the snake Norman drove over, it's huge!" Caleb exclaimed.

His curiosity roused and his injury forgotten, Jason fetched Bastian before following Caleb to the scene of the incident. A small crowd of people were gathered on the side of the street, Norman's wagon abandoned a few feet away. With some effort the three of them made their way to the front.

"Whoa," Jason's eyes widened and Bastian whistled.

A snake of at least a metre and a half in length with pitch-black scales was lying partially curled up in the street. It was not particularly thick, about five centimetres across.

"Do you think it's an adder?" Bastian asked.

"Most likely," Caleb replied.

"It doesn't look very dead to me," Jason said sceptically.

"Don't be daft," Bastian reached out and touched the snake's body. "See?"

Suddenly the snake struck out with lightning speed. The crowd retreated as quickly as possible, stumbling over each other in their haste to get away. The snake was rearing and hissing viciously, but did not otherwise move from the spot.

"Is anyone hurt?" someone asked.

"Oh my—" Jason said weakly, his voice unusually high. Bastian was clutching his left hand. Two marks where the snake's fangs punctured him were clearly visible. His face was contorted and turning red. Caleb rushed to Bastian's side and roughly hauled him to his feet.

"Jason, watch the snake!" Caleb called over his shoulder.

With great difficulty, he half-dragged, half-led Bastian to the house and into Dad's surgery. Jason was in a daze, his mind still recovering from the initial shock. Some detached part of his mind was warning him that he was going into shock and had to calm himself, but this was somewhere in a very vague corner of his mind.

Dad immediately jumped into action. With Caleb's help they got Bastian onto the examination table. After inspecting and cleaning the wound Dad started applying medicines via injections into Bastian's body, which was starting to tremble. His skin was turning grey. Already the area was swelling up and purple vein-like bruises blackened his arm.

"Do you know what snake bit him?" Dad asked calmly.

"An adder I think," Caleb replied his eyes wide and his face frozen.

"No," Dad shook his head. "An adder bite does not react like this. If we know what snake did this, we can help him."

Caleb nodded and ran outside. Jason was standing a wary distance away from the snake, his mind working in overdrive. The incident played over and over in his mind, but no matter how many times he recalled it, it still happened too fast to fully comprehend anything. All he remembered was suddenly being pushed away by Bastian. Some men arrived with shovels and pitchforks to get rid of the snake. Holding their "weapons" a safe distance from their bodies they jabbed at the serpent and it reared and hissed at them. Finally one of the men managed to decapitate the snake and its body writhed about in a sickly fashion. Jason turned away from the scene before he threw up. He heard several more sickening sounds as the men hacked the body apart.

"What snake is this?" Caleb asked.

"I'd guess it's an adder," one of the men replied grimly.

"But my father—" Caleb did not finish because the snake's remains started smoking and dissolved into thick black smoke which rose and curled in the air before it evaporated.

Everyone retreated away from the scene, their hearts pounding at the unnatural phenomena. Sudden and vivid flashes of childhood memories returned to Jason of late nights he stayed up with his brothers when they told each other scary stories.

Jason returned with Caleb to the surgery. Bastian was lying on the table, jerking uncontrollably with froth pouring from his mouth. The urge to run away had never been as great for Jason as he watched his brother suffer. Tears stung the corners of his eyes and he was suddenly overwhelmed by it all. Caleb's comforting arm pulled him closer and he burst into tears into his brother's side. He allowed himself to be led to the kitchen where Caleb informed Mum about what was going on. She ran to check on Bastian, but also returned in tears. Caleb unexpectedly found himself in the role of comforter and rock for the family, a role Dad normally filled.

Eventually they calmed down once the initial shock was over. They sat silently, staring into the middle distance and quietly praying that Bastian was all right and that Dad had a cure. When Dad finally emerged, he looked pale, drained and tired. Sinking into a seat, he took a deep breath before speaking.

"As of yet I cannot say if the medication I applied helps, we will have to see. The snake that bit him is unknown so the correct counter of the venom cannot be given."

"Is he going to die?" Jason barely managed to ask.

"I don't know." The words dropped heavily. They were not what Jason wanted to hear. He had never in his life heard of his father being unsure about someone's condition. He always had rock solid faith in his father that he could cure anything. It seemed there was a first for everything.

"Caleb, can you help me carry Bastian to his room?"

Caleb nodded solemnly.

"Jason?"

"Huh?" he jerked as if he had been woken from a dream.

"May Bastian get your bunk? It's easier to access."

"Oh, yes, of course," Jason blinked.

A few moments later Dad and Caleb carried Bastian in from the surgery. He looked dead. His skin was grey and his left arm was covered in purple webbing. Jason watched expressionlessly, Mum kept her eyes averted, her hands wringing the material of her dress.

"I'll write a letter to Cathy," she said huskily.

Jason was left alone with his thoughts and his fears.

Chapter 2:
Advice From a Stranger

Jason slept fitfully that night. His dreams were nightmarish and filled with black, faceless creatures. But the image that haunted him the most was that of Bastian's cold, lifeless body. He woke often throughout the night, panicking when he forgot where he was and waking Caleb up in the process. Caleb would reassure and comfort Jason until he drifted back to restless sleep.

The following morning Jason rushed to Bastian's room. Dad and Mum were sitting at his bedside. Dad wiped his brow with a damp cloth and Mum held his uninjured hand. Jason crept inside and stood behind Dad, a lump rising in his throat as he watched Bastian.

"How…?" he left the question unfinished. His voice sounded broken, as if he had been up yelling all night.

"The medicines did not seem to have taken any effect, but I have given him some more with variations. I'm going in to Lothair later to buy new medicine and herbs and such. You have to watch him while I'm gone," Dad said in his gentle voice. There were deep shadows under his eyes.

"What if something goes wrong?" Jason croaked.

"You know enough to handle any situation that might take place," Dad said confidently.

"And I'm here if you need me." Mum smiled tiredly.

———⟫◆⟪———

Several days passed, with Bastian's condition neither improving nor worsening. None of the remedies or treatments that Dad tried seemed to work and they were running out of cures. Neighbours and friends often visited or dropped in with their condolences when they passed. To Jason it felt like Bastian was already dead. Everyone else thought so at least. Yet he refused to give up. He could not allow Bastian to die. There must be something! Jason had recently taken up going for long walks when he felt over-whelmed at home. He would walk as far as the hill overlook-ing the Nameless Wood before turning back. For some reason he always walked south, never northward toward the castle.

One morning Jason woke unusually early, the sun was barely up. He rolled over and closed his eyes, trying to return to sleep. Every night for the past few nights Jason had little rest with every moment of slumber stolen by nightmares. The shadows under his eyes deepened and his whole posture became haggard, like a person who had suffered terribly.

For at least half an hour Jason lay with his eyes closed, but sleep would not overtake him. Irritated and bone weary, he decided to get up. Caleb was sleeping gently in his bed when Jason crawled from his mattress to the door and slipped quietly through. The house was quiet, but suddenly the silence was inter-rupted. Though very vague and soft, Jason heard his parents' voices drift toward him from Bastian's room. He snuck down the corridor, quietly across the wooden floorboards and pressed himself against the wall behind the half open door. He heard quiet sobbing (Mum) and warm murmuring (Dad).

"When should we tell the boys?" Mum's voice asked through a sob.

"When they wake up. No need to interrupt their precious sleep."

Jason felt as if an icy claw was clutching his heart. Something happened to Bastian. That was the only explanation he had. But then—

"He's so thin," Mum's voice said quietly.

"If he does not wake from this coma soon he'll starve," came Dad's voice.

Relief mixed with renewed anxiety replaced the icy fear in Jason's chest. Bastian was not dead, but they were running out of time. He felt the familiar constriction of his throat and he quietly slipped back down the corridor.

Jason formed dozens of theories about Bastian's snake bite during the hours he was left to his dark thoughts. Some ranged from far-fetched to impossible to lunacy, yet he had little control of the direction his thoughts took during these times. One theory kept returning over and over and it was one of the most extreme he had thought of. The fact that the snake dissolved into thick black mist supported the idea even further. Maybe, just maybe, the snake was a Shifter. If this was true then many other legends could also be true, and a magical cure for Bastian could be found.

Silently Jason got dressed and went outside. Shops were starting to open and people gradually spilled onto the streets. His feet automatically followed the route southward that would take him to what he in his mind had referred to as Nameless Hill. On the way he passed an Ard-man, a farmer and a merchant driving his mule-drawn caravan.

With Nameless Hill about ten minutes away, Jason became aware of a nagging sense that something or someone was following him. He ignored it until he heard the sound of footsteps. Casually he glanced over his shoulder and saw a thin man, his skin a sickly pale colour and his dark eyes set deep into his sockets. If the man was not walking toward him he would have thought it was a corpse. He looked ahead again and tried to ignore the man, but he became irritably aware of his heavy, wheezy breathing and no matter how fast he walked it sounded as if the man was right behind him. He shortly came to a halt, and the man also stopped. A prickling sensation starting at the base of his neck spread up across his cheeks and his face until his entire head was prickling. His heartbeat quickened and he slowly turned around.

"May I help you sir?" he asked politely, though with some difficulty for his mouth was unexpectedly dry.

"Is it your brother who is ill?" the man asked.

"Why, who are you?" Jason asked, retreating a few steps.

"I am no one important, but I know where you can find a cure for your brother. The cure of all cures!"

Jason's breath caught in his throat. "What are you talking about?" he struggled to speak the words as his throat tightened with suppressed excitement.

"The Dream Keeper knows the answer to anything; he can grant you anything that your heart desires."

"Why are you telling me this?" Jason frowned and retreated a few steps.

"I simply want to help," the man smiled, though his eyes remained mirthless and lifeless. "What could I possibly gain from telling you how to save your brother?"

"How do you know about my brother?"

"Everyone knows; everyone is talking."

Jason felt his cheeks heat up as he realised the stupidity of the question. He tried to back away even further. Something about the man made his skin crawl.

"All right, if you're so keen on helping me, where is this Dream Keeper?" Jason asked feeling a spark of triumph. He expected the man to offer a price in return or name some impossible location. Instead he unexpectedly said,

"South, you must head south. You will know the Dream Keeper's home when you see it." Then the man turned around and walked away. Jason watched after him, his thoughts in a tangled mess now. He did not know what to think or what to do. He could not just leave on the random advice of a complete—and creepy— stranger! Yet, what if he was right? What if—what if—

The journey home had never taken so long before. Jason considered the stranger's words over and over and, as if he had been infected by some parasite, the more he thought about it the more convinced was he that he should leave and find this Dream Keeper. But should he tell Mum and Dad? They would never let him leave and if he told Caleb, Caleb would probably tell them. There was also the matter of transportation; he could not just walk kilometres on end. Bastian would be dead before he even crossed the border. There was also another problem; the stranger never said how far south he had to go. It could mean anything from beyond the hill to beyond the southern edge of the earth. But one thought overruled all the others. Bastian would die anyway, so he might as well try the last chance he had. Jason met no one as he entered the house. Strangely, Caleb's room was also empty. Taking this as a sign of confirmation, Jason made his decision. He would embark on the insane quest to save Bastian. Searching through Caleb's wardrobe he discovered a rucksack and a heavy cloak that he could use. Jason packed the cloak, spare clothes and a blanket. In the kitchen he scouted for food that would not spoil on the journey. When sufficient food for nearly two weeks was packed, he decided he was ready to leave. At the door, he paused however. Going over a mental list of what he might need, Jason realised he might get injured. He ran into Dad's surgery, also empty and packed a small medical aid kit, just in case. He stepped outside, said a quick prayer and took the first step of his life-changing adventure.

Standing on Nameless Hill, Jason knew that once he was beyond the ridge there would be no turning back. He had to be sure. For a long while he stood there with the wind ruffling his hair and tugging at his shirt. "What's it going to be Jason? You wanted to be an explorer and you are about to enter uncharted country." Closing his eyes, he took a single step. After that he opened his eyes and carefully made his way down the hill. Deciding to follow the road as far as it could take him in the desired direction, Jason shouldered his rucksack and determinedly set forth.

Long before the day was done his calves were aching and threatening to cramp, but Jason doggedly pushed on. His muscles ached and screamed for him to stop, but he could not. At the back of his mind he imagined a clock ticking out the time Bastian had left. This fuelled him to continue.

Up ahead in the shadows, Jason noticed a strange creature standing where the road sloped downward. A knot formed in his stomach, but he walked on. As he got closer to the silhouetted mystery, the knot tightened forcing him to stop. Jason's heart raced and his breath sped up. The creature spotted him and started to approach. When the sun was no longer at its back, Jason saw what it was and he almost cried with relief. A pony trotted toward him.

"Hello," Jason breathed and petted her nose. She tossed her head and pawed the ground. "Where's your owner?" Jason asked. Jason wondered if she came from one of the settlements further south, but there was no one to be seen for kilometres in any direction, so he decided that he might as well ride her. Clambering awkwardly onto her saddled back, Jason settled his feet in the stirrups and turned her around with a tug of the rein. He had never ridden a horse or pony before, except once when Caleb's friend Samuel gave him a lesson. But that was six years ago. Uncertainly he tapped his heals into her side and she lurched forward into a trot. Bouncing in the saddle was uncomfortable and sore. What did Samuel teach him again? He stood in the saddle then sat back down and repeated it. He moved in rhythm with the pony's movements and found the riding easier.

They rode through most of the night, boy and pony, until he was so weary he could not keep his eyes open. His head sank lower until it rested against the pony's neck. She trotted on following the road, the sensible creature that she was. But Jason started sliding down her side until he fell onto the side of the road. He was woken up by the fall, but too exhausted to get up and make a proper camp. Almost immediately he fell back to sleep while the pony kept watch.

Jason woke with his face in the ground, breathing grass and tasting earth. It was cold and he was shivering in his thin clothes. He rolled over and gasped as pain shot through every muscle in his body. Shutting his eyes tightly, he suppressed a cry. His body was stiff from the riding and slightly bruised from his fall. How was he to continue in this state? A soft velvety nose prodded his hand and he opened his eyes, looking straight into one of the pony's large eyes. She started prodding him harder in the ribs and he groaned.

"No, leave me alone!"

She ignored him and prodded harder.

"Stop that, it hurts!"

The pony pushed him with enough force to roll him over. Tears sprung into his eyes as his muscles protested. "Go away, let me die!"

The pony tossed her mane and rolled him until he was once more on his back. Jason glared at her along her long nose. "You're an evil pony."

She snorted, spraying something onto his face and he grimaced. Muttering under his breath and groaning with every motion he slowly got to his feet. He tried walking, but stumbled and fell. Gritting his teeth, he stood again. This time the pony caught him with a swing of her head when he stumbled. Leaning against her sturdy body he made his way to the saddle, but the stirrup just seemed too hopelessly high for his leg to reach.

"I can't," he whispered and rested his head against her warm side.

He nearly fell again when she unexpectedly lowered herself to the ground. She waited patiently for him to crawl onto her back. Once he was secure, she rose and continued at a steady walk. They went as far is his body allowed and he whispered. "Stop. No more, I must rest." Once more she lowered her body to the ground and he slid off. His tongue was parched and his stomach grumbled, but he trembled so much he could not open his rucksack.

"Don't be such a weakling!" he scolded himself. With another attempt, he undid the straps and ate a little of the bread and drank water from the bottle. Refreshed and with new strength he got to his feet.

"Just a little more," and he clambered onto the pony's back.

When night fell and he was exhausted again, he steered the pony a little way off the road to make camp. He took the cloak from the rucksack and the blanket. The cloak he clasped at his throat and he started unsaddling the pony. Removing everything was simple and easy, but he worried about re-saddling her again the next day. Jason fell asleep, curled up under a blanket while he watched the pony graze nearby.

Over the course of the next few days Jason gradually got used to the riding and learnt how to steer the pony properly, with some help from her of course. His muscles became harder with the exercise and he could now ride for long stretches without wearying. He had even given the pony a name: Blue, after the pony he rode when Samuel gave him lessons.

The sun had set and they were almost ready to make camp. Blue's ears rotated constantly as she listened to the nightly sounds. Suddenly her ears froze, facing backward. Jason could feel her muscles stiffen beneath him. His insides knotted and he looked from side to side in search of enemies. Blue's ears flattened against her skull and her nostrils flared.

"What is it girl?" Jason whispered.

A loud snort from behind caused them both to jump. He dared not look over his shoulder to see what it was. Blue's nerves gave in and she lunged forward and galloped down the road. Jason flung himself forward and clung to her neck. His heart beat wildly as he listened to the heavier footfalls pursuing them. Once he peeked over his shoulder, his heart leaped into his mouth. A creature twice the size of the pony was bounding after them. It was pitch-black and scaly, with a long tale swinging after it. Its gigantic claws threw clouds of dust into the air, but Jason could see its red eyes glow through the haze. Blue was in an uncontrollable state of terror and he had no way of calming her or steering her. All he could do was to hold on tight to keep from falling off.

A fork was up ahead and he was panicking because he could not control his pony. Blue unexpectedly swerved to the right and he was nearly thrown off. Instead of waiting for the fork, Blue had decided to plunge straight into the Wood. Jason tried to shield his face from the whipping branches with one arm while he held on with the other. His arm and face were bleeding from several small cuts while Blue charged on. He peered over his shoulder every now and then and the monster appeared further away with every glance as its path was hindered by the enclosed space.

Blue raced on even after the pounding of heavy paws could no longer be heard and the monster was gone. Jason whispered into her ear, trying to calm her and finally she slowed to a nervous trot, but her ears were still pulled back. He did not trust the silence either, his pulse was still racing rapidly and he jumped at every sound he heard. They were hopelessly lost. Blue's mindless flight into one of the world's largest forests and being pursued by scaly monsters, left them too frightened to rest in case of an ambush.

The initial adrenaline rush started to wear off and Jason suddenly felt weary to the bone. His lids were heavy and threatened to fall shut. Blue's hooves started dragging and her head was hanging. Suddenly, Jason's head jerked up and he strained his ears to hear the sounds of approaching hoofs. Blue's ears were also pricked, listening for the sound of hoof beats that was not their echo. A rumbling started to their left and was approaching fast. The earth trembled beneath them and the trees shuddered.

Wide awake again, Jason persuaded Blue into a canter and steered her into the opposite direction of the rumbling, but toward the hoof beats. Was this nightmare never going to end? No matter what direction they went they were either pursued by the rumbling or heading for the other horse (at least he hoped it was a horse). Once he could vaguely see the other rider about ten metres away, but it was soon obscured from his view again. The rumbling intensified to the point where he could feel it in his bones. Something or some *things* were getting very near, very fast. Almost out of nowhere, six wild boars the size of his pony with ugly squat things riding them appeared from the left and charged at him while filling the air with high-pitched squeals. Blue made a sound that was between a whinny and a screech, and reared onto her hind legs. Jason just managed to stay on, but failed to see the missile aimed at him. A stone the size of his fist walloped his head, just above his left eyebrow. The force of it threw him from Blue's back and he landed with a thud. Black crept across the edges his vision, but he fought against it. The ugly brutes jumped from the boars' backs and approached with clubs and blades. He held one arm up weakly to protect himself while he struggled to remain conscious.

A dark stallion soared over his head and landed among the squat creatures with earth spraying in all directions. There was a distinct ring of steel as a sword was drawn and the horse's rider jumped from its back. Swiftly and professionally the person cut the creatures down. Their blunt blades and clubs were no match for the rider's gleaming sword.

The last thing Jason saw was the rider finishing off the last creature. As the person pulled the sword from the brute's body, Jason saw his rescuer's face, framed by long dark curls. *It's a girl,* he thought with surprise as darkness overwhelmed him.

For a split second Jason thought he was dead and that he was looking on the face of an angel when he opened his eyes. But the dull throbbing in his head told him otherwise. With a groan, he lifted a hand to his head and felt an apple-sized lump. The girl looked over her shoulder and called to someone, but Jason did not hear the name. A boy the same age with identical dark blue eyes and curly brown hair as the girl approached Jason.

"You took quite a blow to the head there," said the boy. He spoke with a slight, almost indistinguishable accent. .

It took effort, but Jason propped himself up on his elbow and searched about for Blue. She was standing by a glorious dark bay stallion and a black mare. He was very grateful that she did not run away when those creatures attacked the previous night.

"My name's Darryn." The smiling boy held out his hand, which Jason accepted. Darryn had a strong and firm grip. "This is my sister, Rose. We're twins."

Rose dipped her head slightly in acknowledgement. Jason felt his cheeks burn as he recalled mistaking her for an angel.

"I'm Jason Thorn."

"That's a nice name," Darryn said. "Knew a Jason once, he became a famous general in Arden."

Jason managed a smile and slowly got up.

"Steady," Darryn warned. "You don't want to hit your head again, mate."

"What were those things?" Jason asked.

"Goblins, or goblin riders to be exact. As to the black monster, I haven't the faintest idea," Darryn said.

Jason's head whipped. "You saw the thing too?"

Darryn frowned slightly. "Yes."

"It probably stopped chasing me because it smelled you two."
He turned to face Rose and with a shy smile said, "Thank you for
saving my neck last night."

She shrugged and wandered off toward the stallion. Jason
watched her feeling slightly confused. Darryn was also watching
his sister, but then he returned his gaze to Jason. "Don't mind her.
She's just the silent type."

Jason nodded slowly, but kept his gaze fixed on her. She was
stroking the stallion's nose.

"So, Jason, what are you doing in this part of the world?"
Darryn asked.

He hesitated before answering. "I'm heading south," he finally
said.

Darryn lifted a brow and said in a doubting tone, "South?"

Jason nodded and Darryn's blue eyes wandered to the side of
his head. He smiled sympathetically at him. "You look horrible,
mate."

"Do you know where I could find some water?" Jason asked.

"There's a stream of some sorts that way," Darryn pointed.
"And don't worry about your pony; we already took care of her."
Jason thanked him and walked into the indicated direction. After
a short while the merry bubbling of water met his ears and he
came upon a narrow stream barely half a metre wide. He gingerly
dunked his head into the icy water. Carefully he washed his face,
wincing when he touched a sensitive area. When he was finished,
the shoulders and back of his cloak were soaking wet and he had
a headache. When he returned, Darryn was tending to the black
mare. Jason noticed that a sword hung at the boy's side from his
belt. It made him nervous knowing that the strangers were armed
with dangerous weapons and he had nothing.

"Ah, much better!" Darryn grinned over his shoulder. "Though you might catch a cold."

Jason smiled briefly and went to where Blue was sniffing the stallion curiously. While he tended to his pony, he peeked curiously past her at Rose. The girl was expressionlessly tying her sword underneath the saddlebags so as to keep it out of sight. She stopped briefly and returned Jason's glance. Shocked, he dropped his eyes and continued fumbling with Blue's straps.

"Would you mind if we accompany you?" Darryn asked unexpectedly behind him. Jason jumped with fright causing him to yank the stirrup strap too far.

"Don't you have your own plans?" Jason asked.

"Not really," Darryn said and threw Rose a quick look.

"You may come with me if you wish then," Jason said carefully. "But I'm not exactly sure of where I'm going."

The slightest of frowns formed on Rose's brow and her brother also seemed interested. "Curious," Darryn said. "I think then you'll benefit by us travelling with you. After all, there's safety in numbers."

"All right," Jason said and righted Blue's stirrups. He mounted her and waited for the strangers to mount their own horses.

"So you said you were heading south?" Darryn asked.

"Yes," Jason said and turned Blue in the right direction. He clicked his tongue twice and she started out on a trot. Darryn and Rose followed and were soon riding on either side of him and his pony.

"So what are you doing here in one of the wildest parts of Bristan?"

"It's a long story," he replied evasively.

"All right, I understand." Darryn smirked. "You don't know us well enough to trust us yet."

Jason's cheeks flushed, but he remained silent. The forest seemed less menacing now that he was not fleeing for his life. In fact it was rather peaceful with the sound of the stream off to his right and birds singing in the boughs. The soft thudding of the horses' hooves on the ground created a hypnotic rhythm resulting in a drowsy atmosphere. Darryn hummed quietly. It was a merry tune and one Jason did not know.

"I don't know this song," he said. "What's it called?"

Darryn smiled and said, "It is an old Arden folk song about a woman who fell in love with a wolf."

Smiling at the notion, Jason asked, "How does the tale end?"

"Oh they end up marrying and having children," Darryn said with a straight face.

The two boys burst out laughing at the idea.

"What songs do you have here?" Darryn asked.

"Oh lots, er, you don't want me to sing some for you?"

"No, of course not!" Darryn laughed.

Jason felt oddly at ease, he had never felt so comfortable in other people's presence. For the first time in days he felt his heart lighten and his worry for Bastian was less oppressive.

"Earlier you asked me what I'm doing out here, but you haven't told me what you're doing here," Jason said after a while.

"Sorry, I can be a little absent minded. We ran away from home. It became quite stormy back home with my father."

"Is this your first time in Bristan?"

"No, we've been here before, but only on short visits with our father and when we were passing through toward Tiethe."

"You've been to the southern kingdom?"

"Aye."

Again there was awkward silence. Darryn resumed his humming and Jason remained content to admire the scenery. Around noon they stopped for a quick meal before continuing further through the forest. They broke free of the tree cover by late afternoon and travelled westward until they rediscovered the road. They made camp a little way from the road in a dip that kept them from sight. Jason unrolled his blanket and laid it on the yellow grass. He then removed Blue's saddle and tack, and placed them by his rucksack. They could not find any sufficient materials nearby to make a fire so they huddled up in their blankets and stared at the stars. Jason quickly fell asleep, but nightmares were waiting for him.

Darryn and Rose sat some way away and whispered so they would not wake him. The boy slept on until the dawn of the new day. The next day, Jason and Darryn asked more questions of each other's lives and through their conversation learned more of the other.

"Will you tell me now what you are doing out here?" Darryn asked of Jason.

"I don't know what to say," Jason replied truthfully. He wasn't sure why he could not bring himself to share his story.

"Don't worry, everyone has their secrets. You may keep yours as we keep ours."

Jason glanced at Rose where she was riding to Darryn's right. "Don't you have anything to say?" he asked lightly with a smile.

She looked up at him and in her eyes he saw a queer light. "What would you have me say?" she asked. This was the first time he heard her speak properly and her voice sounded to him pure and clear like a bell.

"I just find it weird that a person can go so long in silence."

"Silence is a time of thinking and contemplation," she said. "It's not always evil."

"Talking isn't evil either."

She seemed a little annoyed at him after that.

—◆—

The country around them changed subtly. The forests and trees thinned out and the grass grew greener and more lush, a sign that they were nearing the southern border. Rolling hills appeared the further they went. They were not as sheer and high as the hills surrounding Jason's home, but seemed friendlier and more the type of hill where a flock would graze. The weather warmed, as did the wind. The nights, however, still remained icy in their last hours before the sun returned.

Darryn and Rose started to find their fur-lined clothing more and more uncomfortable. Jason admired their clothing. Though weather-stained, they were obviously of rich materials. His own clothing was becoming rather haggard from days of ceaseless wear, and he was desperately in need of a wash.

"I think we should stay the night at the next town," Darryn said. "I'm starting to miss cooked food."

"I haven't any money," Jason muttered quietly.

Darryn smiled. "We can pay for you."

"But it would be wrong because I won't be able to pay you back."

Darryn looked at him as if had just declared that the sky is pink and the grass purple. "You don't need to pay us back. We'll do it because we want to."

They arrived at the little town Warrenstone when the sun was setting. The town seemed to be built entirely of dark greyish stone, giving it a melancholy atmosphere. The buildings were built so close to the road that they seemed to lean over it. The inn was a homely enough little building consisting of two storeys with stables behind the inn where the animals could be taken care of. Once they had left their mounts in sure hands, they entered the inn. The common room was a pleasant place: men laughed and talked with each other over a mug of beer, while serving girls wove about delivering drinks and plates of food. In the corner, a minstrel quietly plucked at the strings of his harp. There was even a gremlin dozing by the fire.

Darryn looked around with a critical eye, and when satisfied went toward the counter where the owner should be.

"Good evening sir," Darryn greeted. "I would like some lodging for three people. They need not be luxurious, only free of pests."

The man behind the counter had a good-natured face and his cheeks were the colour of a ripe tomato. He smiled at Darryn and said, "Certainly, Young Sir. Would you like meals to be included in the price?"

"Yes."

"How many days would you be a stayin'?"

"Just the night. We'll be leaving in the morning."

"Ah yes, so that would be supper and breakfast plus three rooms?"

"Yes. Thank you, my good man."

"That would be five gold pieces."

Jason's eyes nearly popped out of his head. Five gold pieces! That was about how much his father earned in a month. He watched with his mouth nearly hanging open as Darryn took out a small purse and easily paid the man the five bright yellow coins.

"Kribs will show you your rooms," the owner said. " Kribs!" he bellowed. A small weasel of a man trotted forward. "Yes sah?"

"Take these three customers to their rooms. Here are their keys."

"All right, follow me," said the man and energetically took them up the stairs leading from the common room. A long corridor ran down the length of the building, with doors opposite each other leading to the rooms.

Numbers fourteen, fifteen and sixteen were their rooms. Jason was given the first room, number fourteen and was then followed by Rose and Darryn. "Your baths will be ready for you after supper," Kribs informed them.

"Thank you," Darryn said. He and Jason met down in the common room.

"Where's Rose?" Jason asked.

"Hmm," Darryn shrugged and they sat down by a table near the minstrel.

Soon two steaming plates of roast chicken, mashed potatoes and a variety of cooked vegetables were brought to them. Jason had never eaten so much good food at once in his life. His mother was a good cook, but since their budget was minimal she had to be very creative when preparing their meals. The mashed potatoes melted in his mouth and the vegetables had a wonderful spice applied to them that nipped slightly at the tongue. The roast chicken was divine and he quickly devoured it all. Darryn grinned over his own plate at Jason.

"Have you survived a ten-year famine?"

Jason smiled back at him. "It certainly feels like it."

Darryn chuckled. A very pretty serving girl enquired if they wanted anything to drink.

"Just water, thank you," Jason said shyly.

"I would like to try your beer," Darryn said, and Jason threw him a shocked glance.

"Coming right now, sirs." She smiled and was off with a swish of her skirt.

"You can't drink, you're under age!" Jason whispered.

Darryn threw him an annoyed glance. "I have drunk many a goblet of wine in my life thank you. You are not my parent to tell me what I can and cannot do."

"Sorry," Jason mumbled. "Just don't get drunk."

The pretty girl returned and placed a plain wooden cup with water before Jason and a cup filled with golden, frothing liquid before Darryn. He took an experimental sip and his smile broadened. "This is excellent! Where do you get it?"

"It's specially imported from Targon," the girl said.

Jason was about to say something, but bit his tongue and took a sip from his cup and turned to watch the minstrel. An untouched cup stood on the table while the man lay back with his eyes closed as his fingers found their way across the strings. The lively tune he played was replaced by a melancholy melody that brought tears to the eye. The man opened his eyes and smiled at Jason.

"Are you a musician?" he asked. His voice was soft and as musical as the harp he was playing.

"No," Jason admitted.

"What a shame."

He heard a roar of laughter and turned around to see Darryn had engaged himself in a drinking contest with a bear of a man. He nodded his farewell at the minstrel and went upstairs.

As promised, a tub of steaming water awaited him. Gratefully he stripped down and sunk into the warm water. A faint splash came from the room to his right and he realised with a flush that Rose was bathing in her room. He closed his eyes and tried to ignore the sounds, but he couldn't shake the image in his mind and slipped beneath the water's surface. All sounds, save those caused by him, were blocked out. When he needed air he came up again and involuntarily strained his ears for any other sounds. Thankfully there were none and he lay in the bath until the water cooled down. He climbed out and was about to use his cloak to dry off when there was a knock at the door.

"I'm busy," Jason called.

"Just forgot your towel, sah," Kribs' voice called from the other side.

"All right, er, come in,"

Kribs ran in with his eyes shut tight, dropped the towel and ran back out. Gratefully Jason took the towel and despite its coarse fabric wrapped it around himself. After drying himself off, he changed into the spare clothes he had packed and wondered how he would clean his dirty clothes.

Another loud roar of laughter came from below and Jason recognised Darryn's raised voice. His poor friend was going to be drunk as a skunk before the night was done. Uncertain of what to do, Jason decided to talk with Rose, but he paused by the door.

"She might be lonely," he thought. "But she does not seem like the talkative type."

The next thing he knew he was standing outside her room and raised his fist to knock, but his nerve failed him. For two and a half minutes he stood with a raised fist before her door.

"Come on, Jason, just do it!" he said under his breath.

With a jerk his fist knocked once on the door, and then timidly he knocked a few rapid little taps. He paused and waited feeling very nervous. He did not know this girl very well and did not know what her reaction might be. Light footsteps, barely audible approached and the door opened. A flicker of surprise passed across her face and was replaced by puzzlement.

"Um, hello," Jason said. "I was just wondering if you needed some company."

Her eyes passed briefly down the length of his body and her expression became blank again. "Oh," she said and then seemed unsure of what to do next. "I was not feeling in need of company, but you may come in."

She stood aside for him to enter. The room was identical to his except the curtains were a different colour. She closed the door and walked to the middle of the room, crossing her arms. They stood in awkward silence. One did not know what to say to the other. Jason noticed the faint trace of a lovely perfume in the air. It was floral, but soft and subtle with a certain wild edge to it.

The loud laughter sounded again.

"I think that was Darryn," Jason said uncomfortably.

"Hmm," Rose replied.

Jason desperately searched for something to talk about, but his mind went blank. He was floundering, casting about for anything. "What's your favourite colour?" he blurted out stupidly.

She looked up at him with a slight crease between her brows. "Pardon?"

Surprised by his own question, he repeated meekly. "What's your—favourite—colour?"

"Oh," she said and the frown deepened slightly. For a moment Jason thought she had disapproved of him, but then he realised she was in thought. "I guess it would be red."

"Red," he repeated. "Why?"

She shrugged her shoulders lightly.

Jason suddenly found his bare toes very interesting and examined them intensely. He was feeling that this visit was becoming more and more of a disaster. Finally he looked up and smiled apologetically. "I'm sorry I took up your time, I'll go now."

He left rather hurriedly and imagined seeing a look of loss pass across Rose's face. When he was safely in his room he flopped down on the bed and closed his eyes. He did not intend to fall asleep, but eventually he drifted off. For the first time in days he slept soundly throughout the night. Not a single dream disturbed him.

Chapter 3:
Across the Border

About three hours after the sun rose like a fiery disk above the horizon, Jason, Darryn and Rose were already on the road southward. Darryn was notably quieter and grumpier, due to a headache caused by the previous night's 'fun'. Jason had offered to give him some herbs to take away the pain, but Darryn brushed his offer aside with a growl. For the first time since Jason met them, Rose smiled.

The weather was definitely no longer that of approaching winter and more like the beginning of summer. Jason removed his jerkin and cloak, and tucked them into Blue's saddlebags. Darryn did likewise, but Rose endured the heat, cloak and all. The official border between Bristan and Tiethe was the broad river called the Fiume and a stone bridge guarded by two Tiethan sentries spanned the rushing waters. Jason felt nervous as they approached the two armoured figures. They carried spears and bronze short swords at their sides. On their heads rested helmets with crimson plumes and the tunics beneath their armour was of a slightly darker shade of red. The sentries stood on either side of the bridge, thus allowing traffic to pass through. Darryn nodded to each in turn as they passed by them, but the sentries remained motionless and stared ahead. One did turn his head, however, when Rose passed by prompting his companion to nudge him with his spear.

They arrived at the first Tiethan town by midday and the difference between the neighbouring kingdoms was unmistakable. The architecture was completely different and most of the people wore strange and foreign clothing. Another very notable difference was that the Tiethans all had black hair and dark eyes with olive complexions, so Jason and his companions stood out with their brown hair, fair skin and different clothes.

"I think we'll just pass through," Darryn murmured as dozens of heads turned to watch them curiously.

Near the end of the town they passed a building built of some white stone. Boys of all ages and girls up to about the age of twelve were exiting from it.

"What's that?" Jason asked.

"That's the public school," Darryn replied. "The rich children receive private tutelage paid for by their parents in the capital city of Targon. They learn things like reading and writing, arithmetic, singing, dancing and athletics, well the boys at least. Girls only learn basic arithmetic and reading and writing."

"Why? In Bristan everyone can go to school equally."

Rose answered this time. "Because Tiethe still believes to some extent that men are better than women. It has improved over the years though."

"But that's wrong."

"Well maybe when you get the chance one day you can change it," Darryn said jokingly.

"How?" Jason asked.

"I don't know. It was just a joke, mate."

Jason looked around at the people and despite the unfairness toward the female gender they seemed to be a happier people than he was familiar with. There were many old men with long beards and white robes that reached down to their sandaled feet just standing about or talking earnestly with each other in small groups. Young men went about their work, while women laughed and talked with each other. The wonderful aroma of fresh bread mingled with the sweet scents of exotic fruits.

"Those men with the white robes are the philosophers, the so-called wise men of Tiethe," Darryn pointed out. "They spend all their lives trying to figure out the secrets of the universe." He chuckled then lowered his voice and said, "Some say that they can do magic."

Jason looked over his shoulder at the old men, meeting the eyes of one of them and a shiver ran down his spine.

Wide open, grassy country stretched out like a green blanket beneath the blue sky and warm sun. Sometimes they passed an orchard with rows and rows of trees bearing unknown fruit. Some were orange and others strangely shaped.

The country was very strange to Jason and they often passed people on the road either on foot or riding donkey carts. The following day they passed through another town when Darryn decided that Jason needed a weapon.

"It's dangerous out on the road; you need to be able to defend yourself. I'm not fond of guns, they're a little cowardly, but maybe you could use one."

Jason tried to protest, but Darryn persisted. Later Jason found himself holding a pistol, its smooth wooden barrel fit snugly into his palm. The first chance he had, he put it away in his rucksack.

"It is unbearably hot," Darryn gasped when they stopped for a short break and spread out on the cool grass.

"Hmm," Jason said, his eyelids were hooded and slowly closing. Rose had already fallen asleep not too far from him.

"We shouldn't—fall—asleep—" Darryn yawned as his head sank to the ground.

Hours later they were woken by a loud roar. In an instant Darryn and Rose were on their feet with their swords drawn. The looming creature was enormous and covered in black scales. Its ugly head was rather bat-like and it had enormous teeth that continued snapping menacingly at them. The tail was nearly two and a half meters long and very thick; it kept swishing it about, ready to knock one of them over. Jason was frozen in place, he could not move.

"Jason, get your gun!" Darryn shouted. "Shoot at its eyes!"

Broken from his trance, he nodded quickly and ran toward Blue. He took his pistol and quickly loaded it. In his panic he did not aim very well and his first shot struck the creature's jaw. He took the next aim shakily; well aware that Darryn and Rose were battling for their lives while it swiped at them with its gigantic claws. Again the bullet merely ricocheted from the hard scales around its red eye. Jason repeatedly tried to shoot the tiny targets while also focusing on his friends. Darryn and Rose dodged a swipe of its right claw and Darryn struck out at it with his sword. The blade merely glanced off. It snapped at Rose's face, but she jumped aside. *Bang!* The shot missed again. Sweat was rolling down Darryn's brow and body. He blinked away a few beads and lunged at the creature again. It was impossible to get it from behind because of its vicious swinging tail. But Darryn took the chance and ran in from the side with the intent of stabbing it through the ribs. The tail came around at the same time and struck him hard in the chest. He went flying backward and landed with a thud on his left shoulder. Darryn appeared to be unconscious and Jason anxiously turned his gaze toward Rose. She was quick. She easily dodged the swipes and snaps, and jabbed at its head when the opportunity came. But even she could not see everything. The monster unexpectedly whirled around and the tail slammed into her.

"Ugh!" she grunted and fell. She desperately groped for her sword, but it was out of reach. Just as she was going to roll over, one of the beast's paws crashed down upon her leg and she cried out. It raked its claws slowly down, cutting through her flesh as it went. Red blossomed on her clothing where the material soaked up her blood. The sight horrified Jason and he was once again petrified beyond action. Rose breathed in sharply and she gritted her teeth at the burning pain. She looked fearlessly up at the creature as it lifted its claws for the death blow. Just as it brought its paw down it uttered a loud cry and collapsed onto its side. Darryn's sword was sticking out from between its ribs and Jason was panting wide-eyed, still clinging to the hilt. After he got over the shock, he glanced at Rose.

"Don't worry, I can help," he said and hurried toward Blue (who miraculously did not run away). Rummaging in his rucksack he found the first aid kit and rushed back to Rose. Gently, he lifted the skirt of her dress up to her thigh. His heart was still hammering in his chest from the overdose of action and adrenaline. Nearly her entire leg was soaked in crimson blood. He had tended minor wounds before, but never something as serious as this. Stifling the urge to be sick, Jason hurriedly started to clean the wound. When his water bottle was empty, he fetched Rose's. He had to use all three of their bottles before he got most of the blood washed away, but the wound was still bleeding. He carefully bandaged the leg to staunch the bleeding. The white material was completely soaked before he even finished. After using all his bandages, Jason grabbed his extra shirt and tore it into strips. Rose gripped the grass so that her knuckles turned white, but her face was emotionless. Only her eyes were burning with the intense pain.

Darryn eventually regained consciousness, but his left shoulder was in agony. He watched Jason warily as he worked. "Are you sure you know what you're doing?"

"Yes," Jason said. "But this will help only for now. We must find a professional healer to tend to both of you."

"Thank you," Darryn said. "Could you help her get onto her horse?"

"Of course," Jason said. He knelt down and picked Rose up very carefully as if she were made of glass. That same faint perfume he smelled in her room at the inn was now mixed with the scent of blood and sweat. Together they managed to get her onto the horse so that she was relatively comfortable. Darryn also needed some assistance to mount his mare because of his shoulder. Once everyone was finally settled, Jason led the way down the road at a slow walk.

It was properly dark when they finally arrived at a small village. Jason left Darryn and Rose just outside the village and went in search of a healer by himself. Lights glowed behind drawn curtains and shop owners locked up their stores. But everywhere Jason went he was denied entry. Giving up hope he started to turn around.

"Are you looking for somebody?"

He turned around and faced a young woman with long dark hair on the opposite side of the road. She was carrying a basket with loaves of bread and some other things.

"Yes, do you know where I might find a healer?" Jason asked.

"My friends are in need of attention."

"I am a healer's apprentice," the woman said and Jason's face broke out in a smile of relief. "I will take you to Mistress Mayflower."

"Thank you," Jason said. "I'll fetch my friends."

He hurried back to where he had left Darryn and Rose. Rose looked dangerously pale and was hanging low over her horse's neck. The young woman met them and with a concerned glance at Rose's leg led them through to the other side of the village. A little way away from the other buildings was a quaint little cottage built amid a rocky piece of ground. All sorts of flowers and plants with medicinal properties grew in well-tended little gardens. Jason would have loved to stop and examine them, but there was currently no time for diversion.

With the woman's aid, Jason helped Rose from the horse's saddle and carried her into the little cottage. Darryn slid down his own horse with difficulty and followed them.

An old woman with her grey hair tied back into a bun greeted them in the kitchen. She immediately hastened Jason through a door and down a corridor into a tiny bedroom. He gently laid Rose down then went outside to tend to the horses. The young woman bade Darryn to sit down by the kitchen table so she could look at his shoulder, leaving Jason alone to think.

An hour later the young woman came outside and handed him a wooden bowl filled with stew. He accepted it gratefully and drank straight from the bowl. When he was done he went inside and placed the bowl by the basin. Darryn was seated by the table eating his own supper; his left arm in a sling.

"So what was wrong?" Jason asked sitting down opposite him.

"Broke my collar bone," Darryn grinned.

"How's Rose?"

Darryn's smile disappeared. "I don't know."

Jason got up again and went down the corridor, stopping outside the room where Rose was being tended to. He knocked softly and asked, "May I come in?"

"Yes," Mistress Mayflower called and he opened the door. A lantern was hanging from the ceiling lighting up the whole room. All the bandaging Jason had applied had been removed; the old woman was finishing up her own bandaging. Rose's eyes were closed and her brow glistened with sweat.

"She has lost a lot of blood," the old woman said. "So the girl is weak. I suggest you remain here until she has regained her strength."

Jason nodded.

"I would just like to know how she came upon this injury and why you are unscathed," she said and turned to him with curious eyes. Slowly she rose from her seat, gathered her tools and said, "Come let's talk over a cup of tea. Luciana can show the other young man to his room."

Once comfortably seated and each with a cup of steaming hot tea, Jason told Mistress Mayflower of the attack. She nodded her wizened head every now and then as if she understood some hidden meaning he did not see.

"Tell me child," she said when he was done. "Do you know what this monster was?"

"Yes, a Shadowling."

"And why are they after you?"

"No, but how—"

"I am not entirely ignorant child, but you must be careful on whatever journey you are on. Beyond the borders of humankind lies a terrible world of wonder, magic and danger."

"All right—" Jason said uncertainly. "Well, goodnight ma'am. I think I'm going to bed."

"Goodnight, sweet dreams." She smiled at him over the rim of her cup.

"You can leave and continue without us. I think it's better this way," Darryn said the following morning at the breakfast table to Jason.

"And abandon my friends?" Jason snorted.

"You have been delayed long enough by us. It's time we part ways."

"So you want me gone?"

"No, of course not!"

Jason took a deep breath for a moment to consider if he should reveal the intent of his quest. So far Darryn and his sister had proven trustworthy and good friends. And he did not know if he may be able to complete his mission alone. "I am not leaving without you two."

"But your journey—"

"I'm afraid of continuing alone!" Jason said abruptly. He stared Darryn right in the eye and said, "I need your help."

Darryn looked momentarily taken aback. Then with a smile said, "You have my sword."

Hesitantly, Jason started to tell Darryn about the snake and Bastian's illness and of the strange gaunt man's words.

Shaking his head, Darryn said with a chuckle, "You have gotten yourself into quite an adventure, mate!"

Jason smiled meekly. "Do you still want to come with me?"

"Of course I do! This is an adventure I won't miss."

Relief flooded through Jason and for the first time in days he felt truly at peace. He no longer had to face his troubles alone. After breakfast they decided to visit Rose. When Darryn knocked on her door she called for them to come inside. She was sitting propped up against some pillows in her bed. Jason thought she looked considerably better, though still very pale.

"Good morning. How are you feeling?" Darryn asked and sat down beside her on the bed. Jason stood against the wall, silently observing.

"Better," she answered. Her eyes flashed toward Jason. "Thank you."

Some colour crept into his cheeks and he smiled shyly.

"So how long do you think it will take for your leg to heal?" Darryn continued.

Rose shrugged. "The woman didn't say anything. Though I don't think it will take more than a few weeks."

Darryn threw Jason and anxious glance then he said to Rose. "We will be accompanying Jason on his journey, if that is all right with you."

"May I know where we are going?"

"Jason will explain."

Jason stepped forward and stuttering slightly over his words explained it to her. All the while her dark blue eyes were fixed upon him, making him feel uncomfortable. When he was done he warily searched her face, but whatever she was feeling did not show.

She lifted one hand to brush a stray curl from her face and the sleeve fell slightly down, revealing what appeared to be a solid gold band around her wrist. Jason's eyes widened. Catching his glance she froze for a second, and then quickly pulled the sleeve back up to cover the band. Jason looked quizzically at her, but she suddenly found the view outside her window very fascinating. Darryn watched him with an almost dangerous look in his eye, as if to dare Jason to ask the question that was burning on his tongue.

"I'm going outside," Jason said instead and was well aware of the eyes watching his departure.

He had not noticed it the previous night because of all the excitement, but the air had a distinct salty smell and a refreshingly strong wind buffeted him. Also something he managed to miss was that the entire village was situated only a kilometre from what appeared to be a sheer drop. Curiosity caused him to walk toward the edge and he peered over the side. Contrary to what he had assumed, it was not a straight drop but more of a very steep descent. He glanced over his shoulder to see if Darryn had followed him. Satisfied, he started the slow and careful climb down the side of the cliff side. The going was precarious because the area was very rocky and quite a few times he nearly slipped and tumbled to the ground below. When his feet safely touched the bottom, he started walking in a generally south direction.

Ten minutes into his walk he noticed a strange almost liquid sound, like a strong wind, in the forest. The salt tang on the air was also more prominent. Leaving the route he intended to take, he followed the sound. The ground became progressively harder and the plant life less, yet it was not at all dreary like a desert. Large boulders appeared on his way and he wove his way around them or clambered over them. His biggest challenge was a boulder that reached nearly twice his height with a smooth and difficult surface. Just beyond it he could hear the sound he had been following quite clearly, rising and falling in volume. There was no way around the boulder as others even larger blocked the way and he had not the patience to search for another way around. Gritting his teeth he reached up, searching for hand holds. With a lot of difficulty he managed to get on top of the boulder and the view took his breath away.

Stretching across the horizon, glittering beneath the glaring sun and as blue as the sky above, was the sea. White sand bordered the great waters constantly under assault from waves that broke ceaselessly on the shore. Jason watched with silent amazement that anything could be so…endless was nearly beyond his comprehension. He slid down the other side of the boulder and landed on soft, warm sand. Bending down he removed his boots and stockings and buried his toes in the whiteness. It was pleasant to his travel weary feet to walk upon the warm, soft surface. He made his way to where the waves were falling and very hesitantly felt the water as it pulled back with his feet. It was surprisingly and pleasantly warm. He rolled up his pant legs and entered the water until the waves reach his knees. Impulsively he pulled off his shirt and tossed it onto the beach. With a cry of delight he dove beneath the surface. Resurfacing he swam deeper in, diving under the waves as they threatened to crash upon him or take him back to shore. He swam until the beach was nothing more than a thin white strip in the distance. Deciding he had gone far enough, he turned around as a wave approached and allowed it to carry him all the way back. The experience was exhilarating.

Hunger made Jason get out and change back into his shirt and boots. It was a little unpleasant to walk around in wet trousers and it certainly made the return climb a lot more difficult. The heat of the sun quickly dried both him and his clothing. Playing on a hot day and for a long time in the ocean left Jason incredibly thirsty His tongue felt thick and dry and no amount of swallowing could return moisture to his mouth. He blinked more often than usual because of the salty sting in his eyes caused by the ocean water. When he finally arrived back at the cottage he was tired, thirsty and hungry. Everyone was seated by the kitchen table drinking cool lemonade and eating some delicious fruits from Mistress Mayflower's garden.

"There you are," Darryn said as Jason sat down in the chair next to his. "Where were you?"

"I think the young man has found the ocean," Mistress Mayflower smiled.

He accepted a glass from Luciana (the young woman) and nearly finished it all in seconds. Rose was also at the table, her injured leg wrapped up securely in white bandages. Jason wondered if one of the women had helped her there or if she had made the journey herself. While taking smaller sips he watched her over the edge of his glass. Her eyes met his and a sudden shock travelled down his spine, causing him to shudder. A small crease former between her eyes, but disappeared as soon as it came.

"Good news. Mistress Mayflower says that Rose's leg should be fine in five weeks' time," Darryn informed Jason.

Jason nodded in reply. "Good."

The stay at the healer's house was pleasant and restful. It also filled Jason with more longing for home. At the back of his mind the constant urgency of Bastian's approaching death made him impatient to leave, but he knew very well Rose had to regain her strength first. His agitation increased as the weeks passed by, his temper became shorter and he preferred to be left alone.

Jason was sitting on one of the rocks in Mistress Mayflower's garden. The sea breeze was ruffling his hair. His fingers were lacing and unlacing, elbows resting on his knees. Hearing footsteps, he looked up and was surprised to see Rose. She was limping very slightly, but otherwise seemed fine.

"I am well enough to travel again," she informed him.

His heart leaped in excitement. "Are you sure?"

"Yes."

Jason stood up and walked briskly back to the cottage and straight toward the room he shared with Darryn. He found him already packing. Darryn grinned and straightened up. He still had to wear the sling for another week, but was otherwise fit to go.

"Did you hear the good news?" Darryn asked.

"When do we leave?"

"Tomorrow. As soon as possible,"

"Do we head south then?"

"Yes, I think we should head for Targon and figure things out once we're there. It should be a four day journey from here, three if we hurry."

"The quicker we get there the better."

Darryn laid the hand of his good arm on Jason's shoulder, "He'll be fine, mate. We'll find your Dream Keeper and your brother will be back to health soon."

"I hope so."

Jason did not have a lot of packing to do because he had kept his rucksack as ready as possible in case he needed to leave in a hurry. Once he had checked that he had everything, he went outside to see to the mounts. Blue had become shockingly fat on the sweet short grass that grew here and there. He patted her side and stroked her nose, offering her a sugar cube he snuck from the breakfast table.

"We have some more hard riding ahead for us, girl. Are you ready?"

She tossed her head lightly and he smiled.

Luciana was busy outside tending to the numerous plants in the Mistress's garden. She was kneeling in a patch of some plant Jason did not recognise wearing an earthy-coloured dress. Glancing at him she said with a smile, "Unfortunately, being a healer's apprentice means I also have to do all the lazy jobs."

"I know," he said. "I'm an apprentice myself, but not very advanced. My father is an excellent healer in the area where I come from."

"I've always wanted to see Bristan." She paused thoughtfully. "There are so many interesting plants to examine. I have a passion for all things growing and green."

"The plants aren't as interesting as the things that grow here in the south,"

She rolled her eyes, "To you they seem exotic, to me they are just the everyday trees and shrubs of my life."

Jason pondered this, considering the truth in her words.

"Are you leaving tomorrow?" she asked.

"Yes, since Rose is fit enough we can go."

"Hmm, it will be a little lonely when you go. It was nice to have some new company."

"Don't you have friends in the village?"

"No, most people my age go to the capital to broaden their knowledge or to seek out who knows what."

"Why don't you go to the capital?"

"I grew up there and it's too crowded. I like the quiet countryside."

"Oh, well good luck."

She smiled and resumed her work.

Jason excused himself from her company, deciding to say

farewell to the little beach he often visited. He knew he would see the sea again since they would be travelling mostly along the coast toward Targon, but it would be different, not as private.

He stood waist deep in the ocean, his face lifted to the sky and with his eyes closed. Breathing in deeply he realised he would miss all this back home. Turning around he returned to beach and put on his clothes. His footprints were washed away as if he had never been there in the first place.

———⊳•◇•⊲———

Finally on the road again they started out at a gallop, urgent to get to Targon. The horses and pony were unused to the hard riding and so were the riders. Despite the aches in their muscles they pushed forward. On the second night they were camping on the fringes of a forest. Their little campfire was burning low, hardly giving off light or warmth. Their sleeping forms were scattered around the flames against the cool night.

Jason was roughly woken up by strong arms pulling him from the ground. Confused and frightened he tried to see what was going on in the darkness. Something cold was pressed to his throat and with a lurch in his chest he realised it was a knife. His eyes desperately searched for his friends and he saw they, too, were being held by armed men.

"What have we here?" asked one of the men, apparently the leader. His accent was harsh to their ears. "Three children alone outside? What shall we do with you?"

"You're slave traders!" Darryn exclaimed, which earned him a punch in the jaw.

"You speak only when I say you can, got that?" the leader

pressed his face close to Darryn's, his putrid breath blowing up his nostrils.

Slowly he circled Rose, an ugly grin on his face. "Look at this pretty little thing."

She glared viciously at him.

"We'll fetch a mighty price for her in Umbra!"

"Umbra? That's in Setar!" Jason panicked.

"What should we do with these?" asked another man who was holding all three the steeds by the reigns.

"Take them with, if they die on the way we could always sell the meat," the leader replied.

Their hands were tied with rough ropes behind their backs. The slavers confiscated any weapons they carried and ransacked their saddlebags and food packs. All the while Jason was praying desperately that somehow they would be saved. After the slavers were done with their search, they forced their captives to march with sharp blades pointed at their backs. For what seemed like hours they marched through the night and Jason no longer knew in which direction they were going. He was disoriented and about to collapse from exhaustion.

Sometime later they joined up with the remainder of the group who had strange animals with them. Jason tried to make them out, but through his tired delirium gave up. Finally the leader growled that the party should halt and set up camp. Guarded by three men with broad, curving swords, Jason, Darryn and Rose were forced to sit down. Gratefully, Jason closed his eyes and fell asleep.

It felt as if they had hardly slept at all when they were once again hauled to their feet. In the daylight Jason could see his captors better. They all had dark skin, black hair and black eyes. Their teeth flashed white when they talked or jeered, and nearly all of them had scraggly beards. Their clothing was also completely foreign to Jason: long dirty robe-like garments were worn by most of the men and they all had the same curving swords. The leader wore a thing Jason learned was called a turban, wrapped around his head. He also learned the leader's name was Abdal.

There were five of the strange animals with the slave traders. Their fur was a yellowish colour and they had long, thin legs and wide, flat hooves. On their backs, they had strange humplike formations and they had to carry all the goods belonging to the traders.

If the captives did not walk fast enough a whip would snap at their heels and sometimes crack at their backs. The stinging whip bit at Jason's back, forcing him to speed up. He had the most sympathy for Rose, whose leg was probably giving her a lot of pain, but she showed no emotion whatsoever, except for seething disgust and hatred toward their captors that Jason could read in her eyes.

They became mechanical in their movements, not thinking, just doing. Jason forgot about everything: who he was, why he was there, where he was going. All he could think of was placing one foot in front of the other and the bite of the whip. After a number of days – he had stopped counting how many long ago – they finally crossed the border to the east. For a moment he stopped and raised his head, his mouth so dry that his tongue was swollen and clinging to the roof of his mouth.

Stretching before him like a golden ocean was the desert. Dunes rose and fell like frozen waves. The sun beat down mercilessly, trying to burn them to a crisp. They were in Setar.

Chapter 4:
Diverted

Jason squinted through his lashes and his heart sank at the sheer endlessness of sand. The whip cracked across his back and he suppressed a cry. Blood trickled down the newly made cut, tickling him and staining his already dirty shirt even further.

"Only three more days before we reach Umbra," Jason heard one of the men say.

"I think we're stopping at the camp first before we set out toward the city," said another.

"The sooner we get there, the better."

"I agree. The desert has become a lot more unsafe with the rebels about."

"Don't you worry about them. We are in more danger from Abdal than from a bunch of ragged vermin with knives."

Darryn's head snapped up and a hopeful gleam came to his eye. One of the slavers hit him in the face and sneered, "What are you smiling about? Oh, you think that the exiled prince and his rabble will come and save you! Well let me tell you – boy – no one is saving you, understand?"

Darryn glared after the man, a bead of blood forming on his bottom lip.

When the sun started setting the slavers' moods improved considerably. The captives were soon to discover why. A haphazard collection of tents and rough huts seemed to spring up out of nowhere. Two guards were ordered to take the captives away while the rest went off to relax. Jason was thrown into a small cage along with Darryn and Rose. There were five other people being held captive by the slavers: four Setarans and a young Ard-man. The dark-skinned Setarans paid the newcomers no heed, but the young Ard-man lifted his head from his arms.

"Hello," he smiled sadly. "I'd welcome you but we're being held prisoner at the moment."

Jason crawled beside him and rested his head against the cage bars. "Hello."

The young Ard-man could not be much older than Jason, even though he was nearly two heads taller.

"My name's Gabbro by the way."

"Jason," he replied shortly.

Gabbro looked at Darryn and Rose who were both leaning against the side of the cage.

"This is Darryn and his sister Rose," Jason waved his hand in their direction.

"Pleased to meet you," Gabbro smiled, "Or at least I would be if it weren't in this cage."

"How long have you been here?" Jason asked.

"I don't know," he shrugged. "I'm not very good with numbers."

"How did you get here?"

"Well, I was travelling to my aunt's in Tiethe when a bunch of these thugs ambushed me. You?"

"Pretty much the same story."

Gabbro nodded and looked at Darryn and Rose once again. "Are you two from up north?"

Darryn looked up, "Yeah".

"Thought so, you don't look like you're from Bristan."

"When are they taking us to Umbra?" Darryn asked.

Gabbro scrunched up his face in thought. "I think they said tomorrow, but I can't be sure."

Jason buried his head in his arms and blinked away the tears that threatened to spill. Bastian would die and he would have to live the rest of his life as a slave. A large and heavy hand patted him heavily on the back and he fell forward.

"Don't worry; everything's going to be fine!" Gabbro said and helped Jason back up. "We just have to remain hopeful."

"Would you shut up you stupid giant!" one of the Setarans snapped from the other end of the cage. "We're not getting out of this! We're not going to be magically saved! We're all going to be sold as slaves at Umbra in a few days."

Gabbro looked at the man as if he had been slapped in the face. "Sorry," he mumbled and a huge tear rolled down his cheek, making a track through the dust on his face.

The camp was silent except for the snoring of drunken men and the hushed whispering of the two sentries. Jason could not sleep. He dreaded the arrival of the coming day. Every now and then the cry of a desert hound would sound somewhere outside of the camp causing the hairs on the back of his neck to rise. A horse snorted and he sat up. As far as he knew the horses were being kept on the other side of the camp. A pinpoint of light appeared in the darkness. Jason watched it curiously as it made an arc, coming to land on one of the tents. It immediately caught fire and he realised what the thing was. More flaming arrows flew out of the night, landing on tents and hut roofs. Men poured into the open, scurrying about in panic.

"We're under attack!" cried some.

"Rebels!" cried others.

Men in black clothing swarmed the camp, brandished their weapons and yelled like madmen. The other prisoners woke with a start and frantically tried to see what was going on. The leader was the only one on horseback, the rest were on foot. Jason watched in shock as men fell left and right under the attackers. The Setaran captives cheered and praised their saviours. A slaver dropped dead in front of the cage, an arrow protruded from his back. The entire camp was lit up as flames devoured tents and huts. One of the black clad men opened their cage and the prisoners streamed forth from their captivity.

"This way," Darryn said and ran toward one of the larger huts that had not yet caught fire. The air was thick with smoke causing Jason's eyes to water. The heat of the fires was so intense that they could feel it even inside the hut. Darryn and Rose grabbed their swords and Jason salvaged a pistol. Gabbro followed them happily, the corners of his mouth nearly reaching the rocky bumps on his temples.

"What do we do now?" Gabbro asked eagerly.

"I'm not sure," Darryn said. "But we'd better get out of here before this hut burns down too."

They went outside and all the men in black were gathered at the centre of the camp. Darryn walked toward the leader seated on his horse with one hand gripping the hilt of his sword.

"To whom do we owe our thanks for our freedom?" Darryn asked, but he was not smiling.

The man on the horse looked down at the three fair-skinned teenagers and the young giant with a mixture of amusement and curiosity. "I am Prince Sarrid. I lead the rebels against my brother

Malik."

"I've heard of you," Darryn said. "You were supposed to become king, but your brother stole the throne from you."

"I'm not proud of it, but yes."

"Prince Sarrid could you kindly help us return to Tiethe? We are on an urgent mission."

"Gladly, but we will have to return back to the base camp. We'll leave tomorrow at dawn. We should make it back to the camp by afternoon then."

"Thank you."

Sarrid leaned forward and peered hard at Darryn, "Have I seen you before?"

Darryn looked him square in the eye, "No."

He straightened up, "I could have sworn—never mind. We must go before we suffocate from this smoke."

After retrieving the horses and pony, Sarrid's men set up some tents for their night's sleep. There was two tents for Jason and his friends. After thanking the rebels once again, they retired to their tents and fell asleep. They left at dawn for the rebels' base camp. True to Sarrid's word, they arrived at what the rebels call Pel-Umbra during the afternoon. The 'camp' was mostly city ruins with ragged tents set up in between. The rebels were heavily armed and grim looking men who were either patrolling the camp boundaries or practising with their weapons. A man ran ahead of the group to announce the prince's arrival and everywhere men stopped what they were doing to acknowledge their leader. Some bowed while other shouted their greetings.

"Hail, Prince Sarrid!"

"Glad to see you back, Sire!"

The men stared curiously at Jason and his friends, some glared beneath heavy brows. Jason's skin crawled at the sight of so many uncovered blades glinting in the sunlight. He glanced at Darryn who appeared undaunted by the dangerous men. Darryn's face and clothing were extremely dirty. His own probably looked the same.

There were strange things fluttering about through the air in small swarms. They were small and yellowish, but were definitely not butterflies. When Jason tried to get closer they darted away making strange chirping sounds.

"Don't bother, they're sand pixies," one of the men explained. "They can bite like hell!"

"Sand pixies", Jason mouthed in amazement. *Were all the fairy tales true after all?*

They passed through the camp until they arrived at the ruins of the palace. Sarrid dismounted his horse and handed the reins to one of the men. He walked through what once must have been the palace gate, but was now nothing more than a precarious archway of stone and a pile of rubble. Most of the palace had completely collapsed. Only one small part was still safe and usable. This area was made up of a bedroom, small hall that acted as council chambers, and a dining hall. Sarrid took them into his bedroom and bade them to sit down on the rickety chairs around the small table. He called for some refreshments before taking his own seat. They said nothing until a man brought a tray with a jug, goblets and a bowl of dates.

"Please, help yourselves." Sarrid gestured at the tray.

Gabbro took a date between his large fingers, sniffed it cautiously then popped it into his mouth. He pulled a face and spat it into his hand, yet took another nonetheless. Jason poured some of the amber-coloured liquid into the goblets. They reached out and drank gratefully. The drink was cool and soothing as it flowed down their parched throats.

"I don't know your names," Sarrid leaned back in his chair. "And I'm curious to know how you were captured."

"My name is Darryn and this is my sister Rose. This is Jason and—Gabbro."

Sarrid nodded thoughtfully and looked hard at Darryn's face. Darryn stared back with equal intensity. Finally the exiled prince said, "Continue, please."

"We were travelling through Tiethe when the slave traders attacked us. Gabbro was captured similarly."

"What were three teenagers doing travelling alone in Tiethe?" Sarrid continued.

"Our business is our own, but it is of the utmost importance that we get back."

Sarrid had risen and was walking slowly toward the window with his hands clasped behind his back. "I would like to know a little more than that." His voice had taken on a slight edge.

Jason glanced at Darryn and saw his fingers tighten around the arms of his chair. He looked at Sarrid and felt his insides get knotted up.

"You are not very truthful with me Darryn," Sarrid continued.

"What do you mean?" Darryn asked calmly.

Sarrid turned to look at him, "Forgive me, I'm just a little paranoid."

"I understand," Darryn said carefully. "Times are difficult."

"What exactly happened in Umbra?" Jason asked.

Sarrid sighed. "It happened five months ago. My father had passed away after a long and dreadful illness. My brother and I had just returned after visiting the holy city of Katico. The sages came to us while we were still on the second level. First of all, they bowed low to us and murmured 'My Prince'. Naturally we were shocked and worried, so we hastened ourselves up to the palace. They were carrying his body out to the burial room when we arrived."

Sarrid paused in his narration and took a few deep breaths before he continued.

"We grieved for the required nine nights and days. On the tenth day, I left my chamber for the first time, took a bath, and ate a hearty meal. Malik and I were called to the throne room. It was strange to see the golden chair empty. The sages were waiting for us with my father's sceptre and I knew they were to name the new king. They bowed low before me and whispered 'Our King'. I was given the staff, and I fully accepted the responsibility of ruling the kingdom. Malik was jealous of this. It was no secret that he wanted the throne—"

"Wait," Jason interrupted, but quickly remembered who he was talking to. He flushed a deep shade of red. "Sorry, continue."

"No, you were saying?" Sarrid smiled.

"I thought the eldest always inherits the throne."

"Yes, but here in Setar the sages choose which of the king's children inherits the throne. Malik is my senior by three years. As I said, Malik was not pleased by the decision and devised a plot to dethrone me. He somehow built a great following for himself and violently claimed what he called his 'birth right' back. His first act as king was to exile me, thus making sure that I could not do anything to avenge myself. For weeks I wandered the desert and was on the point of starvation until I re-discovered Pel-Umbra.

"Meanwhile the kingdom started falling into ruin. Malik robbed the people of all their money and reinstated the slave trading. His punishments were cruel. He does not know how to run a kingdom and he feels no compassion for his subjects. Very few of our neighbours still trade with Setar, the rest have withdrawn themselves. Out of desperation, a few men still loyal to me fled the city and found me. Gradually more came until I had a decently sized following. Thus, the idea of winning the kingdom back started. At first—because of our small numbers—we kept our attacks secret, small and simple. But eventually word of my rebellion broke out. This caused a great uproar. Notices for a reward on my head went up all over the kingdom. Soldier patrols were instated and more. But my following still grew. We are not enough to attack Malik in open battle, but I am sure that in time we can cripple him enough for me to reclaim the throne."

Sarrid fell silent. He leaned onto the windowsill and stared at his hands.

"I think you may be able to win the kingdom back with a well thought out plan," Darryn said. "You said that it would be impossible to win the kingdom back in a head-on battle, but what if you were to attack the enemy where he expects it the least?"

"Do you have an idea?" Sarrid asked sceptically. Darryn was after all only a fifteen-year-old boy.

"Maybe, but unfortunately we must go back to Tiethe."

Jason squirmed in his seat and stared guiltily at the bowl. Some absent part of his brain noticed there was only one date left. Gabbro reached out and finished it with a content grin on his face.

"What was this idea of yours?" Sarrid asked anyway.

"If someone could just gain access to the palace then the gates could be opened to let the rebels in without any bloodshed and we can then threaten Malik to hand the kingdom back. It's rather simple really, but the trouble is to get in."

"It does sound like a good idea," Sarrid started to pace across the room. "All we need to do is find a way in."

"Are there no alternative entrances into the palace besides the main gate?"

"No."

Darryn rose and paced along with Sarrid. He paused for a moment to ask, "Would it be possible for someone to sneak in disguised as a slave?"

"I don't know. A lot has changed since I left. I think if we held a meeting with my generals we might form a good plan."

Darryn's expression became troubled. He looked first at Rose then at Jason. "Listen, I know your quest is important to you and I will not ask you to forget it or delay it further, but I think I can help out here. I—I'm staying."

Jason felt like he had been punched in the gut. He could not see how he would be able to continue on his difficult mission alone. Darryn and Rose were a comfort to him and he enjoyed their company on the road. "I understand," he said softly.

Gabbro glanced quickly from Darryn to Jason then patted him on the back until he was nearly on the floor. "Don't worry, I'll come with you! I may not be very bright, but I can still help with other things."

Jason gave him a feeble smile. "Thank you, you are very kind."

Darryn exhaled loudly through his nose in frustration. "Isn't there another way, Jason? Couldn't you stay? When we're done here, Rose and I can go with you to find the Dream Keeper. You said yourself you can't do it alone and we could still be of some valuable help."

"Every day I delay is a day closer to my brother's death." Jason replied. "He doesn't have very much time left as it is! I don't even know if he's already dead," his voice failed on the last word.

"Yes, but if this plan succeeds it shouldn't take more than a week or so."

"And if it fails? I'm not willing to gamble my brother's life!"

Sarrid interrupted them, "What are you talking about? You speak of dreams and apparently someone is dying."

Gabbro sat up in alarm, "Who's dying?"

"My brother," Jason said and glared at Darryn. "And I can stop it from happening if only I could get back to Tiethe."

"What are you looking at me for?" Darryn shouted. "It's not my fault!"

"But you promised to help me!" Jason yelled back. "I thought you were my friend."

Darryn swore and threw his head back with his eyes closed. "Jason this has nothing to do with friendship and such and I never promised you anything! Don't you think that maybe you could save more lives by helping us here than by getting to the Dream Keeper first? It is after all one life compared to thousands."

Jason's blood started to boil and he longed to lunge at the blue-eyed boy across from him. "Are you saying my brother's life is unimportant?"

Darryn did not reply. He merely glared at the floor. Tense silence fell upon the little room. Darryn refused to speak to Jason and Jason refused to speak to Darryn. Sarrid was once again peering out of his window. Rose sat silently and expressionlessly. Not a single word had left her lips and she was now examining everyone in turn.

Gabbro hesitantly asked Jason a question, "Why exactly can't you leave your friends here and go to the—whatever you called it alone? Well not completely alone 'cause I want to come with you, but why do you want them to go so badly?"

Jason stopped his angry thoughts and pondered Gabbro's question. "I'm just too afraid to continue on my own and I need help." He looked up at Darryn. "You said you could help me. I'm just a stupid boy from Bristan." But in his heart Jason knew there was another reason, but he could not figure out what it was. Why was he so unwilling to leave Darryn and Rose behind?

"I remember," Darryn said quietly. "And you're right; you won't be able to handle another of those black monsters without us." He swore again and ran a hand across his face. "Why does everything have to be so difficult?"

Darryn flopped down into his chair and frowned into the distance. Jason's fingers fidgeted with the hem of his shirt as he waited for something to happen. Darryn finally looked up and stared straight at him. "You must decide, Jason."

"Me?" Jason asked and his eyes widened incredulously.

Darryn closed his eyes, "Whatever you decide on, I'll stand by you. *We'll* stand by you."

"Please don't do this to me."

There was a knock on the door and all heads turned.

"Enter," Sarrid commanded.

The door opened to reveal a crudely armoured man with several scars across his dark face. He bowed and brusquely said, "Forgive me for the interruption, Your Highness, but we have intercepted a merchant wagon heading toward the city. It's from Corak."

"I'll come and look."

Jason watched Sarrid leave the room. The weight of the decision he had to make rested heavily on his shoulders. When he looked up he noticed that everyone was staring at him.

Jason said. "I don't know what to say. I don't know what to choose."

"Why don't you think on it," Darryn said.

Jason opened his mouth to protest, but Darryn was already leaving. Rose paused for a moment before following her brother out. Gabbro remained with him, still smiling.

"So what are you going to do?"

"I don't know."

Jason wandered alone through the city ruins. Occasionally he came across some of the rebel sentries patrolling the camp borders. He longed to punch something and swung his fist at a broken wall. The stone crumbled further, but he also split his knuckles open. Suppressing a cry, he cradled his injured hand against his shirt. "Stupid, stupid!" he muttered and kicked at the wall causing it to collapse. "What should I do!" he yelled at the empty air. "Tell me!" He sat down against the rubble pile he created. "Everything's going wrong for me, why can't I do anything right?"

"Jason!"

His body stiffened as he heard his name being called. "Yes?" he called out.

"Where are you?"

Forgetting about everything he jogged to where Rose's voice was coming from. "I went for a walk. I hoped it would clear my head."

"You won't have to choose anymore," she said. "Sarrid just heard from the merchants. The border has been closed off. Only those approved by the king may pass."

"What?"

"We can't pass through."

Sarrid and Darryn looked up as Jason slammed into the little room. "Is it true?" he demanded.

"Afraid so," Darryn said grimly. "The only way for us to head south is if we get the kingdom back and reopen the border."

Jason leaned onto the table, glaring at a crack in the surface. "So what was your plan again?"

"Jason, I'm sorry,"

"It's not your fault. Let's just try to fix this as quickly as possible."

"Jason!" Darryn said loudly.

He looked up.

"You have to stop worrying about everything that you can't do anything about. Focus on the things you can change. Now what were you saying, Your Highness?"

"I am holding a council with my generals tonight. You can tell them of your idea then."

"Thank you. Jason, do you want to come?"

"I'll come," he said.

�==◆==⟩

Five rugged men, two teenage boys, a girl, a giant and a prince were gathered around a table in the council chambers. Sarrid was standing at the head of the table looking at the people he called together. A stray pixie had fluttered into the room and was circling Gabbro's head. He tried to swat it away, but it nimbly dodged his hand and continued pestering him.

"Thank you for coming, my good generals," Sarrid said. "I have ordered this meeting for the purpose of formulating an invasion plan against Umbra."

Gabbro leaned toward Jason and whispered, "What does

'formulate' mean?"

Jason opened his mouth to explain, but fell silent as he caught a glare from the nearest general. He had an eye patch.

"As you know it is futile to attack Malik in direct combat, so Darryn here proposed that we somehow gain entry to the palace which would give us an advantage over my brother. Darryn do you mind explaining?"

Darryn rose and Sarrid took his own seat. Looking completely confident and undaunted by the several gazes directed at him he cleared his throat. "As the prince said, it would be a great feat for us if we get into the palace. We could easily avoid battle and a lot of bloodshed, and still win the throne over by either kidnapping Malik or forcing him to hand the kingdom back. Now we have to figure out how to get into the palace without raising suspicion. Taking the palace by siege is completely out of the question and sneaking in is impossible. So we will have to go in disguise."

"We could sneak in as servants," Gabbro suggested.

Darryn opened his mouth to say something, but paused and stared incredulously at him. Instead he asked "What are you doing here?"

"I just thought as long as I'm stuck here I might as well help." Gabbro grinned.

Darryn looked to Sarrid for help who merely shrugged.

"Okay you can help."

The general with the eye patch rose and asked, "May I say something?"

"Certainly, General," Darryn sat down.

"I think to sneak in as servants will be too risky. Ever since one of our spies was found out they have been watched like hawks. Another way would be safer."

"Thank you, General," Darryn said and a crease formed on his brow. "We must find a way that Malik would not suspect or distrust. Maybe even make him welcome us with open arms, like a—dignitary."

Sarrid snapped his fingers enthusiastically. "Exactly! But not just any visitor, an exotic guest from far away who has heard of the mighty Setaran Empire and wishes to pay him respects and shower him with gifts. Malik cannot resist."

"But who must play the part?" asked another general with a vicious scar running from his left temple down to his jaw.

"Someone that Malik will immediately welcome—someone who knows how to play the part and still be able to carry out the mission," Sarrid said and starting pacing up and down the room.

"I know someone who could play the part," Darryn said carefully. "But she's not going to like it."

Rose's normally impassive countenance was disrupted. Her eyes widened and her lips parted slightly. "No," she said firmly. "No, absolutely not! I am not going to seduce some tyrant into handing the throne over."

Darryn looked pleadingly at her. "Please Rose. The king won't be able to resist welcoming you into the palace!"

"That's what I'm worried about."

"And it won't be that simple for her to persuade him to hand over the throne," Sarrid interjected. "At least we have a way into the palace now."

The thinnest of the generals rose. "I have an idea."

"Please, continue General Anjay." Sarrid dipped his head.

"We could send some of our forces with her into the palace posing as her guard. Then, they could open the palace gates for the rest of us and we can take the throne back."

"Excellent idea," Sarrid said.

Darryn nodded his approval. "I don't see what could go wrong."

"We would just have to make sure that the attack doesn't happen too soon," Sarrid said. "We must win Malik's confidence first."

"Now it only leaves—" Darryn turned to Rose who was glaring at him.

"All right, I will do it," she sighed. "But don't get carried away with your idea."

Darryn hugged her with one arm. "I knew you would help us!"

"What are we going to do?" Jason asked.

"Well, the princess will need a personal guard," Darryn grinned. "You, Gabbro and I should stay with her as extra protection."

"I'll arrange for the armour and the men," said General Eye Patch.

"Thank you," Sarrid said. "We will have to steal some clothing for her to wear," he added.

"I'll help with that!" Darryn said eagerly.

"As soon as the preparations are done we start with the invasion," Sarrid said. "Council dismissed."

The generals left, but Sarrid called Darryn back. "Since you are strangers to Setar, I think I should show you the vague outline of Umbra." He produced a map from inside his shirt and unrolled it onto the table. Darryn leaned curiously over it. "As you can see it is fairly simple to reach the palace. Umbra is built in a conical fashion on a set of five levels. The bottom level is where the poor live and where their market is and where the slave trading, fish mongering, begging and so forth happens. The conditions are poor and the environment less than hygienic. It becomes better the further up you travel. The second level is where the real marketplace is. Though not much better in terms of cleanliness and over-crowdedness, it is where all the businesses and trading of Umbra are conducted. The third level is where the middle class citizens of Umbra live and the fourth where the rich, noble and high in rank live. On the very top is the palace."

"Thank you," Darryn said.

Jason followed Darryn outside and a thought occurred to him. "What happens if the plan fails?"

"Don't be so negative, the plan won't fail."

"I'm not negative. I just want to know what happens when an actual fight starts. I don't exactly know how to use a sword."

"I see," Darryn paused. "How about I teach you some of the basics? Let's start tomorrow morning."

"I don't know. I'm sort of a pacifist."

Darryn stared uncomprehendingly at him.

"I don't like fighting," Jason tried to explain.

"I know what it means," Darryn snapped. "I just can't believe it. We'll find you a sword and you will learn to fight. I'm sure the blacksmith will have one. We'll all need new swords anyway if we want to play our parts convincingly."

"Will we have curved swords?" Gabbro asked.

"They're called scimitars and yes we will."

"I hope they'll have a big enough sword for me."

Darryn examined him from head to toe and said. "I hope so too."

Now that it was dark, the pixies were glowing noticeably, looking like giant fireflies. Their yellow lights floated serenely past them and Jason could just make out the tiny, vaguely humanoid bodies. They were undeniably beautiful in their own way. He could not help but admire them.

A female pixie the size of his forefinger floated right up to his face, hovering before his eyes. Nearly everything about her was golden in colour, from her hair to her eyes. Her skin was a lighter shade of gold and it was from there that the light came. She cocked her head curiously as she watched Jason and hesitantly reached out with a tiny slender arm. Jason smiled as he felt the tiny hand on his nose and she smiled back. She then took a lock of his hair in one hand and chirped something. A male pixie approached, chirped at her and she followed him back to the rest of the pixies.

"The fairy tales are real," Jason murmured. He was no longer so sure that it was a bad thing.

Chapter 5:
The Princess of Jaba

The following morning Jason went with Darryn to the rebels' blacksmith to get a sword. The blacksmith was a large and very hairy man who reminded Jason of a bear he once saw passing through the Nameless Wood. He was busy sharpening a vicious war axe when Jason timidly approached. The man looked up at him, glowering from beneath a heavy brow.

"Hmph?" he said.

Jason looked uncertainly at Darryn who gestured for him to continue. "Er, you might not have a sword for me—sir?"

"Harrumph." The man got up with some difficulty and gave the axe to Jason to hold it for the moment. He disappeared into his tent to the sound of metals banging about. Jason eyed the axe's sharp edge nervously and held it away from his body. Darryn leaned against what had once probably been a door frame and grinned at him.

The man returned with several swords, some curving and some not. They appeared to be newly forged and, though unattractive, they were undeniably practical. He put the swords down in a pile and took the axe from Jason. He grunted and gestured at the pile for Jason to pick one up. Jason chose a slim blade with a slightly curving edge and looked uncertainly at the blacksmith.

"How does it feel?" Darryn called.

"Er."

"A sword must feel comfortable in your hand. It has to feel like a part of you and not just as a tool."

"I don't really feel anything," Jason answered and waved the sword vaguely above his head.

"Does it feel too heavy? Is the balance wrong?"

"It does feel like the end is heavier than the handle."

"Hilt," Darryn corrected. "Try another."

Jason picked up another, but it was far too heavy. The next felt unbalanced. He tried sword after sword, but none felt right to him. Eventually he just decided on a light scimitar and, though it still did not feel a part of him like Darryn explained, it was still better than the other blades he had tried. Darryn also chose a scimitar for himself and then led Jason off to a secluded area between the ruins.

"Try to block my attacks. I'll start slowly," Darryn said.

Jason wiped some sweat from his brow and nodded. He awkwardly took on what he thought was a ready stance and held the sword out at arm's length. Darryn sighed and stepped forward. "You look as if you're afraid the sword's going to bite you. You have to be more confident in yourself."

Jason adjusted his grip on the sword and glanced at Darryn, "Like this?"

"That's a little better. Now block my attacks."

Jason blocked the first blow by accident because he instinctively lifted his own blade to protect his face.

"Very good," Darryn said and aimed a blow at Jason's legs. Jason brought his sword down vertically and Darryn's blade made contact and a loud metallic clang. Darryn moved progressively faster and Jason had to concentrate to block each and every one.

When he missed, Darryn would touch him lightly on the spot and say "dead" or "lost your arm" or "lost your leg". But Jason was fast, so he did rather well.

"Move your feet more, see if you can dodge the blows," Darryn said.

Jason lithely ducked beneath a thrust at his throat then stopped a blow aimed at his stomach. Darryn grinned and moved even faster. Soon Jason was out of breath and sweat was pouring down his body. The sun was burning mercilessly down upon them. He started to miss the attacks more frequently and his head started throbbing from fatigue and the heat.

"Let's stop for a while," Darryn said. "I'll see if I can find some practice swords for us."

Jason collapsed onto a large yellow stone, gasping for breath. He felt sticky and hot and his shirt clung uncomfortably to his chest and back. Darryn soon returned with a bottle of water and Jason drunk eagerly. Water dribbled over his chin, rolling down his throat and into his shirt. It was wonderfully refreshing and cooled him off. Then it was back to his training. Darryn had discovered two rusty old swords so blunt they couldn't even cut through bread. They sufficed as training swords for the moment.

"I don't have very long to teach you so you have to work hard and remember everything I tell you," Darryn said. "If you are ever uncertain about an attack, don't do it. The time you spend wondering about it is time where you could lose your life. Try to attack me."

Jason lunged uncertainly at Darryn's chest. The other easily blocked his blow with such ease that the shock caused Jason to drop his sword.

"Another piece of advice: never drop your weapon! No matter

how much your hand smarts. If you can't use your sword hand, switch your weapon to the other. You have a much better chance of surviving than when you have no weapon at all."

Over and over Jason tried to hit Darryn, but all of his blows were deflected as if they were no challenge at all. Jason grew frustrated and moved faster and faster, hitting harder each time.

"Keep your temper in check, Jason. Your attacks are growing wild and reckless."

Jason stopped abruptly and slumped onto his sword. "It's no —use—I can't—do it!"

"Nonsense," Darryn snapped. "You have a lot of talent. And how do you expect to beat me in one morning? It takes practice to be good. I've been training nearly all my life."

"Why?" Jason looked up through his tangled locks.

Darryn ignored the question and said, "Come on, get up. Try again."

With a groan Jason got to his feet and swung weakly at Darryn's stomach. Darryn flicked his sword tip away. "Again, try harder, Jason! Reach within yourself. You haven't shown me your best yet! Try to combine accuracy, speed and power in one blow."

Accuracy, speed and power, Jason said to himself. Accuracy, speed and power. He repeated the phrase over and over. He tucked his sword in close to his body and tensed his muscles like bowstrings. He focussed on the spot that he wanted to strike: Darryn's chest. Jason calmed his breathing and focussed everything on that spot. Darryn's eyes twinkled merrily as he grinned back at Jason. In Jason's mind his friend had become his enemy. He was no longer Darryn, but an evil that must be destroyed. Jason released all the cropped up tension inside of him and shot the sword forward. It was like an arrow being released from the bow. Darryn's eyes widened, his grin transformed into a gasp of surprise. His blade moved up instinctively and just managed to catch Jason's attack, but the force of it knocked him back and he stumbled. It all happened too fast for their minds to fully comprehend.

"That was amazing!" Darryn exclaimed. "How did you move so fast?"

Jason shrugged and stared in wide-eyed astonishment at the blade in his hands.

"If you fight like that you definitely stand a chance against a regular soldier. How about we have a proper sparring match now? Don't worry, I'll go easy on you."

Encouraged by his unexpected performance, Jason's confidence grew. He moved a lot more and struck out without hesitation. The sparring was a little more difficult because Jason had to focus on both blocking and attacking. Several times they stopped with Darryn's sword point tickling Jason's throat or prodding his stomach. He received several bruises and cuts as well. Though Darryn was only putting in a quarter of his usual effort, he was still merciless in his attacks.

"Enough, please!" Jason cried out as his legs buckled beneath him for the sixth time after Darryn rapped him on the shins.

"We'll practise again later today." Darryn waved. "I'll come and fetch you. Right now I have to focus on getting Rose some clothes for her role as a princess."

Jason watched Darryn walk away and tried to get up. He groaned as his legs protested painfully. It was like horse riding all over, except now his front hurt as much as his back. He limped back to the palace ruins and put his sword and practice sword away with his other things. The stench of his own sweat nauseated him and he longed for a bath and change of clothing. Unfortunately, he had no clean clothes left. Looking about the room as if he expected some clothes to appear, he wondered where he could wash up.

"Looking for something?" someone asked and he quickly turned around. Gabbro stepped into the ruinous room.

"You might not know where I could get a wash, do you?"

"I asked one of the men earlier, there's a sort of oasis not far from here. I'll take you."

"Thanks."

"Wouldn't you like some new clothes?" Gabbro wrinkled his nose.

"I would, but I don't have any."

"I'm sure some of the guys will have a spare set of shirts and trousers for you."

Gabbro took Jason out to the scorching heat and walked confidently through the maze of tents and rubble. On the way, he asked a Setaran if he had some spare clothes. He glanced at Jason and nodded.

"They're a little worn out though," he said.

"That's all right," Jason said. "I don't mind."

The man disappeared into his tent and brought out a beige shirt and faded brown trousers. "Here you go."

"Thank you very much," Jason accepted the clothing. "How can I repay you?"

The man blinked in surprise. "I—er, I'll call you."

"Thank you!" Jason called over his shoulder as he followed Gabbro away.

The tents abruptly stopped even though the ruins continued on for some time. Gabbro followed a rocky route that must have been a street once. It was a five-minute walk until they reached an old crumbling fountain. Miraculously, water still bubbled forth from the weird stone creatures' mouths.

"Gabbro, this isn't an oasis," Jason started to say, but thought better of it. Jason took off his shirt and was about to remove the rest of his clothes when he turned around. "Could you please, er, not watch?" he asked.

"Oops, sorry," Gabbro giggled and turned his back on Jason.

He quickly stripped down and stepped into the fountain's pool. The water was surprisingly cool despite the rays of the sun beating down upon the earth. Jason took care not to take too long taking Gabbro in consideration. He scrubbed himself from head to toe as best as he could without soap. When he was done he pulled the clothes on. They felt strange and scratchy to his skin but he ignored this as best as he could. The shirt reached down to his knees and had long sleeves, while the trousers only reached halfway down his calves. He wondered if this was a Setaran fashion.

"I'm done now," he called to Gabbro.

Jason searched about briefly for a tub or anything similar to wash his clothes in. He searched the ruined houses and shops and found a large bucket under a pile of rotting cloth. Filling the bucket at the fountain pool he started to wash his shirt. The moment the cloth made contact with the liquid, the water turned brown. He had to refill the bucket three times just to get his shirt cleansed of all the grime and blood. The process had to be repeated with his trousers and stockings. By the time he was done, he was sweaty and hot again.

"Forget it," he muttered and pulled his boots on, but the leather had become hot in the sun. "Ouch!"

"Looks like you need sandals too."

Back at the palace ruins, one of the generals was busy explaining the plan to the fifteen men chosen to accompany them to Umbra. Jason watched them and felt slightly more at ease about invading the city. These men looked like hardened and tough warriors. In the council chambers Darryn was discussing something with Sarrid, and Rose listened intently.

Later in the day, Darryn found Jason and another sword lesson took place. It went slightly better than the morning lesson, but only slightly. The session stretched on until the sun started setting and they were summoned to dinner. Jason's appetite hand grown tremendously from the hard exercise and ate twice as much food as he normally did. The fare was simple, but satisfying: bread, salted meat and fruit.

The following day, Jason had to practice on his own because Darryn had left at dawn with the raiding party. A caravan from Quatal was sighted moving north-westward toward Umbra. It was a fortunate raid because the caravan was filled with royal clothing. That evening Rose spent most of her time trying on different outfits for her time in Umbra. Jason did not see her in her princess finery yet; they were still being chosen and adjusted to fit her exactly.

It took five days for all the preparations to be finished. All fifteen men chosen for the mission had matching armour that fit them. Darryn, Jason and Gabbro all had their own customised armour to wear and Rose had sufficient clothing for her role.

Finally, the day came that they would set out for Umbra. A royal litter was specially constructed and it waited outside the palace for Rose to climb in. Jason fidgeted nervously with his sword hilt. His armour was heavy and uncomfortable and made him only hotter. Because the armour left his arms and shoulders bare, Jason had to put a special ointment on to protect his skin.

"Here she comes," Darryn said and Jason looked curiously over his shoulder toward the palace entrance.

Rose stepped into the sunlight and Jason's eyes nearly popped out. He had to restrain his jaw from dropping open. The men gathered there started fidgeting and murmuring among each other, and for a reason. Rose was scantily dressed in a silk top that left most of her slim waist exposed and a skirt with cuts running up to her thighs, exposing her long legs. Golden bands glinted around her wrists and other jewellery glittered around her throat and on her breast. Her long hair curled loosely about her face and down her back, giving her an extra exotic appearance. And she was scowling.

"You went too far," she muttered to Darryn before she settled onto the litter. She drew the curtains closed around her so that the men could stop gawking at her. Jason tried to forget the image and turned his attention to the task ahead, but his efforts were futile. His heart was playing drums in his chest, but for the first time not out of fear. Gabbro heaved the litter onto his broad shoulders with little trouble.

"Good luck," Sarrid said. "We'll be outside the palace gates in five days at exactly three hours before dawn."

"I'll remember," Darryn nodded in affirmation. He turned his gaze to the horizon and one of the men shouted, "Let's move!"

Jason walked alongside Darryn at the head of the procession. Behind them was Gabbro with Rose inside the litter. The fifteen warriors followed after them. Someone struck up a marching song somewhere at the back. So far so good, Jason thought.

The armour tired Jason out much quicker, but he pushed on.

He tried to focus on images of Bastian to keep his resolve strong, but his thoughts wandered constantly to the litter being carried behind them.

At midday, a halt was called and everyone had a quick drink of water. Rose did not emerge from her litter, but did accept a water bottle through the folds of one of the curtains. When everyone was slightly more refreshed, they continued north-eastward to Umbra. A warm, dry wind picked up and whipped sand into their eyes. Jason wiped them wearily and peered at the horizon in the hopes that the city might appear. A while later, however, the city emerged in the distance, as if out of nowhere. In the late afternoon, as the sun began to set in the west, they arrived at the wide-open gates of Umbra. Constant traffic moved in and out, beggars, merchants, dignitaries, slaves and more were swarming about the city. Flowing past the city's eastern end was a broad river along which several farms were arranged. Stately boats sailed slowly along the green waters, while smaller fishing boats dotted it everywhere.

Jason admired the vastness of the city in open-mouthed awe, only to remember he was supposed to be a guard a moment later. The top two levels glittered white and gold in the sun with palm trees and other foliage growing so thickly that it looked like a jungle. The palace itself was a magnificently golden domed building with several towers and turrets and more. In sharp contrast to it all, they passed into the streets of Low Umbra. The stench of sweat and rotting food filled the air and people packed the space tightly. Jason struggled to stay calm as thin, raggedly clothed people clawed at him for charity and jostled him about.

Darryn cleared his throat and roared, "Make way peasants! Make way for the Princess of Jaba!"

The effect was instantaneous. The crowds parted, people

trampling each other in the effort to get out of the way, expecting the bite of a whip on their sparsely clad backs. They were very well accustomed to important people passing through, important people with merciless guards. Despite the scattering, the people peered curiously at the litter being carried by what appeared to be a young green-skinned giant. Their voices buzzed loudly as they chattered among themselves. It's like a bees' nest, Jason thought.

Many of the crowd followed the procession through the streets and up to the next level. Word had spread of the exotic princess and soon everyone was clamouring around them to see, while still keeping a respectable space between them and the grim guards. The Umbra Marketplace was as busy as Low Umbra, but notably cleaner and the people were better clothed and fed. Servants doing their masters' shopping stared curiously from the shops and stalls, while the merchants and shop owners admired the expensive armour and accessories greedily. They passed further through until they came to the third level, Middle Umbra.

As they moved through the streets and passed row upon row of houses, Jason noticed that the people following them now were only those that must be of the middle class. That Middle Umbra was intended for housing was obvious. It was quieter here and washing lines stretched high above across the streets between houses. As they progressively climbed higher the houses became more luxurious and the number of storeys increased. The second last level, High Umbra, was green, beautiful and prosperous. Miniature palaces with vast and exotic gardens flanked the paved road. They passed many other important people along the way, who gazed curiously at the drawn curtains of the litter. Jason was disgusted by the fact that people could live in such obvious pleasure and comfort while others suffered extreme poverty not too far away. He could not dwell on the fact, however, for the winding street had brought them before the palace gates.

Darryn and Jason approached the gates and Darryn called out, "Open up for the Princess Shasti of Jaba!"

The guards on the wall leered down at him. "No one is allowed without an appointment."

"The Princess has heard of King Malik's prosperity and wisdom and wishes to grace him with her presence!" Darryn growled at them. "You will open your gates."

The men held their spears ready to throw and the one said, "You had better be careful with that cheeky tongue of yours!"

There was some stirring from within the confines of the litter. "Why have we stopped?" Rose called in a commanding voice with a strange, but alluring accent.

Darryn pretended to be frightened and hurried back to the litter, leaving Jason alone with two spears directed at him. He swallowed nervously, but kept his expression blank, trying to keep his legs from shaking. "My Lady, the sentries refuse you entry," Darryn said in a pathetic voice to the drawn curtains.

"Let me speak to the idiots," Rose said loudly enough for the sentries to hear. They scowled and pointed their spears at the litter.

"But my Lady—"

"Silence, servant!" Rose snapped. She drew the curtains aside and glared up at the sentries. They nearly dropped their spears in astonishment and stared unashamedly at her. "Why won't you let us pass through?" she asked in a dangerously low voice.

"My apologies, Your Highness!" stuttered one of the guards.

"Forgive us, Your Grace!" said the other. Then he snapped, "Open the gates!"

Slowly the great wooden gates creaked open and the procession filed in. The palace grounds were intricately decorated with all sorts of shrubs, trees and plant life, and beautiful statues and ornate fountains. They passed through until they reached the palace building itself. There were several guards everywhere, patrolling through the garden or on the palace wall. At first the guards at the bottom of the steps leading up to the palace stopped them, but after a glance at Rose they nearly fell over each other to open the door. Rose ordered Gabbro to set her down and she climbed graciously out of the litter. From there she walked with Jason and Darryn before her, Gabbro behind her and the remainder of the guard after him into the palace. They found themselves directly in the throne room, from where three doors led off into the rest of the palace. Sitting on the elaborate gold throne, was an immensely fat, short man. He was dressed in lilac silks and wore a strange pink thing on his head sprouting a white feather.

King Malik looked up grumpily and shouted in a ridiculously shrill voice. "Who dares to disturb the king? You have no invitation or appointment!"

The procession halted in the centre of the hall. Jason and Darryn each stepped aside so that Malik could have a clear look at Rose. His tiny eyes widened and a red tongue darted out of his small mouth to wet his lips. Rose gracefully, yet with an air of command, strode toward the little man with her chin high. She stopped a metre from the throne and in a ringing tone said, "Three times now I have been treated with disrespect. I have travelled very far to meet the wise king of the mighty Setar, but it seems I have been poorly misinformed."

With great difficulty the man got out of his throne and waddled toward Rose. He took her right hand in his own pudgy hand. Each finger had at least two golden rings on them. He kissed her delicately (or what he considered to be delicately) on the hand and a flicker of disgust crossed Rose's face. "Please accept my apologies, Dear Princess. These are difficult times for me. My brother is leading a rebellion against me so you must forgive my paranoia."

"I understand," Rose agreed loftily. "Rebellion has always been the thorn in all the great empires' sides."

A small chuckle escaped Gabbro's lips and Darryn kicked him inconspicuously. No one else seemed to have noticed. Jason allowed himself to briefly admire the throne room. It was rather empty of furniture, with only the golden throne and a low table next to it. The walls were of some sort of white stone and were decorated with gold and precious stones in floral patterns.

"You are probably weary after your long journey," the king said. "The servants shall take you to your quarters so that you may freshen up. You are welcome to join me for dinner in my private garden. Ask a servant to show you the way when you are ready."

Rose nodded stiffly, and then said, "And for my guards?"

"They may stay in the barracks for the time being." The king clapped his hands and two maidservants hurried into the hall. They bowed quickly to the king and then to Rose. "You, take the princess to our best room and you, take the guards to the barracks."

The servants bobbed their heads and one left with the fifteen men to the barracks. The other waited with Rose and murmured, "This way, my Lady."

The king interrupted, "What about these three, do they not wish to rest?"

Rose glanced at Jason and the others and said, "These are my personal guards, they never leave my side."

"Hmm, yes." The king smiled, but Jason saw a strange look in his eyes that caused his temper to rise.

The four of them followed the maidservant through the door on the right and down the hallway. When they reached a stairway, she led them up and then left into another hallway. The palace had a horrible sense of endlessness to it, making Jason even more nervous. After a maze of stairways, hallways and corridors, the servant finally stopped outside a set of double doors and bowed. Jason opened the doors and bowed before Rose, and she walked inside. "Bring my luggage," she called out and Gabbro bowed low.

"Yes, My Lady," he turned to leave, but paused uncertainly. Lowering his head to the servant girl's level he whispered, "How do I get back outside?"

She giggled, but quickly composed herself. "This way."

Darryn and Jason positioned themselves outside Rose's door, pretending to keep watch.

"We're finally inside," Darryn whispered. "Now all we have to do is wait for five days before we continue with the plan."

"This is going better than I imagined," Jason admitted.

Darryn peered at him through the corner of his eyes and asked in an amused tone, "Really?"

"I thought it would be harder to get in."

"Me too, looks like Malik is denser than I thought."

"What are we going to do next?"

"We'll go to Malik's dinner and afterward, when he'd gone to sleep, I'll look for the gatehouse or whatever they use to open the gates."

"What if someone sees you?"

"I'll think of something."

A guard walked past them without throwing them a glance

and Jason felt a little more at ease. He fidgeted with the hilt of his sword and looked up and down the corridor. It was lined with doorways on one side, while the other was filled with windows looking out onto the palace gardens. The heat was stifling despite the open windows. A warm breeze ruffled his hair and he sighed. Rose opened the door, disturbing the air. Jason could actually feel it move and shift across his skin. Maybe he was just becoming drowsy—

"Shall we go?" Darryn asked.

Rose nodded but looked like she would rather stay in her room. A servant took them to the garden, which had a lovely view to the east of the city and the river that stretched like a serpent to the northeast beyond the city walls. The garden itself was a sensual delight of scents, sights and sounds. Brightly coloured birds with long tails roosted in bizarre looking trees with aromatic blossoms or mouth-watering fruits hanging from the branches and boughs. The whole scene contrasted with the dry, lifeless waste of desert within view from the little paradise. An artificial stream gurgled through the garden, adding to the din of the birds and the faint noise of the city below. Beside the stream, a blanket was laid out on the lush grass with velvet pillows and a low table set upon it. King Malik was seated on one side with four guards flanking him and he gestured toward the other seat. Rose sat down with obvious dignity and folded her hands in her lap.

"Please, help yourself," Malik smiled and waved his hand at the food piled on the table.

Rose reached for her goblet that was filled with red wine and took a sip. Suppressing the urge to spit out the foul tasting liquid she returned the goblet to the table. Her expression had not shifted from the cool arrogance for one moment. While she dined, the king himself only nibbled on a chicken leg, his piggy eyes watching her every move like a cat would watch a small bird. She ate very little, whether this was just the custom of royalty or whether she was afraid of poisoning or for some other reason Jason did not know. His stomach rumbled a few times, but he ignored it.

Soon, small talk ensued between the king and Rose. They spoke of the politics in other countries and the economical state they found themselves in. Jason was highly impressed by her improvisation skills. If he had not known who she was, he would have easily been fooled into believing she was a princess.

The hour passed with agonizing slowness, as if time had decided to take a nap and return to reality later. Jason almost sighed when Malik finally rose (with great difficulty as you can imagine) and signalled for his guards to follow. Rose stood up and followed him back inside, with Jason and Darryn at her side. Instead of waiting outside her chamber, they went inside with her at her bidding. Jason noticed she was holding something like a rolled up handkerchief. This was unrolled onto her bed, revealing two chicken legs, a strange orange and green fruit, a loaf of bread and some cheese.

"How—?" Jason could not recall seeing her sneak things under the table.

"It doesn't matter," she interrupted.

"I agree," Darryn said with his mouth already full of chicken.

The meal was small, but filling enough to satisfy the boys.

"Thanks," Jason grinned at her.

She answered with a brief smile that did not reach her eyes and went to stand by the window. A little crestfallen by her reply, Jason resumed his position outside the door. Darryn joined him a little while later.

"Don't be bothered," Darryn said. "It's just her way."

Jason shrugged. "I don't mind."

"We'll keep watch in shifts through the night so that they won't get suspicious and so that we both can get some rest. I'll take first watch."

"I thought you were going to explore the palace."

"I would have if Gabbro showed up. Where is he anyway?"

"Maybe he thought he should stay in the barracks."

"Maybe. Tomorrow, I'll speak with him and try to look around. You can also keep an eye out."

"All right. Er, if you're taking first watch, where am I supposed to sleep?"

"On the floor in Rose's room," Darryn said as if it was the most obvious answer in the world.

Jason swallowed and whispered to himself, "Of course."

Chapter 6:
Flight

Darryn had discovered the location of the gatehouse the next day and was hastily making plans for the invasion night. He frequently visited the barracks to keep the rebels updated and to hold quick council with the more experienced men. It was on these outings that Jason was either left alone with Rose or on guard with Gabbro. Sometimes when Rose was in her chamber and Gabbro was "guarding" her, Jason could take some time off and wander through the palace. No one even glanced his way, thinking he was on some errand or patrolling the corridor. He enjoyed his solitary excursions. It gave him the chance to orientate himself in the palace and to think. Often his thoughts strayed to Bastian. How was he? Had his condition worsened, or was he already dead?

It was the day before the invasion was to take place and Darryn was noticeably tense. He had taken on the nasty habit of rapping his hands against his thighs whenever he thought or spoke about the invasion. Jason unexpectedly found himself in the position of the calm, reassuring role that Darryn usually wore.

"Don't worry. Everything will be fine," he told his friend again for what felt like the twentieth time.

"Yes, it will," Darryn nodded and rapped against thigh. "What could go wrong?"

Jason soon found out.

On one of his explorations, Jason found himself in a new part of the palace he had not been to before. Filled with curiosity, he walked down the corridor. He passed a doorway opened to a crack and heard voices inside. He changed his pace so as not to disturb the occupants, but a phrase drifted out and caught his attention.

"What do you mean she's not a princess?"

Jason froze.

"I'm telling you, there's no such place as Jaba," said another voice. "She is a fake."

Jason leaned closer, his face almost touching the wood.

"But why would she—?"

"Don't you see, idiot? It is a trap, cleverly set by the rebels. And they're going to succeed if we don't do anything."

"What are you going to do, march up to His Highness? It's madness—you'll be killed! You're just a guard, remember. Let the rebels take over, they can't be worse than him, can they?"

"Where is your honour?" the first spat. "You are a member of the palace guard and you took an oath!"

"I was *forced* to take an oath. You can take your honour and your king. I couldn't care less if he ends pinned up against the wall by a spear."

Jason's eyes widened as he heard the sickening sound of a blade piercing through armour and flesh. The second man made an odd sound and he could hear the dull thump as his body hit the floor. Luckily he had enough common sense to leave despite his shock at what he overheard. The nearest hiding place was behind one of the tapestries hanging from the walls. He leaped for the nearest, but decided on one further away. The moment the last of him disappeared behind the tapestry, he could hear the door creak open. There was some grunting and the sound of something being dragged across the floor. Jason realised the murderer was going to hide the body of his unfortunate victim behind the tapestry he initially wanted to hide behind. His heart hammered away in his chest as he waited for the man to leave. When he heard nothing but his own breathing, he slipped out. Cautiously, he approached the tapestry across the doorway and peered behind it. The murdered man stared at him with glazed eyes and he felt bile rise in his throat. Forcing his ill feeling down with a shudder, he ran back the way he came to find Darryn.

Jason ran as if one of the Shifters was behind him. Fortune was with him and met no one during his mad dash. The murderer could be anywhere by now, he could even be telling Malik what he thought at that very moment. He burst into Rose's room and through his gasps for air managed to say,

"Must—leave—now! They—after—us—any—moment—quick!"

Gabbro stared blankly at him, but Rose immediately grasped what was going on. She grabbed her pack and rushed into the corridor with Jason.

"What's going on?" Gabbro asked, his brow wrinkling beneath his rocky knobs.

"We have to get out of the city, now!" Jason cried out. "Where's Darryn?"

"I'll go tell him," Gabbro volunteered. "You two go on, we'll catch up with you. If not, see you at camp."

Before either Jason or Rose could protest, Gabbro was gone, loping down the corridor.

"This way," Jason led the way toward the southern part of the palace where he knew there was a window where the palace and palace wall became one. If they could just climb out of the window, they would be outside the palace walls and they could then run toward the city gates. "Act naturally," he advised in a low tone. "We don't know if they know yet."

They nearly reached the stairway leading to the corridor with the window when the sound of footsteps rushing in their direction started from behind.

"Run!" Jason cried and they leaped down the stairway. They jumped the last dozen and tore down the corridor. Harsh voices cried behind them, but they did not stop. The window loomed up and Jason waited for Rose to climb out while he peered anxiously over his shoulder. When she was completely outside he swung himself down, holding onto the windowsill alongside her. They listened to the footsteps die away after they rushed past. Jason sighed and bizarrely wanted to laugh. He chuckled under his breath before peering down. His breath was pulled in sharply. He had not realised the window was so far from the ground. They would have to climb somehow. Rose had already started feeling about for foot and handholds. Slowly they made their way down, carefully searching the wall for cracks or anything that could aid in their descent.

Jason stretched down to feel for the next foothold when he unexpectedly slipped and fell. He cried out and reached blindly. His fingers closed around something similar to a gargoyle and he hung for a few seconds, his eyes wide with fright. Finally after what felt like an eternity of scaling the wall, they were close enough to drop to the street below. Jason landed awkwardly, spraining his left ankle. He was about to celebrate silently when he heard shouts and more feet running toward them. About a dozen soldiers appeared around the corner and ran toward them. Leaping forward he ran after Rose, with his rapidly swelling and painful ankle. They ran until the roofs of the houses from the street below appeared a meter or so from the roadway. A sudden idea came to him and he called out, "This way!"

He jumped across the gap and ended his landing in a quick tumble. Immediately after he got back to his feet and was running down the street leaping from house to house with Rose at his heels. The thundering of the guards' feet and their yelling followed them, neither falling away nor getting closer. The street gradually grew narrower so that the houses on the opposite side were within reach. Changing tactics he flew over the larger gap across the street, hoping that Rose had done the same. On the other side rooftops stretched out for quite a distance, but he did not tarry long. Like strange deer, they bounded toward what they hoped was the city gate along the roofs. The sun was setting behind the horizon like a fiery red orb. The lengthening shadows and increasing darkness scrambled the guards' sense for space, and quite a few times they nearly fell to their deaths onto the dirty streets below.

What are the people below thinking? Jason thought in a detached part of his mind.

The sea of roofs ended abruptly. A street further below distanced the next level's rooftops from them. Jason panicked and looked around desperately. He peered over his shoulder and his heart sank as the guards gained on them by the second. His left hand reached for the sword at his side, but he knew he stood no chance against so many on his own. Mentally he measured the distance between the house they were currently standing on and the one on the other side of the broad gap.

A surge of courage moved through his body out of nowhere and he turned once more to face the guards. No. They would have to risk the jump. He grabbed Rose's wrist and ran a little away from the edge to get a running start. The guards were almost upon them when he released her hand, wheeled around and ran full speed for the edge.

"What are you doing?" Rose yelled, but there was no fear in her voice.

"Trust me!"

He kicked away as hard as he could and he soared. His ankle was throbbing but he no longer noticed it. They flew—and then gravity kicked in and they dropped. Jason yelled and shut his eyes tight as they collapsed onto the opposite roof, rolling a little way after they crashed. Turning around he saw the guards had reached the edge of the other house. Some were peering down at the street, while the others watched them angrily, yelling threats and cursing.

Uncontrollable laughter spilled from Jason's lips. He laughed long and hard until his sides were aching and tears were rolling down his cheeks. They escaped the guards and now they only had to reach the gate before it closed. Once they calmed down, they stood up and continued at a more relaxed pace. Jason could not resist the temptation to turn around and wave at the fuming guards. But they were already running back the way they came to call reinforcements or to chase them by another route.

By the time the guards had reached the house where the two had escaped them, they were long gone and probably already past the gate.

———⊳◆⊲———

Gabbro thundered down the corridor, knocking man and woman out of his way. He nearly crashed into Darryn as he was coming up to see them.

"We have to leave!" Gabbro exclaimed.

"Why? We're so close now!"

"Jason said we must, he sounded really serious."

"Are you sure?" Darryn asked and lifted a brow.

"Yes, now let's tell the others!" Gabbro grabbed him by the arm and started dragging him back downstairs, but Darryn struggled and squirmed in his grip.

"Let me go! Why should we leave?"

A couple of guards came running down the corridor towards them yelling, "Halt!"

Darryn needed no more explanation or persuasion. But instead of running, he and Gabbro rushed at the guards. A brief fight ensued, but the five guards stood no chance. Afraid of what might be going on down at the barracks, Darryn and Gabbro rushed down stairs and through corridors. They sneaked past a room where a group of guards were discussing how to cut off the exits before continuing the race. The palace grounds were swarming with guards and the two barely had time to duck into a nearby bush outside the scullery's door. The thorns pricked their skin and tore their clothes, but they hardly noticed the discomfort as they tried to see the barracks.

"It's hopeless; they're probably all captured by now. We have to warn Sarrid," Darryn whispered.

"But how will we get out of the city?"

"Let's wait until its dark. It'll be easier to sneak away then."

They did not have to wait that long. A loud racket caused them to jump and nearly give their positions away. All the guards ran into the direction of the noise. Darryn and Gabbro took the opportunity to rush for the palace gatehouse. Once inside the little room, they bolted the door. While Darryn worked the mechanism, Gabbro peered through the window.

"Hey, it's the others!" Gabbro called.

"What?" Darryn paused and tried to look past Gabbro's bulky frame.

Sure enough, the rebel soldiers escaped the barracks and valiantly fought their way through the guards. They were now fighting for their lives.

"We need to open the gate!" Darryn grunted as he leaned all his weight against a lever.

"Let me," Gabbro gently pushed him away, throwing him across the room. The lever shifted easily under his persuasion and the gate opened. Unbolting the door they ran outside, yelling to the rebels, "The gate! Go through the gate!"

Some heard and others just followed them. Breaking free from the fighting, they ran through with guards in hot pursuit. People scattered out of the way in the streets, watching the strange chase wide-eyed with great interest. Some even ran after them, cheering the rebels on. One or two guards broke away to punish these unfortunates, but the race continued.

"We can't possibly make it!" Darryn yelled, yet he was grinning broadly.

Gabbro just nodded, too out of breath to speak.

What they needed was a miracle. Unexpectedly, that miracle came in the form of a cart piled high with goat manure. Gabbro accidentally stumbled into the poor man pushing it, who lost control and sent the cart flying into the ranks of the pursuers. They scattered to avoid the smelly missiles, but most of them crashed straight into the cart. Utterly disgusted and with their pride wounded, the guards abandoned the chase for the moment to complain or grumble loudly about the state of their uniforms and the smell.

"Great work, Rocky!" Darryn called out.

Gabbro just smiled.

The crowds swallowed them up and the guards struggled to find them in the throng. Darryn took advantage of this and weaved toward the city gates where the news of the imposter princess had not yet reached. The gates stood wide open. Gabbro followed as best as he could, but he stood out among the bustling bodies which made him an easy target. The rebels had slipped outside along with the outgoing traffic and ran into the desert toward camp. Darryn was inside the gateway and he glanced over his shoulder. Gabbro was close behind wading through the throng like a swimmer battling a strong current. Once the young Ard-man reached him they ran outside together, leaving the smelly city behind along with their hopes of victory against Malik.

It was well after sunset when Darryn, Gabbro and the fifteen rebels arrived at Sarrid's camp. At first they were denied entry, but when their identities were sorted out they were taken to see Sarrid. Darryn briefly informed him of what happened. Sarrid was quiet for a long while after Darryn had finished.

"Our situation has not improved then," he said finally. "I do not blame you at all. It was just a stroke of misfortune against us. We'll just have to form a new plan."

"I must also warn you, Prince," Darryn said urgently. "We have to leave as soon as possible before Malik sends his men after us. If they find us here, we will be slaughtered."

"Yes," Sarrid stared blankly into the distance. "We'll leave tomorrow at dawn."

"Has my sister arrived with Jason yet?"

"Who?" Sarrid blinked and looked at Darryn.

"My sister, Rose, and Jason, have they arrived yet?"

"Oh, no, they have not. I thought they were with you."

"No," Darryn's brow creased with worry. "But they're probably on their way."

"If they do not return by the second hour after dawn, then I am afraid we must leave without them."

"I know," Darryn walked away.

———◆———

Jason was quite certain that they were lost. Nothing but the desert could be seen, stretching endlessly in all directions. Because the sun had set he no longer could rely on her bright face for direction. The stars in the sky could not help him either. They were so alien in this dry, sandy world that he could not even find familiar constellations, much less figure out which way was north. Far behind them, like some bizarre glowing beehive, Umbra glittered faintly. They had managed to slip out of the city gates with little difficulty and started running in the direction where they guessed Sarrid's camp lay.

Stumbling a little, Jason winced as his left ankle shot out waves of pain. Every step he took worsened the swelling. Soon he would be unable to walk.

"Can we find somewhere to rest for the night?" he asked.

Rose nodded, glancing at his ankle. "It will need to be bound,"

"I know," he said through gritted teeth as he brought the injured foot down again.

They were about to settle down at the foot of a large dune, when Jason's sharp eyes caught something not too far off.

"What's that?"

Rose peered into the gloom in an effort to see what he was pointing at. Curiosity won over fatigue and pain. Jason limped toward the oddity to see it up close. When they neared it, they saw it was a collection of pillars and stone slabs. Their surfaces were smooth from centuries of wind and sand blowing across them. In the poor light of the moon the boulders looked eerie and black against the almost ghostly mist twining about at their feet.

"What is this place?" Jason whispered. A shiver travelled up his spine as the wind started to blow.

"The Spirit Mists," Rose replied in a low voice. "The Setarans believe that spirits dwell in these mists and that the gateway to the spirit world lies in places such as this."

Goose bumps formed on Jason's arms and legs and he rubbed them to shake away the uneasy feeling.

"What are these table things?"

"It is rumoured that a barbaric people made human sacrifices on them."

Jason peered uneasily at the nearest slab and he almost imagined seeing a dark stain on the surface. He swallowed and managed to ask, "How is the mist formed?"

Rose shrugged.

"Shall we rest here until morning?" she asked when no more questions came.

"Here?"

"Yes, it is a little sheltered from the wind."

"All right," Jason said with false bravado.

They settled with their backs against one of the slabs. The mist curled around their legs and around their middles, causing them to shiver slightly. Even though Rose seemed unaffected by the ghostly place, Jason was fairly spooked. His ears were strained to catch any sounds and his eyes darted about. Normally he did not believe in ghosts, but something about the place, the mist, the pillars – was almost unhealthy, unwholesome.

"You never told me your favourite colour," Rose said unexpectedly, causing him to jump.

"What?"

"You asked me what my favourite colour was," she said, with a hint of humour in her voice.

"Oh yes, at the tavern," Jason recalled.

"So— ?"

"Er," he mentally went through all the colours he knew and then he replied, "green, I suppose."

"Why?"

"Maybe because this place has so little of it, so little life, so little colour."

They fell into silence once more. Jason shivered a little from the cold and wished that he had his cloak with him. "What am I doing here?" he asked himself silently. "I set out to save Bastian and now I am stuck in a desert with no way out. I don't think I've known what to do since the moment I started this mad quest." He inhaled deeply, then released the air with a large sigh.

A tiny pinprick of light appeared and floated toward them. It was a sand pixie, its tiny body shining brightly from within. Jason reached out toward it and it fluttered away.

A small smile appeared on Rose's face, though he did not see it. In a serious tone he asked, "Do you think I can succeed, that the Dream Keeper exists?"

Her smile faded and she regarded him with her dark, intense eyes. "I don't know."

He hugged his knees to his chest and rested his chin on them. "It's just so hard," he closed his eyes and his posture relaxed. Soon he was fast asleep despite the mists pouring around him with ghostly tendrils.

"Jason," Rose whispered beside his ear and he lifted his head. Bright sunlight shone down upon them. Even in daylight the pillars and slabs were dark and threatening and dark stains covered them on all sides. The sand glittered with a blinding intensity so that Jason had to screw his eyes to see. Sitting up he looked around and his gaze fell upon a very strange sight.

Five odd men stood before them. What made them so strange was that they were all made of sand. Everything from their heads, limbs and body to their robe-like clothing was made of constantly moving and shifting sand. Rose was facing the strange figures and holding a knife with a long thin blade. Jason scrambled to his feet and drew his weapon. His scalp prickled and his pulse quickened. The foremost creature lifted its hand and a spray of sand erupted from its palm. Jason dodged to the side while keeping his gaze fixed on them. One of them lunged at Rose and she swiped at its right arm. The severed part fell and the sand grains blew away on the breeze before they could touch the ground. The creature looked at the sandy stump and slowly an arm started to rebuild itself.

"What the hell!" Jason yelled.

"They're Sand Weavers," Rose said calmly. "They can control the sand."

"So I've noticed! What do we do?"

"Survive."

"What?" His voice went up an octave. One of the Sand Weavers threw a solid-looking ball of sand toward him, but Jason knocked it aside with his blade. "We can't kill them?"

She did not answer. She was too busy battling the Sand Weaver that had re-grown its arm. Jason defended himself from thick yellow limbs and missiles of compacted sand thrown at him. His muscles were tiring, the heat and the armour taking their toll on him.

"I can't – do – this – much – longer!" he gasped. His eyes were full of sand, his hair was full of sand and he tasted nothing but sand on his parched tongue.

The sand beneath his feet suddenly started shifting and his balance wavered. Looking down, he saw to his horror that he was slowly sinking into the desert. Struggling violently against the pull he forgot about the Sand Weavers. Suddenly it went black and he struggled no more.

Rose was concentrating on both the Sand Weavers and her rapidly disappearing lower body. The sand burned her bare legs and chafed her skin as she struggled. She knew that soon she would also be knocked unconscious like Jason, but she was going down fighting. One of the Sand Weavers extended its arm and hit her in face. The rough texture had cut her skin, but she hardly flinched. With lightning speed, she was hacking, slashing, cutting, and severing limbs left and right only for them to return with a vengeance. Her throat was dry and raw from breathing and swallowing sand. Every breath burned.

She was nearly down to her knees in sand. With her mobility restricted, her chances of survival were slim. The Sand Weavers towered over her and Jason was nearly completely buried in sand. She just hoped he could breathe.

The Spirit Mists, though no longer the place of gruesome rituals and neither the dwelling of ghosts, was the abode of the Sand Weavers. And they hated intruders.

Further and further Rose sank until she no longer could use her arms. She glared at the creatures standing over her, already feeling her chest become constricted by the weight of the sand. Jason was out of sight and was soon going to die from lack of air if not from sand in his lungs. One of the Weavers knelt down before her, appearing as if it was sinking itself. She knew what was coming and closed her eyes, gritting her teeth.

The Weaver rose back to its full height and stared at the unconscious girl. Turning around it and its kin walked away, dissolving into thin air as they went.

Chapter 7:
The Forgotten Palace

Coughing and gasping for air, Jason woke up on a smooth cold floor. He was completely disorientated. Expecting sand and heat, he was met with a distinct and comforting coolness both from the air and the floor. After rubbing his eyes to get rid of the sand and the scratchy irritation, he looked around. He was in a wide hall of some sorts, with nothing but a wide stone basin at its centre. The floor was tiled with large black squares, veined with white and the walls were ribbed with emerald green pillars leading up to the high ceiling. The ceiling was a magnificent feat of workmanship, masterfully created with various shades of blue and it had a strange sort of depth to it. It was like staring into space.

When Jason had completed the examination of his surroundings, his thoughts returned to the fight with the Sand Weavers. What happened after he was knocked out? Where was Rose and was she all right? How did he get into the strange hall?

Stiffly and shakily he got to his feet, sand pouring from within the folds of his clothes and from underneath his armour. He winced when he touched his sprained foot to the floor. His side felt unusually light and he found that the curved sword was gone. Limping toward the basin he found it filled to the brim with water. A little way beyond the basin was something previously obscured from his view. His heart leaped inside of his chest and he shuffled toward the heap on the floor.

Rose was still unconscious, but breathing. Her body was dusty with sand and her face and arms scratched from the fight, with a particularly nasty cut just above her right brow. Despite all of this she was still breathtakingly beautiful. Jason sat down before her and wondered if he should wake her. Her face looked different without the usual hardness and guarded expression. He liked it better this way. She looked younger, more her age. *I wonder how old she is*, he thought. *Probably not much older than I am.* Absentmindedly, he reached out to brush a curl away that had fallen across her face. His fingers left a trail through the dust on her brow.

Rose stirred and her eyes opened, two dark blue pools that could pierce the soul with their intensity. She blinked a few times and slowly sat up. Her face took on the usual hard expressionless mask as she took in her surroundings. It took a while for her gaze to settle upon Jason. He smiled at her, but she did not return the gesture.

"How did we get here?" she asked.

Jason shrugged. "I just woke a moment ago myself."

She looked around her again, this time looking up at the ceiling. He followed her gaze and stared at the blue space. Looking away he started limping back to the basin. Dipping his hand into the cool water he scooped some of it into his mouth. He almost groaned with pleasure as the delicious liquid rolled across his tongue and down his throat. Dunking his head into the water he drank greedily until his stomach was about to burst. When he finally withdrew, his chin was dribbling and his shirt beneath the armour was soaked. Rose had not left her spot; she was still gazing at the ceiling. An idea came to Jason and he started removing his armour. Once the heavy things were off he tore a strip from his shirt and dipped it into the water. He rinsed the piece of cloth out to wash away most of the sand before taking it back to Rose.

"Here, you should clean that cut before it gets infected."

She accepted the dripping token and stared at it for a second or two before looking up at him. "Thank you," her tone had a hint of surprise in it.

"What are friends for?" he smiled.

"Friends?"

Once again his smile was wiped away by her strange behaviour. "We're not exactly strangers and I hope we're not enemies, so we must be friends," he said.

She started dabbing at the cut on her brow with a thoughtful expression on her face, a nice change from the usual blankness.

"I've never really had friends before," she said quietly.

"Why not," Jason leaned a little closer.

"Circumstances," she shrugged. "My father..." her voice trailed off.

"He must be an unpleasant person from what I hear."

"Unpleasant is an understatement. He rules my life, decides my every action and if I disobey, his punishments are severe. That's why we run away so much."

"You ran away before?" Jason urged her to continue.

"Darryn and I have been running away since we were twelve years old," a small smile appeared as she reminisced. "Our uncle found us while he was out on a—" she interrupted herself. "While he was out on a trip. We were punished for our misbehaviour, but soon we ran off again."

"But you were caught?"

"The first few times yes, but we started travelling farther

away and we got better at not getting caught. We always go back though," and she fell silent.

Jason contemplated her words. The little insight he gained on her life only increased his curiosity. "Why do you keep going back? Why don't you just stay away?"

She sighed heavily, her hands in her lap, fumbling with the now dirty cloth. "It's—complicated."

When no more came forth he decided to leave her alone. Slowly he got to his feet and re-examined the room. There appeared to be no doors or windows or any other visible exits. How they got there was a mystery. Jason looked up at the ceiling as if to find an answer among the swirling shades of red.

"The ceiling is changing colour!"

Rose followed his gaze upward, "I know. I've been watching it."

"I wonder what it's made of because I don't think its stone."

He limped around in search of any hidden doorways or anything that could help them get out of the strange hall. After he circled the basin for the tenth time he gave up and sat back down. Rose was cupping something in her hands close to her face and was staring at it with a faraway look on her face.

"What's that?" Jason asked.

"My locket," she replied and opened it. A pretty lullaby started playing softly.

At the back of Jason's mind his memory tugged annoyingly at him.

I know that song, he thought and his brow creased in concentration. *Where did I hear it?*

Somehow the music started echoing around the hall, growing in volume and intensity. But it no longer sounded like the notes of a tiny music box, but more like a glorious melody. Jason listened in awe as the music flowed around him. The air was full of it, moving in rhythm to it. The music had a sad undertone and the melody was haunting, it still echoed on through the mind even after it stopped.

"How?" Jason whispered.

How? How? How? HOW? His voice echoed all around, but instead of like a regular echo it started softly, growing in volume until it was thundering from the walls and ceiling.

"ECHO!" he bellowed. Nothing happened.

"How strange, it only echoes soft sounds." He softly hummed a tune and slowly the sound started to be thrown back at them, growing louder, but also somehow more complex. His voice was magically transformed into a symphony of melodies entwining each other, creating a more complex tune around the original. It sounded deeper, richer. "A Hall of Music," he breathed and the words became tangled amidst the still resonant music.

When the last note died out, the silence felt oppressing and heavy on their ears. A sudden surge of fear travelled through Jason from out of nowhere. Where were they? How did they get stuck in such an obviously magical place?

"How do we get out of here?" he asked Rose.

"The same way we got in I suppose,"

"Yes, but from where was that?"

They started walking through the hall, feeling the walls, touching the pillars, scanning the floor. Nothing. Their search proved futile. Jason grew agitated; his limp became pronouncedly impatient. It was a riddle they had to solve, without any clues to guide them. Finally he stopped, leaning with his head against a pillar and his eyes closed. *The basin.* A random thought directed him. He turned his head until the stone basin was visible in the corner of his eye. Maybe there was something underneath it. He approached it and knelt down to look underneath it. There did not appear to be anything, but he had to know for certain. Pressing his back against it, he braced himself and pushed with all his might without using his sprained ankle. Inch by inch it moved. He pushed until he collapsed from exhaustion. Looking around he saw the basin had moved several centimetres, revealing a black slit in the floor beneath it.

"Rose," he called. "Come look at this!"

When she looked, they pushed the basin together. With the extra help it moved a little faster. Water sloshed over the sides, making the floor dangerously slippery. Jason slid once and landed on his back with a grunt. Eventually they managed to clear the opening halfway of the basin. They could not push it any further for fear of falling down the black hole.

"This can't possibly lead outside," Jason panted.

"Still, it's a way."

"It can't be safe though, what if it's a straight drop? We could break our necks."

Rose crouched beside the hole and tried to see through the darkness. Looking over her shoulder at him she said; "I'm going to lower myself down, hold onto me so that I don't fall."

"No," Jason said sharply before he even registered the thought.

A flicker of annoyance passed over her features.

"I'll do it, besides I'm a little taller," he added lamely.

She stared at him for a few seconds and he was afraid that she might object. But she rose fluidly and stepped aside. He took her place and lay down on his stomach with his feet just protruding over the edge. Slowly he pushed himself backwards, lowering his body down. Rose kneeled in front of him and grasped one of his hands in case he fell. Her fingers were cool and smooth against his skin. As he made his way he carefully groped about with his feet, gritting his teeth every time the injured foot met the hole's wall.

"I think I can feel a sort of bend," he said after his entire body from the chest downward was in the hole. "It's definitely sloping, maybe it's a tun— AAGH!" His feet slipped against the side of the sloping, slippery smooth tunnel and he fell. Rose's grip tightened painfully, but even so his hand slipped away and he was gone down the hole. She hurried forward and peered vainly into the blackness where he just disappeared.

"Jason?" she called.

Only his rapidly disappearing cry answered. With a sigh, she nimbly lowered herself down until her feet touched the side. She too slipped and was suddenly shooting down a tunnel of darkness that twisted and turned maddeningly. All of a sudden the tunnel opened out into a wide empty space with bluish light, nearly five meters from the ground. The ground below approached rapidly, too fast for her to even assume the correct position to increase her chances of survival. Instinctively her arms went up to protect her face. *Thump!* She crashed into something unexpectedly soft and warm.

"Ouch," Jason wheezed.

Rose quickly got to her feet and helped him up. "Are you all right?"

He nodded but his eyes were out of focus.

"What happened, did I fall on you?"

He nodded dazedly and rubbed his stomach.

"Why didn't you move? I could have killed you."

He ran a hand through his hair a little embarrassedly. "I sort of found out."

In the dim blue light, Rose noticed the entire left side of his face was grazed and bruised. Catching her glance, he said, "I landed on the sand heap over there," and pointed at a large mound of sand that appeared white in the strange light.

The place they found themselves in was something like a mixture between a large hall and a cave, where the natural and the constructed wove into each other as one. The walls were made of large blue (or maybe it was some other colour, they could not tell) slabs of stone, the floor had an icy appearance to it, stalagmites grew from the ground, transforming into pillars which then merged with the stalactites hanging down. Not all of the stalagmites became pillars and not all of the pillars joined with stalactites. The blue light seemed to be coming from the floor, giving everything a surreal appearance. This room was larger than the one they came from, the furthest wall could not be seen through the forest of stone.

Out of curiosity, they started to explore the place, admiring the extreme delicacy of the carvings that adorned the pillars or wandering like a person locked in a dream among the stalagmites. Rose approached the sand mound and circled it while Jason was progressively making his way to the other side of the cavernous hall. They rejoined near the centre and continued to the far side together.

A large, gilded archway at the mouth of a large tunnel signalled their exit, but as they approached it shadows appeared on the walls of the corridor beyond it. Jason froze with chills running up his spine and Rose had to drag him behind a stalagmite before he was seen. From their hiding place, they watched a curious assembly of Sand Weavers enter. They differed slightly in height, but these were both taller and leaner than the Weavers that had attacked them previously. They moved with an odd grace, sand falling onto the floor like droplets of water from a duck. There were probably two dozen in total. When they disappeared from sight, Jason and Rose crept forward toward the next stalagmite while keeping an eye out for the creatures. They darted from hiding place to hiding place until they were parallel with the archway. Jason was about to make a run for it, but Rose stopped him.

"Let's see what they're doing," she whispered, forgetting that the previous hall echoed such sounds. Fortunately nothing happened.

"Why?"

"I don't know," she replied and crawled forward. Without a choice, he followed her.

They went forward until they were very close to the sand mound. From their hiding place they could see the Sand Weavers stand in a circle around the mound. Leaning slightly forward with their arms outstretched, sand started leaving their bodies into the mound. All of it was being channelled through their arms, where the sand poured like water from a fountain. The mound grew ever so slightly as the creatures poured their substance into it.

Jason's eyes were fixed on the bizarre ritual. What did the creatures look like under all of the sand? Were they invisible phantoms that need the sand to take on a visible shape? The idea made his skin crawl.

A bare foot became visible with the figure standing the nearest. Soon sand was also travelling up its other leg. Two bare legs protruding from beneath a sand body looked rather odd. Then the sand started creeping along its legs, up its middle and down its arms until its whole body was clear from the stomach downward. The sand from its head started to move down its neck and shoulders toward its arms. The same was happening with all of the others.

With all the sand gone, the figures looked very different. They were dressed in simple tunics and leggings with their feet bare. All of them had the same athletic lean build. Their faces were different, yet somehow also alike. Their features were sharp and beautiful, above their intelligent eyes their brows slanted slightly downward. Nearly all of them had long, straight sand coloured hair. Some of them had their hair tied back, revealing slightly pointed ears. There were both males and females among the group.

A light hand touched Jason's shoulder. He turned around, expecting to see Rose. His blood ran cold and his throat tightened. A robed figure towered over him, his other hand on Rose's shoulder. It was one of the pointy-eared creatures around the sand mound. Though his face appeared ageless, wisdom radiated from his grey eyes. Slowly Jason stood up, aware that the attentions of the other creatures were now upon him.

"Who are you?" asked the person in a calm even voice.

"Jason, sir," he managed to say.

"And you?" he asked of Rose.

She did not answer.

"Very well," the person sighed. "You do not have to answer."

"Please sir," Jason stuttered. "Don't kill us."

A chuckle bubbled over his lips. It was a lovely sound like a brook in a forest glade. Jason felt some of his tension disappear.

"Why would we kill you?" asked the person with genuine curiosity on his face.

Jason's mouth flapped open and shut, but no words came out.

"You are hurt, come." The person gently pushed them back toward the archway while the other creatures followed.

The tunnel was lit by spark cylinders in sconces on the walls. Jason marvelled at their beauty, though he could not stare directly at one too long before his eyes hurt from the brightness. The robed figure's hands were deathly white on their shoulders, whether because of the lighting or if it was naturally so, Jason did not know. They stepped into another hall, but it was more like the Music Hall in appearance than the blue hall. Several doorways branched out of this room into various directions.

"We'll speak in the library," the robed person said. The other creatures went their own ways while Jason and Rose were led away.

The person's skin was indeed very fair, but not unhealthily now that Jason could see him in natural light.

The library was an enormous room, made up of three storeys that stretched seemingly into infinity. Rows upon rows of shelves stood lined with books, scrolls, tomes and any other form of written word. In the centre of the spacious library was a circular open space with tables for reading. The room was well lit, but the source of the light could not be identified by Jason.

The light pressure on his shoulder disappeared as the person stepped around the table and took a seat on the other side. Jason and Rose sat down opposite him and looked around at the magnificent collection of knowledge around them.

"I am Fven," the person smiled at them.

"Fven," Jason repeated, feeling the odd word on his tongue. Hesitantly he ventured a question. "Pardon me for asking, are you fairies?"

Fven laughed as if Jason had told a hilarious joke, but then he stopped so suddenly and a very queer look came into his eyes. "No, we are not fairy. We are called the Fae."

"Fae means fairy in the old Arden tongue," Rose said quietly.

"Indeed, but then we must look further," Fven said eagerly. "For in the old Arden tongue, which I believe is still spoken in some of the more remote regions of the kingdom, correct?"

He waited for Rose's affirmative nod before he continued. "The word originally meant magical or of magic which was later interpreted as fairy-like, as the humans for a time believed only fairies possess magic which led to the overall naming of any creature of magic a fairy. This influenced the western speech which is why you humans so easily make the mistake."

"All right…" Jason said slowly. "So, you can use magic?"

"In a certain sense, but not as you humans consider or think magic to be. We do not say incantations or draw magical circles, which are rituals of Dark Magic anyway. We are things of magic, we are made up of it, it is in our blood, our hearts, our minds and souls. Humans believe magic is the control over supernatural abilities, but in truth, true magic is the communication between a creature of magic and the element of magic it is most closely related toward. Do you understand?"

"Not really," Jason admitted.

"Think of magic as a living creature. You can ask it to do something and it will do it for you. But only if you have a relation to that specific element of magic, otherwise it will not do anything or even turn on you."

"What of Dark Magic?"

"No," Fven became grave and serious so suddenly that it was almost as if he had put on a mask. "That is a dark subject we are forbidden to delve into."

"Are Shifters Dark Magicians?"

"No, they are things of Shadow. It is unclear whether the stuff is magic or if it is some other form of power since it is not from our world. Their ability to shape shift is part of their anatomy as Shadow Beings. Also, magicians cannot do or use magic. They only create the illusion. And wizards are not human. I have forgotten what humans are called who can speak magic…"

"Where exactly are we?" Rose asked.

"In the Forgotten Palace."

"Forgotten?" Jason asked.

"You are the first living beings aside from us to enter here. We are estranged from all life outside the palace, including our own kin who reside to the west."

"There are more of you?"

"Oh yes, the others are hidden just as we are. Their civilizations are protected and out of reach from humans. To tell the truth, you are trusted very little by most magical people."

"Why are you estranged?"

Fven sighed a deep and sorrowful sigh, "This palace was once a great and glorious building. I and a select few have been chosen to find the legendary Great Library of the desert, for many secrets are contained in these shelves. Through travelling and exploring we located this temple. Beautiful it was to behold and we decided to reside in it. One day a vicious sandstorm like none Setar had seen before swept across most of the desert accompanied by earthquakes. The palace was swallowed and us with it. We had to adapt and gradually we started to learn the language of sand."

"We're under the sand?"

"Yes."

Now made aware of the tons of sand weighing down on them

Jason felt as if his lungs were not getting enough air.

"The other Fae probably think we are dead," Fven concluded sadly.

"Why don't you visit them?" Rose asked.

"The border is closed off for all creatures. We cannot return."

"We have the same problem; we can't get past the border either," Jason muttered.

"The Glassmaker does not stop humans from passing," Fven frowned.

"What's the Glassmaker?"

"It is the creature that guards the border. We name it so because it breathes flames of such intense heat that several Sand Weavers and Fae have been turned to glass."

Jason pondered Fven's words. "Do you think Malik can control this Glassmaker?" he asked Rose. "He could be using it to close the border."

"That is possible," Fven interjected.

An idea started to take root in Jason's mind, but he did not say anything yet. Hesitantly and carefully he ventured another question.

"Do you know about the Dream Keeper?"

Fven's expression changed into something unreadable. He scrutinised Jason's face intently and was silent for a long time. In the corner of his eye Jason saw Rose's knuckles whiten ever so slightly around the arm of her chair.

"The Dream Keeper is a well-known legend among my race. How have you come to know of it?"

"A stranger told me."

Fven's eyes narrowed slightly. "This is interesting…"

"What exactly is it?"

Fven rose from the table and walked toward one of the numerous bookcases. He silently scanned the shelves before moving on to the next. Eventually he stopped, closing his eyes. He placed his left fore and middle fingers to his brow, creasing in deep thought. Jason became aware of a distant whispering sound that seemed to be coming from everywhere. His hair was ruffled by a faint breeze and some dust particles on the table surface moved. Rose's posture stiffened beside him and her eyes were fixed upon Fven.

"What's going on?" he whispered.

"Magic," Rose replied.

A small tornado gradually formed from the swirling winds and hovered a few feet above the ground. Suddenly it whizzed off into the bowels of the library. Occasionally it returned, only to speed off into another direction. After some time it returned, slowly, with a thick book floating centimetres above it. The tornado hovered before Fven, and as he opened his eyes the winds disappeared and the book dropped into his expecting hands. The Fae put it before Jason on the table.

The book was beautifully bound in a dark leather-like material. A glowing symbol etched into the cover threw a blue pattern onto Jason's face from its glow. He reached out and gently opened it. The pages seemed to radiate with their own light, the words glowing in golden ink. At first they seemed to be written in a different language, but the letters shifted and changed and became recognizable. *The Isle of Dreams*, he read. Just after he finished reading the title, the letters swirled and formed two new words, a name to be exact: *Jason Thorn*. He breathed in sharply and sat back in his chair while the letters moved across the page again. He glanced at Fven who nodded for him to continue. Looking down he saw something new was written; *The Keeper opens and closes the gate. Dreamer you must discover your Fate.* He waited for the words to change again, but they did not so he turned the page. The next page was also covered with golden lettering. They quivered and morphed into words: *The Wish Tree.* Before Jason could read the rest, the letters crawled onto the opposite page, joining with the others and formed a beautiful illustration.

"The Wish Tree is a supposedly magical thing that can grant anyone a single wish if they pay the right price," Fven said.

"And the price is?"

"Some legends say that the wisher must pay the price of its own blood to make a wish, others say that a whole sacrifice must be made."

Jason shivered and looked down at his hands. Taking a deep breath he turned the page, which showed various illustrations of wishes granted. The opposite page was blank until he fixed his attention on it. A golden picture of a compass appeared to burn itself onto the page, the southern mark glowed the brightest. So he was heading in the right direction! Excitement bubbled in his stomach and he quickly turned the page. A map started to draw itself. The map depicted Greater Balisme and some of Eastern Balisme. Tiethe was the southernmost kingdom, along the coast-line. The other kingdoms' capitals were filled in with tiny pictures and their names. The remainder of the map depicted the ocean and several islands. Jason searched until he found a small golden dot with the name 'Isle of Dreams' alongside it. But a black inky mass leaked out of the page and obscured the island. A new name formed: The Blacks.

Fven leaned forward, peering at the map. "This has never happened before," he looked at Jason with wide eyes. "How did you make the book reveal the island's location?"

Jason leaned away from Fven's face, which was a little too close for comfort. "I don't know what you're talking about."

"I must do some research," Fven dragged the book toward his side of the table and started reading in earnest. Jason and Rose sat opposite him, uncertain of what to do. Eventually Fven glanced at them, a slight crease on his brow. "I am terribly sorry!" he jumped up. "You are probably in need of refreshment. What sort of host am I to forget my guests? Please forgive me. We are a very easily distracted race."

While Fven led the way, Jason grasped the chance to exchange a few words with Rose.

"I need to get to the Glassmaker to free the border."

"How are you going to do that?"

"I don't know, but I have to get to this island."

"How exactly are you planning to get to the island? Are you going to swim the whole way?"

"I'll think of something."

Rose was silent for a while, before she said, "What about the rebels?"

"They will be fine without me. What difference can I make after all? You can stay if you want to, but I have to get to the Dream Keeper. Maybe he'll show me where this Wish Tree is."

"The Dream Keeper might not be a he or she, it is most likely not even human."

"I don't care."

Later on, after Jason and Rose were fed and washed they returned to the library and found Fven along with another Fae speaking quickly in hushed tones. Jason subtly cleared his throat and they looked up abruptly.

"Hello!" Fven beamed, but his companion glared at them.

"Please, sit down."

Jason did so, keeping an eye on the hostile creature. His eyes were like twin pinpoints of ice, fixed on them as if they had done him some great injustice. When he walked out, his stride was that of someone in a hurry to get away, but refusing to run.

"What—?" Jason started to ask, but Fven waved the question away.

"Do not mind him. It is only because you are human that he is so hostile."

"Because we are human?"

"Humans—and Fae have never been the greatest of allies. You do not trust us because we have magic and are, well, not human."

"And you hate us?"

"Most of my race does. Long ago, the land of Balisme was under the rule of the Fae, but the humans came and drove us out. We were forced to go into hiding and there has been war between out races ever since."

"I'm sorry," Jason said. Rose, however, looked even less at ease.

"It's not your fault. Besides, the humans seem to have forgotten us and leave us alone. I can only dream of a world where we do not have to hide or fight constantly. This war between our races is pointless, but I fear the wounds on both sides are too deep to be forgotten."

"Is there no way for humans and Fae to get along?"

"If there is then I do not know of it."

"What if," Jason said slowly, "I find a way to open the border?"

Fven smiled and shook his head. "One little human against the Glassmaker? Even if you succeed, it will take a lot more for all hurts to be forgiven."

"I still need to open the border somehow," Jason rested his chin in his hands.

"The Glassmaker is a great beast; you will need a miracle to defeat it."

"I have been lucky so far," Jason straightened up. "Maybe I have some luck left."

Fven opened his mouth to protest further, but a sigh escaped instead. He rose and paced up and down, shaking his head. He sighed again and turned to face the teenagers. "If it is your wish, I will take you to the Glassmaker's lair. But that is the limit of it. You bring your deaths upon yourselves."

"Thank you," Jason beamed. "When the border is open, you will be the first to know."

Chapter 8:
Glassmaker

"This is the furthest I will go," Fven stopped short.

They were at the foot of a mountain range quite close to the Tiethe/Setar border. Fven had taken them along a route under the sand through the palace for some way before they emerged into the scorching heat. The moment they were in open air, sand swirled up and gathered around Fven until a small funnel was spinning around him, growing tighter and tighter until the sand settled on every single part of his body. Jason would have easily mistaken him for a Sand Weaver.

"The Glassmaker lives up there," Fven pointed at a gaping hole near the top of the mountain. "Good luck." He turned and quickly sank into sand before their eyes.

Jason stared at the hole, looking so much like the gaping mouth of a hungry beast. He took a deep breath and tightened his hands into fists. Now that the danger was so close, he was less certain about what he was going to do. He did not even have a weapon. His left fist lay uselessly against his side, missing the blade that provided him some protection earlier.

"Are you afraid?" he asked softly of Rose, grateful that she was standing there beside him.

"No."

"Good," his voice rose in pitch. "Because I'm terrified."

"What do we do now?"

He shut his eyes tightly before looking up again, afraid of his own words. "I suppose we climb."

Reaching above his head, his fingers grasped into a crevice and he pulled himself up, reaching for the next hold. The sun burned his back and neck. Sweat rolled down his overheated body and into his eyes, making the climb more difficult. Rose toiled alongside him. She was at a greater disadvantage because of her princess outfit, which was not made for climbing and running away.

"It seems we've been climbing up and down since we came here," Jason gasped.

Rose smiled and a breathless chuckle escaped her lips. "It does seem like it."

Jason's muscles ached and his limbs trembled from the effort of pulling his weight along. His fingers groped for another hold and as he pulled himself up he rolled over onto a ledge. Rose collapsed a second after him onto the ledge and turned onto her back, her chest heaving.

"How—much—further?" Jason panted.

Rose struggled onto her elbow and looked up the steep mountain face. About five metres away the hole yawned blackly at them, waiting to devour them. "Not much—we're almost—there."

Jason shakily got to his hands and knees and settled into a sitting position. He checked the binding around his injured foot and tightened it a little further.

"How do you know how to do that?" Rose watched him.

"My father is a healer," he shrugged. "He taught me a few things."

"Is that why you don't like fighting?"

"I don't know," shading his eyes he peered at the sun, which was become lower in the sky. "Let's go."

The short rest renewed their energy and enthusiasm to finish the last stretch. It took less time than Jason expected so when he suddenly tumbled into the dark space he bit down in his fright, and bit his tongue. Suppressing the start of a whimper he crawled a little way to the side of the cave mouth, sitting on the short shelf-like ledge just outside of it. With his head leaning against the mountain wall he kept his ears pricked to listen for any sounds from within.

"Do you think it's in there?" Jason asked in a voice barely louder than a puff of breath.

"I'll go see," Rose started making her way into the cave, but he grabbed her by the arm.

"No, wait!"

She obeyed and glared at him over her shoulder. "Why?"

He floundered for words. "I'll—come with."

Confusion flickered across her face as she turned away from him. Furious at himself, Jason sneaked after her. With their hands on the cave wall to guide them, they inched blindly inward. Jason's chest tightened with every step and every instinct screamed at him to turn around. He stumbled over something and automatically reached out to steady himself. His hand grasped Rose's shoulder and they froze. Quickly he withdrew his hand and stepped more carefully. Gradually his eyes adjusted to the gloom and he could identify pale objects littering the floor. His foot brushed one and he recoiled as two gaping holes stared at him from within a bleached, grinning skull. Tearing his gaze away, he focussed on Rose's reassuring outline in front of him. A horrible queasy feeling formed in his stomach and the wide, dead smiles of unknown victims in the corners of his eyes did not help.

When Rose stopped, he nearly collided with her. His breath died in his throat as he distinguished the vast hulking shape of a great beast, a little more than a metre away. Deep, rumbling breaths rose and fell from somewhere to the bulk's left lower end, blowing hot air into their faces. It smelled like a severely smoking fire, tinged with rotting flesh. Jason pinched his nose and blinked a few tears away. Now that they were before the creature, he still had no idea what to do. He tapped Rose on the shoulder and mimed for them to return outside. She nodded and they turned around. Just as Jason took his first step, the rumbling stopped. Slowly, involuntarily he turned his head. High above their heads, against the cave ceiling, a pair of amber eyes glowered.

"Don't move," Rose warned in a harsh whisper.

Some smoke billowed across its eyes and its face became illuminated by its glowing nostrils. It opened its mouth slightly. It was like the opening of a furnace.

"Please, can't we just run?" Jason squeaked.

The creature's jaw dropped and from behind the rows of glittering sharp teeth a ball of flame sped toward them. Jason and Rose tore toward the exit with lightning speed. The cave was now brightly lit and the skeletons of long dead things were bathed in a pinkish light. A burning inferno pursued them, singeing their hair and scorching any uncovered skin. They flung themselves to either side of the cave opening and flames gushed past, missing them by millimetres.

"Of course it's a fire-breathing dragon!" Jason groaned.

The flames seemed to exhaust themselves and tremors carried through the earth as the dragon made its way to the cave entrance. A black head snaked its way into the open, with vicious horns curling from its skull and several smaller sharp spikes along its jaw, brow and neck.

"Who dares ta disturb ma slumber?" rumbled the creature. It brought its enormous head to within an inch of Jason's. "Come on, ye have tongues. Speak! Before I et ye."

"M–my name is J–Jason," he managed to stutter.

"And the lass?"

Jason tried to peer past the creature, but it opened its maw, showing off its white fangs.

"Her n–name is Rose," Jason rapidly ejected.

"Pretty name," its head weaved toward Rose in serpentine manner. "Fer a pretty lass!"

A sound like boulders tumbling down a hillside travelled along the creature's body as it chuckled. "What are ye doin' here humans? I was ordered to keep ye from crossin' the border, not ta et ye."

"Who ordered you?" Jason called out.

"Who ordered—" the dragon's head whipped back to Jason. "Who ordered me? The king ye wee twit! Who else?"

"Well," Jason hesitated. "You're so big, and the king is—not."

The dragon's eyes narrowed and Jason gulped. Its head withdrew and it stepped a little way back into the cave. "Come away from there before ye fall ta yer deaths," it called. "A'm not gonna et ye."

Slowly Jason and Rose slipped into the cave opening. The dragon towered over them, its bulk a mass of power, speed and muscle. Its great talons were nearly the length of one of Jason's forearms. Now that Jason could properly see the creature, his breath was taken away. Despite the danger of the situation, he admired the magnificent majesty of the dragon. But instead of scales like in all the stories, it was covered all over in thick black fur. He also spied a thick golden collar around its neck, close to its base at the shoulders.

"Does Malik control you with that?" Jason asked.

The dragon's head turned and it tugged at the collar with its teeth. With a great sigh it buried its head under one of its wings. "Aye, A'm nothin' more than a pet. My every decision, every move is dictated by that tyrant. I jus' want to go home! Back to the sweet highlands of Ansfrid!"

In all of Jason's dreams, he never imagined that he would ever experience sympathy for a dragon. "I'm really sorry. Is there nothing we can do?"

"Nay, unless ye wield mighty powerful magic."

"The collar is magical? Where did Malik get a magic collar?"

"How am I ta know? A'm jus' a dragon."

"Can I see it?"

"All right, mind the spines."

Jason clambered along the dragon's muscular foreleg up onto its back and seated himself just behind the wings. He had to stoop slightly so that his head did not bump against the ceiling. The collar was smooth and cool to touch as he slid his finger along it. The flesh around the collar was heavily scarred and torn. The dragon's skin rippled as he accidentally touched the tender places. Placing both hands on the collar he tried to pry fingers beneath the golden ring, without success and the dragon twitched uncontrollably from the pain. It was as if the band had melted into the dragon's flesh, becoming a part of its hide.

Unexpectedly the collar began to feel warmer under Jason's palms and a faint vibration ran through it. He leaned closer to peer at it, but saw nothing unusual. The heat intensified, but Jason could not remove his hands, it felt like they were glued to the collar's golden surface. He wanted to cry out but his throat tightened and panic threatened to erupt in his chest. A single, blue symbol took shape seemingly deep within the metal and started to glow. Jason was struck by its familiar appearance, where had he seen something like it before?

From where she was standing Rose could not see what was happening on the dragon's back. All she saw was Jason hunched over the dragon's neck with a strange expression on his face. It was a mixture of terror and fascination, his eyes wide and glassy and his body taut and quivering. What was going on up there?

Snick! There was the faintest of sounds and the collar opened at an invisible seam. Jason regained control of his bodily functions and removed his hands as if the collar had bitten him. He inspected his palms and though they were red, they appeared not to have burned. Suddenly the dragon moved beneath him, or at least it rolled its shoulder muscles, but the motion was enough to nearly throw Jason from his perch. He fell forward instinctively, causing one of the smaller spines to press into his chest. A rumble ran the length of the dragon's body, erupting in roars of joy from between rows of glistening fangs. With a clang the collar dropped and landed in the dust.

"A'm free! FREEDOM!" the dragon roared and stomped and victorious flames erupted from its throat. Rose sought refuge from the inferno and stomping claws at the back of the cave while Jason clung desperately to its back like a baby baboon would to its mother's back.

"Mr Dragon!" Jason called out. "Could you maybe celebrate after I've climbed off your back?"

"Sorry lad!" the dragon chuckled. "A'm jus' so happy! How'd ye do it?"

"I don't know, but please can I come down?"

"Why don't ye stay there and I fly you and the lass where ye want?"

"I don't—" Jason started to protest, but Rose was already climbing along its scaly hide. She settled herself between two large spines close behind him.

"Do you know where the ruins of Pel-Umbra are?" Rose asked.

"Aye, but why by the beard of ma granddaddy do ye want to go there?"

"Our friends are there," she stated simply.

"All right, hang on tight!"

The dragon galloped toward the edge and pushed itself into empty air with its powerful limbs. Jason shut his eyes and clung to the dragon's neck. The enormous wings folded open and flapped down in one mighty motion. Gradually, after Jason got used to the rhythmic movement of the dragon's body, he opened his eyes to slits and his breath was caught by the wind rushing past his head. The desert was stretched beneath them like a child's sandbox. It looked so small and insignificant from such a height. In the distance was Umbra, with the river winding eastward close by it.

"Ma name is Gamon by the way!" the dragon roared across its shoulder. "Thank ye a hundred times over and by the bones of ma kin! Ye have given me freedom!"

"You're welcome!"

The kilometres passed beneath them by the second and the distance between them and the rebel camp was rapidly growing less. The sun was setting at their backs: a blood red disk nearly resting upon the horizon, bathing the land in its light causing it to look like a glorious glittering ocean of molten gold.

"We're nearly there!" Gamon called to them, but the words

were snatched away on the wind.

Glancing down Jason saw a sight that caused his chest to tighten and he almost yelled for Gamon to turn around. Tiny figures were battling down below, their weapons glinting every now and then as the sun's last rays caught the metal. They were too high up to hear anything, but Jason could only imagine the cacophony going on beneath them. Somehow Malik's soldiers had found the rebels, and judging by what he saw Jason guessed that the battle was almost over and the rebels were losing.

"A'm takin' ye down!" Gamon roared and dived straight downward. Jason had to shut his eyes against the force of the wind battering his face and he was nearly torn from Gamon's back, but he held on bravely.

The closer they got, the more audible the sounds. The ringing of steel, the shouts and cries of men, and a general confusion of noise floated up to the three of them. The fighters started to spot them and some cried out in alarm, while others roared and cheered in triumph. The idiots, Jason thought. Malik's men think the dragon's here to help them!

—————◆————

Early morning just before dawn, Darryn was unpleasantly shaken awake. Opening his eyes his gaze fell upon the dark face of one of the soldiers leaning over him, his expression screwed into one of intense urgency. He raised himself onto one elbow and rubbed his eyes wearily.

"Yes?"

"Come quickly, there is something you must see!"

"All right," Darryn waved. "Wait outside. I'm just going to

change."

The man pushed the tent flap aside and stepped into the rapidly receding gloom. With a groan Darryn rose and pulled his chain-mail over his shirt and fastened his sword belt around his middle. With some difficulty he pulled on his boots, nearly throwing the whole tent onto its side. Finally, he clambered through the tent flap and followed the anxious soldier.

The entire camp was a bustling nest of activity. Scouts ran around delivering reports and so forth, while others prepared their weapons and hurried to the north-western part of the camp.

"What's going on?" Darryn asked as he trotted after his guide.

"Troupes from Umbra," the man replied bluntly.

What? How? Darryn's brow creased in worry. A gentle thumping approached him across the ground and he turned to see Gabbro loping toward them. He was holding a large club-like weapon studded with stones like the ridges around his bald head.

"What's all the hubbub about?" he asked of Darryn, easily keeping in time to with them with long strides.

"Malik's troupes have found us. They're marching here at this moment."

Gabbro abruptly fell behind as he stopped. "That means we're going to have to fight them. I've never been in battle before!"

"There is a first time for everyone," Darryn called over his shoulder.

Sarrid was standing at the fringes of the camp, staring into the distance where he expected the enemy army to appear. The rebels were organizing themselves as best as they can, but they were not trained in battle tactics and formations. Darryn watched them with a sinking heart. What chance had they against a properly trained army?

"I see you're up," Sarrid greeted grimly.

"How did they find us? A traitor?"

"Most likely," Sarrid's hands balled into fists and tightened until the veins stood out against his dark skin. "I want you to stay here where it is safe among the ruins. I do not wish to have your blood on my hands over this battle."

Darryn felt the wild blood of the north boil in his body and their red hot heat crawled up his face reddening his cheeks. "I want to fight."

"You are just a boy."

"I am fifteen and I can fight! I have fought in battles before. I am no mere novice."

"I did not wish to dishonour you and I do not question your valour, but a war is no place for one as young as you."

"I have as much right as you!" Darryn said with his voice steadily rising in volume. "I can use a sword just as well as you and your men, maybe even better than some. I have fought against goblins and have slain a mountain troll when I was fourteen. You have not only insulted my pride, but also the pride of my entire family."

Sarrid regarded him coldly. "It is best that you should remember that I am the crown prince of this kingdom and that such a tongue deserves severe punishment."

Flames danced in Darryn's dark-blue eyes and for an instant he strongly resembled his sister. He reached into his clothing and withdrew a chain on which a slender silver ring hung. Engraved into it was an eagle in flight. He held this before Sarrid's eyes, who regarded it in surprise.

"Forgive me," he said after a while. "I did not know."

"And it is better so," Darryn said, tucking it back out of sight.

"May I ask that it still remains a secret?"

"You have my word."

After a spell of silence Darryn asked calmly as if he was enquiring after the time. "When should they be here?"

"As soon as the sun is above the horizon."

The sun's red fingers reached beyond the horizon, plucking stars from the velvet sky and chasing the moon away in its fiery brilliance.

Malik's army arrived with a shouted challenge in numbers far greater than the meagre rebel army. Despite the grave situation Darryn's heart raced with excitement and a thrill born of his northern heritage. The crimson banners and tunics of the enemy army appeared like a wave of blood rolling down upon them, threatening to engulf them. Sunlight glinted off spear tips, helmets, breastplates, and naked scimitars and sabres. For a brief moment there was silence as the armies faced each other. For a very brief moment men said their prayers and silent farewells knowing that in seconds they would be pitted against their former kinsmen to fight to the bloody death.

There seemed little hope for the rebels; they were heavily outnumbered. The king's army was well equipped and far more experienced. It would take a miracle to save them.

"Remember what we stand and fight for," Sarrid called for his men to hear. "Remember why you are standing here with me. Remember that we fight for freedom and what is right, against a tyrant who rules by stealing the money out of your pockets and the food from your mouths!" he roared a brutal battle cry and charged at the enemy ranks. His men followed suit, yelling and shouting as they went.

The armies clashed violently, swords met swords and shields

battered against bodies. Arrows rained from both sides slaying and maiming where they landed. With the northern spirit properly roused inside of him, Darryn fought like a deadly whirlwind. He hacked, slashed, and stabbed left and right, while deflecting attacks with equal ferocity. Anyone who looked upon his face was struck with terror, and none would have thought that he was but a boy. So fierce was his expression that even his allies stayed clear of his destructive path. An unfortunate swipe cut his arm, causing warm blood to flow from the open wound, but he hardly noticed it and continued on his rampage.

The fierceness of the rebels' attack surprised the king's soldiers and they were slightly taken aback at first, but they slowly regained the upper hand. The sheer volume of the fighters began to wear the rebels down and overpower them. The sun scorched them and beat down from above, shouting silent taunts at the pitiful humans below. Sweat mingled with blood and sand stung their eyes, filled their mouths and stained their clothes.

Darryn received several other small cuts across his body and his initial rage was starting to die down. His arms and shoulders ached and the sword started to feel heavier and heavier. His dark hair clung to his neck and forehead, drenched by sweat, and he constantly had to wipe it out of his eyes. How much longer he would hold out he knew not, but his strength would fail eventually and death would follow. Bodies littered the ground, making movement difficult. Several were the crimson-clothed soldiers, but there were also rebels biting the dust. No matter how hard the rebels fought, they were just too outnumbered.

At least Rose is safe, Darryn thought. Gabbro crashed through a battalion of soldiers like an enraged bull, trampling them beneath his giant feet and whacking the brains out of others with his weapon. Gabbro was still relatively unharmed, except for a vicious cut on his left arm, thanks to his tough Ard-man skin. Soldiers tried to pull him down by their combined weight, clinging to him and hanging from him nearly a dozen at a time, but the giant just swatted them off like flies.

The sun climbed higher and higher as the battle continued. The rebels were spent and tired, but doggedly kept fighting. The numbers on both sides were dramatically less, with new recruits joining the legions of the dead every minute. Eventually the sun grew tired of watching the men and started her descent. A few dozen rebels remained and they gathered for a final stand as the sun was nearly touching the horizon. Darryn found himself alongside Gabbro, whose shadow provided a rather brief respite from the deadly last rays of the sun.

Then an even greater dark shadow fell across them.

Everyone looked up and the rebels cried out in fear as a great dragon swooped down toward them. The king's soldiers cheered and laughed. Darryn's heart first jumped to his throat, then slid down into his stomach as despair finally came. The battle was lost, there was no hope left.

The dragon landed amidst the fighters with the sun behind it so that no one could look directly at it. Gabbro stretched to his full seven feet and shielded his eyes against the bright light while the last of the rebels' arrows whizzed over their heads at the creature.

"There's something on its back," he reported loudly for whoever wanted to hear. "Two *somethings*. Humans I think. The one looks a lot like Jason and the other like Rose."

Darryn froze, his mind doing somersaults as he peered at the dragon's back. Sure enough, two figures were waving frantically from the dragon's spiny back. "Stop shooting!" Darryn yelled at the top of his lungs. "It's on our side, stop shooting!"

The dragon let out a great roar and a fearsome inferno erupted from its maw engulfing five nearby soldiers. The rebels cheered, and with their newfound hope came new strength and they hacked at the ranks of their enemies.

⇒·⇐

The moment they landed Jason realised the danger of their position. The rebels knew nothing of the dragon and naturally started firing at Gamon. Jason and Rose stood up, balancing on Gamon's back, and waved for all they were worth to make them stop. It must have helped because the arrows stopped and the king's soldiers stood terrified and the rebels roared. Realizing where they were, Jason's heart missed a beat as he watched the violence in wide-eyed terror. Gamon lurched beneath them and he slipped, landing with a thud to the horrible screams of men being roasted alive.

Jason regained his balance and turned around, looking to Rose for guidance. She stood up, and to his astonishment, leaped from Gamon's back and gracefully crashed down upon one of the enemy soldiers. In a single quick move she punched him in the jaw with her elbow and grabbed his weapon before entering the fray. Jason watched in amazement as she weaved and danced her way gracefully about the battlefield. It would have been very beautiful to watch if it was not so bloody and violent.

Jason now faced a decision. Should he stay where he was safe but felt like a coward, or should he jump down and risk his life to help his friends? His insides were in turmoil with conflict, but loyalty won over as he jumped down, grabbed a fallen sword and charged madly at the nearest red uniform he saw.

The clamour and ferocity of the battle was an immense shock to Jason and he began to regret being a part of it. He barely ducked from a swipe aimed at his neck and deflected a bone jarring blow. Everything was moving too fast, blows were aimed at him, blows to kill. Somehow he managed to dodge and deflect most of these and finally, almost by their own accord, his hands thrust the blade through an opening in his enemy's defences and cut straight through his armour, skin and flesh. Jason stepped back in horror, yanking the blade free and the man dropped lifeless to the ground. Blood stained the metal of his weapon and he felt sick to his stomach. *I just killed someone!* The thought nauseated him, but before he could dwell anymore he instinctively whirled around and his sword slashed through a soldier's stomach. Jason wanted to flee, but there was always another enemy in his path and to survive, he had to defend himself with his sword. "Why won't it end!" he silently screamed. Finally Jason managed to get away. He watched as soldiers fell everywhere, their blood flowing away with their lives. Then one by one the soldiers cried out for mercy and threw their weapons down. They surrendered!

Jason dropped to his knees and sobs erupted; his shoulders shook and his tears flowed. He cried for all the needless blood that was spilled and for all the men that were killed by his and everyone else's hand. With his face twisting into helpless rage he flung the sword away from him and continued sobbing. A friendly hand gripped his shoulder and pulled him upright. Darryn's grimy and bloodstained face smiled sadly at him, and as he patted Jason on the back and squeezed his shoulder he said, "I know mate, I know."

"Why am I crying?" Jason asked between sobs.

"You're not weak, if that's what you think. It's the shock, that's all. I also cried after my first battle. But you get used to it."

Jason abruptly pulled away and aghast cried out, "How can you get used to it! I don't want to get used to killing and stealing lives. I don't want to be a hero."

"You don't have to be, it's all over. We'll find the Dream Keeper and save your brother."

"Bastian," Jason said softly and with a shock he realised that he had forgotten his brother amidst all the drama.

"C'mon, let's go get cleaned up." Darryn put his arm around Jason's shoulders and led him back to camp.

Chapter 9:
The King of Umbra/
Back on Track

At noon the following day Sarrid and his company of rebels, soldiers from Umbra and Darryn, Rose, Gabbro, Jason and Gamon all marched for Umbra. They had dragged all the bodies out of the sun into a cool space in the ruins so they could receive proper burial later when they returned. Jason walked with his head bowed, arms swinging lifelessly by his sides. His belt was absent of any weapons since had refused to take up a sword again. They expected little resistance when they arrived at Umbra.

Most of Malik's army was defeated and the rest eagerly accepted Sarrid as their true king in exchange for their lives. Now they marched along with the rebels and hailed Sarrid as if they had been loyal to him throughout the war. When they arrived at the city gates, the soldiers called out: "Hail King Sarrid! Make way for the true king!" No one dared oppose them. The people crowded around the procession, though keeping clear of Gamon, cheering and crying out blessings to their new king.

At the palace gates, they were briefly stopped and their entry denied by two terrified sentries, but Gamon easily swatted them from the wall and burst through the timber gates that barred the way. Guards scattered out of the dragon's way as he graciously made his way up the palace steps, playfully shooting flames after the retreating men.

Malik was cowering in his throne. A spy had just informed him that his brother had won the battle and was on his way to the palace. Who knew what terrible punishment he would receive? He should run away! Get as far away from the palace as possible before—*BANG!* He leaped into the air. *BANG! SNAP! CRASH!* The entire door gave way and a long, black, furry neck snaked its way through followed by muscular shoulders and the rest of its bulk. A strange squeak was uttered by Malik from somewhere at the back of his throat and he scrambled behind his throne, quivering in terror.

"Oi, kingy!" Gamon called out. "Look who's here!"

Next to enter the throne room was a tall, slender figure with dark hair curling wildly around her face like a vengeful goddess of war.

"You!" Malik cried out in a mixture of a screech and a squeak, trembling with indignant fury and terror. "Y-you lied to me!"

Rose just smiled and shrugged as Sarrid and the rest of the rebels poured into the hall. Jason stood quietly beside Rose while Sarrid marched with dignity toward his brother. Two of the rebels lifted Malik from behind the throne and placed him at Sarrid's feet where he fell flat on his face and shook like a nervous guinea pig.

"Look at me!" Sarrid roared. Malik squeaked again, but remained as he was. Bending over, and in a dangerously soft voice Sarrid repeated, "Look at me."

Slowly Malik lifted his head, his eyes riveted upon Sarrid's sandaled feet. He dared not meet his brother's eyes. Waves of fury leaked out into the space between them, licking his skin and smelling his fear. Suddenly he let out a long and terrible wail.

"Don't kill me! I'm sorry. Please have mercy, forgive me!" and he collapsed into a pitiful sobbing heap.

"Take him away," Sarrid pulled a face and looked away as two rebels dragged his screeching sibling to the dungeon. He regarded the throne thoughtfully before beckoning a servant closer.

"Have the throne destroyed and send for a chair."

The servant bobbed and nodded and scurried off. Soon the throne was carried away by eager hands and replaced by a modest wooden chair. With a sigh Sarrid eased himself into it and closed his eyes. "Home."

Jason felt a twinge of sadness as images of lush fields of wheat and green meadows dotted with cattle and sheep came to his mind. How long before he too could finally return home, if at all? Was Bastian still alive or already gone past the veil to eternity? A deep longing for his comfortable bed and the company of his family ached in his chest like an open wound. Blinking a few times he tried to push these thoughts and feelings away and took a deep breath. To either side of him were the reassuring presences of his friends without whom he could never have come so far.

He glanced at Rose and was once more struck by her beauty and he felt heat rush along his cheeks. He quickly looked away in case she returned his glance. A small crease formed on his brow as his insides twisted around. Maybe it was an after-effect from the battle? His gaze was unconsciously drawn back to Rose and his heartbeat went wild. His blush deepened and he focussed intently on the floor.

A small feast was held that night along with celebrations all over the city. Fireworks thundered long into the night in colourful displays of green, blue, purple, yellow and more. Despite the joyful mood and happy celebrating all around, Jason hardly enjoyed himself. His thoughts were far away, across the golden sands beyond the blue ocean. Even Darryn's jokes could only bring a small smile to his face.

"What's the matter?" Darryn finally asked. "Join the fun, laugh a little. You're alive and we won!"

"I know and I'm sorry. I just don't feel like celebrating."

"Hmm—If I promise we can leave tomorrow morning will you cheer up?"

"All right," Jason finally smiled.

"That's the spirit!" Darryn patted him on the back and left to tell his jokes to someone else.

Jason let his gaze wander along the table. All sorts of exotic foods were laid out on golden and silver platters and there was enough wine to keep everyone's goblet filled. Everyone was laughing, chatting or dancing except two: Jason and the person whose seat was currently empty. He cast about for the missing person and discovered her standing forlornly by a window. An urge to go to her caused him to stand up and the next moment he blinked in surprise, finding himself unexpectedly alongside her. His mind felt terribly blank; he could not think of a single thing to say. How could he have forgotten how to speak?

"Why aren't you over there enjoying the feast?" Rose asked quietly.

"That's what I wanted to ask you," he managed.

She shrugged, her face an expressionless mask.

Jason started to sway his body to-and-fro on the balls of his feet, still desperately trying to think of something to say. The motion distracted her and she turned her head slightly to watch him while he frowned into space.

"What are you thinking so hard about?" she asked and a little amusement had crept into her tone.

"Huh? Oh, er—" He didn't know what to say to her. "Nothing in particular, I was just daydreaming."

Her gaze wandered back outside and he took the liberty to stare at her for a brief while. When she returned his gaze he pretended to be admiring the ceiling. He was looking everywhere, but at her and was intensely aware that she was watching him. His face heated up and he prayed that she would not notice.

"Are you all right?" she asked. "Your face is terribly red."

She noticed.

"It's the—the heat, I can't stand it." He was a little impressed by this impromptu explanation. It seemed plausible.

"The heat—?" she lifted her brow.

He nodded dumbly. After more awkward silence, he gazed outside with her, letting his thoughts wander. "Isn't it strange that it is so extremely hot here, when it is probably winter back home?" He thought out loud.

"It is a little strange," she mused. "Where I come from is almost the exact opposite of Setar."

"What is your home like?" Jason asked in fascination. "I mean Arden, of course."

"It snows the whole year, except for three months in summer. The people call the seasons 'winter' and 'not-winter' as a joke. Because it's so cold we can't really grow crops, so we import food in case the crops die. Mostly we farm with mountain goats."

"How big are they? I've heard they can be as big as cows."

"The rams can grow bigger than that. I've seen one as big as a horse once."

"Where do you live?"

She paused for a moment before answering. "In Ansfrid, the capital city."

"What's it like?"

"It's quite large with thick walls all around and it is right against the Black Mountains. Once it must have been grand, but nowadays it's falling to ruin under the current king's rule. It seems that the great wild Arden is fading into legend."

"Maybe I'll visit you in Ansfrid someday," Jason said. "You can show me all the legendary monuments and places I've heard of in the stories."

"Maybe," she said softly and leaned on the windowsill.

After a lazy and hearty breakfast, among many thank yous and come agains, Jason, Darryn, Rose and Gabbro set off across the vast desert for Tiethe. Before they left, Jason asked Gamon to fulfil his promise to Fven by informing the Fae that the border was free. The dragon agreed to do this one last errand before flying home himself.

They were led by a group of experienced desert travellers on Sarrid's orders. They walked alongside their horses (and in the Setarans' cases, camels) because they were carrying supplies for the long trek. With one hand resting against Blue's neck, Jason marched eagerly. He longed to see green grass again and to feel a cool breeze against his face. The others were also excited about leaving the arid land behind. Gabbro would accompany them as far as the border, from where he would go on his own path to visit his aunt.

The journey was long and Jason's unease increased with each step. Often he would unconsciously increase his pace and storm ahead of the rest while they struggled to keep up. But gradually the distance grew less and the earth harder. When they crossed the border, they found themselves in a dry, rocky area with small shrubs growing here and there. The Setarans bid them farewell and turned around to make the long journey back.

"I guess this is goodbye for us then," Gabbro smiled sadly. "I had a lot of fun, thank you."

"Goodbye, Gabbro," Jason shook his hand and was drawn into a back-breaking hug.

"Listen, Rocky," Darryn grinned. "You'd better stay in practice with that mace of yours in case I need you again in the future."

"I will," Gabbro beamed. He awkwardly scratched the back of his head when he stood before Rose. "Goodbye Rose," he said. "I'll miss you, too."

To everyone's surprise—Gabbro's most of all—Rose gave him a quick hug. "I'll miss you, too."

They waved until the tall frame of the young Ard-man was beyond their vision. A little sadness was felt at his absence, but was quickly pushed aside with the renewed urgency of the journey. They travelled a great deal of the day and took only fleeting breaks to make up for lost time. At the back of Jason's mind the image of Bastian's tortured body loomed over his conscience, constricting his thoughts and depriving him of rest. He pushed his body to the point of collapse and even then would only stop when Darryn insisted.

Some days after crossing the border, they once again came upon Mistress Mayflower and Luciana's village. They considered stopping to greet them, but decided against delay and passed through. A cloud blew in from the south and with evening came rain. Wishing that they had remained in the village, they huddled miserably under the meagre cover of a tree and became soaking wet. Eventually the rain lessened to a light drizzle, which died out in the early hours of the morning. Stiff, exhausted and soaked to the bone, the trio mounted their steeds and continued for a small stretch before stopping for a quick nap.

At one point in their journey, nearly two days from Targon, the road started following the course of a stream that widened and turned into a river. On both sides the banks were lush and green with tiny yellow flowers and lazy bees droning away. The water was clear and crystal blue, so that they could see all the way to the riverbed where schools of glittering fish swam. An otter casually dove beneath the surface when they passed by, its sleek and slender body moving fluidly through the water. That night they made camp by the river's side and slept soundly on the soft grass. With only a day between them and their destination they increased the pace to try and make it in shorter time. Their spirits lifted the following morning as they knew that Targon was within reach.

Ahead of the three, a green hill covered by the same little flowers by the river rose from the earth. They passed a few people coming from the city, but most went toward it. A sudden urge caused Jason to spur Blue on and they cantered ahead. When they reached the top and the country beyond was revealed, his breath was taken away. A dazzling city stretching for miles in both directions lay before him. It was built entirely of white stone, the buildings, the streets and the surrounding walls. But what made it exceptional was that it also extended its reach out to sea. Half of the city was built upon gigantic pillars that stretched down to the ocean floor, making it appear to float on the great blue mass. Gigantic scarlet birds with long, trailing tails swerved over the city and the wide bridges that stretched across the waters. Enormous black and white creatures with fins and flippers would occasionally break through the surface and dive majestically back under. It was a whole new world.

Darryn and Rose caught up to Jason and gazed with him at the city below.

"It's…" Jason murmured, lost for words.

"I know," Darryn said. "Hang on a second," he dismounted his horse and withdrew his cloak, which he clasped around his throat. Rose did likewise. Jason watched in confusion, uncertain of what could cause the strange behaviour.

"What are you doing?" he asked.

"It's just a—precaution," Darryn said. "It is best not to ask questions."

The continued downhill until they arrived at the city gates. Beyond, endless crowds of people went about their daily business. Soldiers in scarlet tunics and plumed helmets guarded the walls, holding standards with the symbol of Tiethe: a bright yellow sun on a red background. Just before they reached the gates, Darryn and Rose drew their heads up so that their faces were partially obscured. The question burned on Jason's tongue, but he wisely did not enquire further.

The noise inside the city was cacophonic, yet somehow wonderfully foreign. Strange music from unknown instruments floated through the air, mingling with the loud laughter of men and the chatter of women. The scents ranged from wonderfully sweet, to the unmistakable smell of fish, to other unidentifiable aromas. The people did not look strangely at them as the villagers did. They were more used to foreign visitors and merchants.

"We should head toward the docks," Darryn said. "If we need to find an island, we'll need a ship."

"But how will we get a ship?" Jason asked.

"Don't worry, we'll think of something." Darryn winked, but glanced nervously around.

"Which way are the docks?"

"We follow the main road southward, this way."

The horses' hooves clip-clopped on the cobbled streets, making their way through traffic and following a cart smelling suspiciously foul. To escape the mad throng, they slipped into a smaller side street where the buildings were so close the horses could only pass in single file. The portion of the city that was built on the ocean was more spacious and seemed to be reserved for entertainment. People leaned on railings and watched the waves lap at the sturdy pillars below or pointed as another of the black and white beasts emerged from the water. One of the scarlet birds flew low enough for its tail to brush the dark heads of the Tiethans. Jason, Darryn and Rose dismounted to lead their steeds by the rein, making it more manoeuvrable for them among all the people.

The harbour was the furthest out at sea and it was divided into four parts: the royal fleet, the navy, the merchant harbour and the fishing port. They started to make their way for it when a fanfare sounded. Eagerly heads craned and eyes roved to see who the important person was. A contingent consisting of a score of foot soldiers, a banner carrier, a herald and on a brilliant grey stallion, the source of the excitement.

"Who is it?" Jason asked. While crowds gathered around the person, Darryn and Rose desperately tried to withdraw into the throng.

With all the pushing and shoving, the trio unexpectedly found themselves at the very front of the bystanders with the contingent passing right by them. Darryn and Rose held their hoods firmly in place and tried to flee, but someone was impatient and shoved Darryn away. He stumbled and fell, his hood also falling back, before the white stallion's hooves. The horse reared and retreated and the rider pulled at the reins to gain control. When he saw Darryn, he dismounted and knelt by him.

"Are you all right?" he asked in a lilting accent.

"Yes, I'm fine," Darryn protested and tried to hide his face.

"Let me help you," said the young man and took Darryn's arm. Suddenly his eyes widened and his jaw dropped. "Darryn?"

Now Jason's eyes widened and his jaw dropped.

The young man grinned and hauled Darryn to his feet. "What on earth are you doing here? And dressed as a commoner! Why didn't you tell me you were coming? I would have arranged rooms for you. Where's your sister?"

Rose stepped forward, dropping her hood. "Here I am, Marcus."

His dark eyes sparkled with merriment. "What are you two up to? You must tell me. But come, I'm on my way to the palace."

Jason was frozen in shocked silence. He had no idea of what was going on. It was like the whole world was thrown upside down and would not make sense.

"Is this your friend?" the man asked and smiled at Jason.

"Yes, may we please hurry to the palace?" Darryn said through clenched teeth, glancing uneasily at the curious faces around them.

"Certainly! Just fall in."

The next moment Jason was riding on Blue behind the young man between Rose and Darryn.

"What's going on?" he whispered harshly.

"I'll explain later," Darryn replied.

"Is he the king?" Jason asked, indicating the young man with the dark curls.

"No, he's the prince."

"How—"

"Not now!"

The palace was an enormous and beautiful building guarded by men in black tunics instead of red. The palace differed from the one in Setar in its architecture and it had a lighter atmosphere about it.

The prince led them toward the palace stables where the horses and Blue could be taken care of. Three young grooms immediately took charge of an animal each and Jason was satisfied to see the gentle care they were given. Then the friends were taken into the palace. Inside was surprisingly light and airy, with large open windows in all the rooms. The prince led them to a veranda overlooking the garden with plush sofas and a table full of fruit. He made himself comfortable on a sofa among the brightly coloured cushions and stared expectantly at Darryn. He and Rose had both taken their seats and Jason followed their suit hesitantly. Was he the only one who noticed the unusual amount of company he was spending among royalty?

"Marcus, this is our friend Jason," Darryn introduced him. "Jason, this is Prince Marcus Verillius, our cousin."

"Cousin?"

Darryn sighed and said, "My full name is Darryn Weylin Conall."

Jason felt his blood turn to ice. Conall was the family name of the royal house of Arden. "So you're...?"

Darryn nodded. "Crown Prince of the Northern Throne."

"So that means," Jason turned to look at Rose. "You're a princess?"

"Well, she is my sister," Darryn said. "She's Princess Rosaline Eirwen Conall."

"Why didn't you tell me?" Jason exploded. "I told you everything!"

"Jason, please," Darryn said, starting to become angry. "It's not something you just tell someone! We had to keep it secret."

"I trusted you!" Jason got to his feet. "I thought you were my friends."

"We are your friends. Just because you suddenly know who we are doesn't change that!"

"You don't understand," Jason glared. "I'm just a commoner, a peasant. I can't be here. It's not allowed. It's unheard of!"

"That's why we run away all the time," Darryn interjected. "We didn't choose to be born royal."

Marcus watched everything with an amused expression. "What precisely is going on?" he asked.

"I'll explain momentarily," Darryn said impatiently turning back to his friend. "Jason, trust us, we really want to help you."

"That's all very well and good, but as soon as all this is over we won't ever be able to see each other again," Jason said. He sat down and stared into space, breathing heavily.

"I know," Darryn said, also calming down. "And I hate it. But let's look at it like this, at least we did meet and are friends."

They were quiet for a while, allowing Jason to control his conflicting feelings. His brow creased and he looked at Darryn. Unexpectedly he asked, "How is Prince Marcus your cousin? You're nothing alike!"

Darryn stood for a moment in confusion before replying, "All the royal families of Greater Balisme are distantly related."

"Oh."

Darryn resumed his seat and Rose looked from one to the other and thought: *boys are strange.*

Darryn briefly and vaguely told Marcus of their adventures so far and emphasised their need for a ship. Marcus listened intently, his eyes sparkled and his mouth turned to a half-grin. When Darryn finished, he waited anxiously for Marcus to speak.

"I may be able to organise a ship for you," Marcus mused. "And I wish you would tell me why you need one, but I won't press the matter further. How soon would you like to leave?"

"As soon as possible," Darryn said.

"It's that urgent? All right, I'll pull a few strings down at the docks."

Jason could not believe his ears. A ship was being organised without any effort on their part and relief flooded him.

"When is the soonest we can leave?" Darryn enquired.

"I'll be able to tell you once I've organised the ship," Marcus said. "I suppose I'll have to go now before everyone retires to a tavern," he said. "If you need anything, ask a servant," he called over his shoulder before he left.

"I told you so," Darryn grinned at Jason.

Jason smiled and shook his head.

Why did he get mad at Darryn?

Marcus returned that evening with good news. One of Targon's esteemed merchants was travelling southward to trade with the Distant Isles and had agreed to take them along as passengers. It took some coaxing and bribing (and a little threatening) on Marcus' part to convince the merchant to pass through the Blacks instead of the usual route.

"Hector said that he and his crew will leave in two days and that you should meet him on the *Bella Donna*."

"Thank you, Marcus. How can I repay you?"

"By telling me the whole story when you get back!"

"All right." Darryn smiled and shook his hand.

Chapter 10:
Bella Donna

The three friends made their way through the crowds toward the harbour. Large, muscular sailors carried cargo across their broad shoulders, and husbands and wives said tearful goodbyes before the men departed on their long voyage.

"Where is our ship?" Jason asked, standing on his toes and peering around.

"Stop that," Darryn yanked him down. "You're not a child."

"Actually—" Jason started, but Darryn's look silenced him.

They walked along the pier watching the different ships. The ships docked were all shapes and sizes; some from foreign countries, others from neighbouring cities; small fishing boats to full-sized warships.

"Good day to you, Lady and Gentlemen," a round man greeted, tipping his hat. "May I help you?"

"It depends, who are you?" Darryn cocked and eyebrow.

"My name is Alfonso, self-appointed tour guide of Targon," the man chuckled.

"Do you know where the *Bella Donna* is?" Jason asked before Darryn could even open his mouth. "It's a merchant ship."

"Right this way, Sirs! And lady." Alfonso grinned and took them through the throngs until he stopped before a magnificent ship. Her prow rose metres above them and the masts several more. Great square sails billowed in the wind and gentle waves rocked her from side to side. Painted in black, red and gold, she was a magnificent craft. "There she is, the *Bella Donna*, the finest merchant ship in the whole known world."

They walked down the dock where the ship was moored and saw a man in rich clothing yelling instructions at sailors who were steadily loading crates and barrels onto the ship. In contrast to the Tiethans, his hair was golden and his eyes a bright blue. His skin was brown from long hours in the sun and had a leathery look about it. A young man who closely resembled him stood next to him, hands on hips and gazing at the horizon.

"'Ello Cap'n!" Alfonso waved his hat. "What a fine day it 'tis to set out on the big blue."

"What do you want Alfonso?" the man asked in a strange, flowing accent.

"Oh, I'm deeply insulted Cap'n, deeply insulted!"

"Shut up and get to your point man!"

Alfonso chuckled, holding his vast belly as if to keep it from falling off. "I was simply showin' these young gentlemen and lady your gorgeous ship."

The man flashed them a quick smile and a nod of acknowledgment. Darryn stepped forward and shook his hand, wincing at the crushing force with which he was greeted.

"Hello Captain, I am Darryn. This is my sister Rosaline and our friend Jason."

"Ah, the special passengers," the captain nodded. "My name is Captain James Swift This is my son Roan." The youth nodded and smiled, his eyes fixed on Rose. Jason felt a roaring sensation in his chest and the urge to hit someone had never been so strong before.

"Roan will show you your quarters. I just have to finish up here." The captain waved them toward the gangplank. "You should also be leaving Alfonso before an officer spots you."

"That I will do sir! An' thank you sir!" Alfonso bowed low, flourishing his hat. He winked at the trio and walked away whistling tunelessly.

"Roan, please give our guests a tour of the ship."

"Yes, Father." Roan led them to the gangplank where he smartly stepped aside and bowed, "After the lady."

Rose passed him without a glance. He did, however, suffer the wrath of Jason's glare. With a face like a thundercloud, Jason took up the rear of the party, out of sight and forgotten. First they were taken below deck to the cabins. They were each shown where they would sleep and were then shown the rest of the ship. When the tour was over, Jason left the others and walked to the ship railings. Looking out at the lapping waves, his thoughts were first occupied by images of Bastian, but were soon replaced by Rose. Without realizing it, Jason gripped the railing with increasing force as his blood boiled. Roan was flirting shamelessly with her. Not only that, Roan was also more handsome, more muscular and older than Jason.

Darryn approached him and leaned alongside him. "Well, here goes the last leg of the journey eh? Roan said we're casting off in about fifteen minutes."

Jason replied by exhaling loudly through his nose. Darryn raised his brows quizzically, then shrugged and walked away. *Forget Roan*, he scolded himself. *It's not like you ever had a chance with Rose anyway. Focus on Bastian, he's the most important thing right now.*

"All aboard!" someone roared.

Jason was suddenly caught up in the flurry and excitement of ship about to set sail. Sailors moved like acrobats along the rigging as they checked that everything was all right, while the helmsman took his place at the tiller. The captain shouted orders that Jason did not understand, but the sailors did and they obeyed them swiftly and effectively. He ran to the ship's prow, all thoughts of Roan and Bastian forgotten. For the moment, he was an explorer on an adventure into the unknown! Slowly the ship made her way into open waters, until the sails caught the wind and increased her speed. Fine salty spray shot up into Jason's face. It was cool and refreshing.

The good wind held well over three days before it slackened slightly. It had taken some time for Jason to hold his balance on the rocking boat, but once he discovered his sea legs he was hardly ever still. If he wasn't in the crow's nest, he was watching the helmsman or clambering up the rigging.

On the fifth day of the voyage, they encountered a school of odd fish-like creatures except they had skin, not scales and tiny holes on top of their heads. They playfully swam beside the ship, easily keeping up while jumping in and out of the waves. Jason leaned too far over the side and got squirted with a jet of water in the face to the roar of laughter. Spluttering and coughing while laughing at the same time, he wiped his eyes and face and blinked against the salty sting.

The sixth day they officially passed through Tiethan waters into the ocean beyond. There was a strange feel in the air that Jason could not explain. He felt it on his skin and his scalp. He remembered a phrase from earlier in his adventures: *Beyond the borders of humankind lies a world of wonder, magic and danger*. Later that evening, a large scaly tail was spotted just as it disappeared beneath the water's surface.

Several more days passed with nothing but empty waters stretching from horizon to horizon. This was a different sort of desolation from the desert, Jason thought. They were both so different, yet so strangely alike. Seemingly void of life, yet if you were willing to look far enough you might find it far too lively than you would wish.

The days blended into each other as they followed the same lazy pattern: eat, work, sleep. Jason found it maddening. The space was too confined for him. Everywhere he went, someone was there. To make it all worse, Roan was spending most of his free time with Rose, trying to win her over. Jason gleaned some satisfaction to see that none of Roan's attempts seemed successful. It gave him a warm fuzzy feeling in his stomach, like a nice hot meal on a cold winter's day.

Then there came a day where the wind was silent. The sails were furled and the sailors rowing down below. They rowed in shifts to make sure that they were fresh for any unpleasant surprises. Jason and Darryn helped with the rowing, Rose had offered to help too, but was refused.

"You just stay comfortable, Princess," Roan said with a stupid grin. "We'll take care of it."

When she passed Jason, he saw the flames roaring in her eyes. She did not like being given special treatment. After their rowing shift was over, Jason's arms and back muscles were aching and on the verge of cramping. Walking onto the deck, he rolled his shoulders and stretched his back to ease the aches when he saw something on the distant horizon. He had no idea in what direction it was, but it was there. Rose's attention also seemed to be fixed upon it and no one else noticed.

"Do you see it?" she asked quietly as Jason came to stand next to her.

"Yes, but what is it?"

"I don't know, but if it gets closer we have to tell the captain."

"Why?"

She fixed her intense gaze on him and his thoughts scattered. Had he ever seen such eyes before? Through the haze, her words somehow made it to his brain. "These are wild waters and that could be a pirate ship."

"Pirates?" he asked trying not to squeak.

Anxiously he stood watch with her, willing the thing to go away. He could still feel the cold steel of a knife pressed to his throat from when they were captured by the slave traders. It made his chest constrict. *Please no, please God!* he prayed. *Not again, please no!*

The watchman in the crow's nest called out, "Ship approaching from the south-south-west Cap'n!"

Captain James Swift took a spyglass from inside his coat and peered through it. Roan jumped to his side like an eager puppy. He lowered the spyglass, brow creasing and mouth pulled in a grim line. "It could be nothing. I can't see her colours yet, but everyone should remain on the alert."

Weapons were issued among the crew members, and Jason unexpectedly found himself in the possession of a pistol and rapier. He felt no safer with the weapons because of his little knowledge of how to use them. The pistol felt the least safe. He was afraid it might go off by itself at any moment. The captain continued to observe the approaching vessel until he cried out, "She's flown the black flag! It's pirates!"

Jason's hands were sweaty and shaking as he took the pistol

from his belt. Obeying the instructions of the sailor who gave him the weapon, he removed the safety and checked that it was loaded. It contained six rounds, far too few against possibly dozens of bloodthirsty corsairs. Rose also had her sword drawn and had somehow changed from her sleeveless dress into leggings and a shirt. Jason only vaguely registered this as he watched with growing dread as the pirate ship grew steadily closer. When it was close enough for the pirate flag to be seen by the naked eye, a loud boom thundered. A cannonball crashed into the ship's railings, splintering them with a crack and sending tiny projectiles around. The *Bella Donna* answered with her own canon fire, trying to keep the ship a safe distance from the pirates. If the pirates were to board the ship, they would be as good as lost.

Like some scary scene from a nightmare, the pirate ship continued to approach, despite the several gaping holes in her hull from successful hits.

"Open fire!" The captain roared and fired three rounds at the pirates. The sailors followed his example and the rapid fire of guns and canons rang out.

Jason nearly jumped out of his skin with terror as he saw the pirates. Not all of them were human. Some were scaly lizard-like creatures with purple tongues darting in and out of their reptilian snouts, while others were simply monstrous. The few that were human were only barely so. They bared their teeth and roared insults like animals. The ship shuddered and rocked as another shot found its target, but the hit felt different. Jason was nearly thrown off his feet as the ship shuddered. Suddenly and shockingly the *Bella Donna* began to move in the wrong direction.

"They have a bloody harpoon!" someone cried out.

Sailors ran to the port side of the ship and peered over. Jason joined them and saw a giant metal spear-like contraption imbedded in the ship. It was attached to a chain that was slowly dragging them toward the pirates.

"Get ready men!" the captain cried out.

The ships met with a jarring blow, their hulls scraping against each other. Like howling savages, the pirates boarded the *Bella Donna* with guns blazing and swords glittering. Jason wasted all six of his rounds on a single troll-like pirate before he fled. Dodging swipes and ducking every time he heard a gun fire, Jason just ran. Panic had completely taken over; he had no control over himself.

By sheer numbers, the pirate crew over powered the crew of the *Bella Donna*. They were either killed or captured and tied up. In the end, only Rose, Darryn, Roan and the captain remained fighting. They fought bravely, surrounded and greatly outnumbered by heartless cutthroats. Meanwhile, Jason was fleeing for his life with six vicious *things* after him. He ran the length of the ship until he ran out of space. Turning around, he saw the pirates quickly gaining. Desperately, he threw the nearest object at them, which unfortunately was just an empty glass bottle. It hit one in the head, but did little damage. When they got too close for comfort, he madly ran toward them, catching them off guard. Leaping up and using the ugly brute's head for leverage, Jason launched himself over their heads and ran madly below deck where other pirates were already looting the place. Once spotted, he turned tail and flew back on deck, nearly running into the *other* pirates for the second time. Instinctively, he lashed out with a kick, catching one in the gut and then fled.

Now eleven pirates were after him while his friends were slowly being captured. Jason ran right around the ship until he was cut off by the ugliest, hairiest man he had ever seen. With a whimper he took a few steps back, right into the arms of one of his pursuers.

"This one's been givin' us some trouble. Cap'n," his captor said in an earthy deep voice which was oddly nasal.

"Yeah, this one's fast."

The captain leaned in close, his breath so bad it was almost visible. The fumes drifted across the small space between their two faces and collided with Jason's nostrils. He deeply desired to cover his mouth and nose but could not. He struggled desperately, but in vain. The hands—or paws—that held him were not letting go.

"What will we do with you, boy?" He spat the word "boy" as if it was a disease he did not want to catch. He reached out and squeezed Jason's upper arm with his thumb and forefinger. "Not much muscle on this one, and running won't be useful to me."

Jason's eyes threatened to fall out if he widened them any further. His heart was pounding his ribs and his throat was so constricted that he could hardly breathe. He could see his friends, bound and held like him by thick, muscular pirates, at the edges of his vision.

"He's not of much use to me, and seeing as he's given you some trouble, I'll make an example of him." The pirate chuckled. His crew laughed unnecessarily aloud with him. "Tie him up with something heavy and throw him to the fishes."

"No!" Darryn yelled. "Let him go!" He struggled more violently than before. Rose kicked and wriggled as hard as she could.

"Please no!" Jason cried out as rough hands bound his hands behind his back and wrapped more rope around his body. He could not see what they tied behind his back but its weight dragged painfully at his arms. He was hauled up and taken to the side where he was gagged before they launched him over the side.

"JASON!" Darryn roared. Rose watched in shocked silence, her eyes wide.

He met the water with a loud splash, his back burning from the hard impact. The weight carried him further down and he struggled pitifully against his bonds. Tiny bubbles floated upward before his eyes, seeking to escape. His head was pounding from the pressure of being so deep and from the lack of oxygen. He was surrounded by nothing but blue darkness. His throat impulsively convulsed and his lungs pleaded for air. Darkness invaded the edges of his vision, closing in and robbing him of consciousness.

Darryn stared in shock at the spot where Jason was moments before. His limbs went limp and his life force was drained. The whole purpose for their mission was now lost beneath the waves sinking to his death. The pirates dragged them effortlessly onto their ship and after they finished looting the *Bella Donna* of her precious cargo, they set her ablaze. The flames were reflected in the glassy stares of her crew.

"Take the prisoners down to the cages," the captain ordered.

Below deck on the pirate ship were three more levels, the bottom level below the surface acted as a dungeon. The prisoners were thrown in there and the door locked behind them. Darryn stared blankly at the wood beneath them, not really seeing it. Gone. Just like that, gone. Jason, who had such a contagious smile, who was so spontaneous in everything he did. He blinked and tears spilled across his face. He sniffed and wiped them away.

Rose was alone in the corner, hugging her knees. She stared just as blankly at nothing in particular. Their adventure was over, the ending far from what they had foreseen.

As the shock slowly faded, the sadness Darryn felt was slowly being replaced by seething hate and anger. A beast was awakening in his chest and was roaring to be released. Once again the furious blood of his ancestors boiled in his veins. He sought revenge.

When the door was unlocked and opened Darryn was upon the unfortunate man like a panther. He bit, punched, kicked and scratched like a berserk animal. The man threw him off and kicked him in the face and the ribs.

"That will teach you, you bloody rat!" He wiped the blood from his face and stalked off to the corner where Rose was sitting. She jumped up and faced him fiercely, her eyes ablaze. "Now, now," the man hissed. "Try anything funny and the boy will get worse than a gentle telling off. The cap'n wants to see you."

Shivering on the floor Darryn glared through his tangled hair at the pirate as he led Rose away. Roan leaped at him with a loud yell, but the man was too quick and spun around and hit him in the gut. Roan collapsed clutching his stomach.

Darryn must have dozed off or lost consciousness, but he jerked awake when the cell door was reopened and Rose thrown inside. He hurried to her side and saw that she was clutching her throat with her right hand. "Are you all right? What happened?" he demanded.

"Nothing," she said a little harshly.

He pried her fingers away from her throat to reveal a shallow cut across her throat, blood trickling down across her collar.

"It's just a scratch," she said and pushed his hand away.

"What happened?" he hissed.

She did not reply and turned her back on him. He cursed and looked at the blood on his fingers.

"We'll get out of this somehow," he said. "And when we do, we'll finish Jason's mission for him."

Rose looked sharply over her shoulder at him, her dark blue eyes flickering dangerously.

Chapter 11:
Into the Deep End

Some hours later while the prisoners were sleeping, a strange shark/frog hybrid *thing* brought them food and dirty water. They eyed the poor fare with sinking hearts and bravely started to nibble at the grey-brown lumps that they hoped was stale bread. Darryn did not eat anything. He was sitting away from the rest, brows knitted in thought. He was a strategist, a planner, a man of action. He simply could not accept their fate as prisoners (again) for the rest of their lives. If no one else wanted to do something *he* certainly would. He scanned the bare cell walls for the hundredth time and for the hundredth time found nothing useful. The door was too sturdy to break down—he had tested it earlier—and there were no weaknesses that he could find anywhere else.

The door banged open again, causing everyone to jump. Another pirate entered the cell and with several grunts and gestures indicated for Rose to follow him.

"What's the matter ugly, can't talk?" Roan called hoarsely.

The pirate faced him and roared, revealing a little black stub in his mouth that once must have been a tongue.

Darryn could only watch as his sister was led away for further torture. He tried not to imagine what they would do to her and forced himself to think other thoughts. Much sooner than he expected he heard the pirates heavy footsteps return along with another sound that made his heart leap to his throat. There was the sound of something heavy being dragged across wood. Instead of opening their cell, the pirate seemed to move to the next cell. The door creaked open and then there was a thump as something was thrown inside. As soon as the pirate's footsteps had gone, Darryn scurried to the wall shared by the next cell and pressed his ear to a small crack. There was too much other noise for him to hear anything so he called out in a harsh whisper,

"Rose, Rose!"

Something stirred on the other side but no answer came.

"Rose, answer me! Are you all right?"

He slumped against the wall and a strange hopelessness settled over him. His heart sunk down to his feet and his limbs felt heavy. He had never done anything without his sister; she was always there. She can't be gone too! Taking a deep shuddering breath he got to his feet and began pacing. No more negative thoughts, he had to focus. Up and down, up and down he walked easily balanced as the boat rocked beneath his feet. He racked his mind until he was weary to the bone. Maybe sleep would reveal something to him. He crawled up against the cell wall close to the spot where he estimated Rose was lying injured or otherwise.

A brutal explosion blew most of the cell wall to smithereens, sending small wooden projectiles in all directions. Darryn flew up, dazed and confused, shielding his head from sharp wood splinters and other harmful objects.

"What in the blazes happened?" one of the sailors yelled.

Darryn stepped through the broken wall and saw that the cell next door was—no more. The door was nothing but a scorched frame standing amidst the wreckage. He frowned, what could have done this? When realization dawned, he ran as fast as he could up the stairs into the pirates' living quarters, which had turned into a battleground. At the centre of the wreckage, Rose was like a whirlwind of death and destruction. Her hands were chained behind her back, but she was kicking and slamming pirates around left and right.

Darryn was stunned for a few seconds as his mind struggled to process what he was seeing, but the present caught up and he grabbed a fallen pirate's sword and entered the fray. He hacked and slashed his way until he reached his sister. The look on her face sent shivers up his spine; it was cold and focussed and wild flames danced in her dark eyes. Just above her left brow was a harsh gash, but it must have been an old wound because the blood was already caked around it.

"Hello, Rose!" Darryn called over the noise.

"Hi!" she replied and bent backward to dodge a stab directed at her throat.

The other sailors had arrived on the scene in the meanwhile and just like Darryn watched in frozen, surprised silence before grabbing weapons themselves.

"Could you—" Rose began, but was interrupted when she had to dodge another swipe, "—free my hands?"

Darryn hacked away at her manacles until they broke off. In celebration of her freed hands Rose grabbed a sword and stabbed a pirate in the gut. "Thanks!"

"Don't mention it!" Darryn replied while disarming another pirate.

Caught completely off guard, recovering from a night of serious drinking, the pirates stood no chance against the prisoners. Soon they were throwing down their weapons and pleading for mercy. Darryn left the captain in charge, while he and Rose bounded up on deck and swiftly dealt with any remaining pirates before bursting into the pirate captain's cabin.

Imagine waking up with two dirty and bloodied teenagers holding sharp and dangerous weapons against your throat. You would probably feel like the pirate captain felt right at that moment; terrified out of your wits.

"Hello captain!" Darryn grinned wickedly.

All the pirates were tied up and thrown into the remaining cells under strict watch. Captain James promptly took over the pirate ship and changed the course back to their original destination.

Roan had just finished inspecting the pirate ship and was impressed. Despite some cleaning issues, it was a sound and beautiful craft. He stood at the helm, breathing in the fresh salty air. He spotted Rose at the prow, her long hair blowing in the wind. The corners of his mouth twitched into a smile and he walked with long confident strides toward her. He stood beside her, hands on hips and through the corner of his eye appreciated her beauty. Despite the bandage now wrapped around her brow, her appearance was unmarred. In fact, it made her look like a goddess of war. He stretched, slightly flexing his arms to get her attention, but her gaze remained on the water.

Disappointed by the little affect his first approach had, his smile faltered only a bit. He leaned against the railing, now openly staring at her. When he still received no reaction he said, "Silver for your thoughts?"

Her eyes flickered briefly upon him, and then back to the ocean.

"Your eyes look like the ocean at night," he said.

Her eyes returned to him, but her expression was unreadable.

"Why are you so serious all the time?" he asked. "If I make

you smile will you kiss me?"

A slight crease formed between her brows and she said, "Roan I hope you are aware that I am a princess of Arden."

"Yes, but I believe in destiny, Princess," he said and took one of her hands. Her eyes flickered down and the crease deepened.

"Even if I were not a princess," she pulled her hand away. "I still wouldn't advise that you continue to try and win me over. I know you do not believe me, but you and I can never be together."

"I don't understand."

She did not say anything. He sighed in frustration. What more could he do to convince her? A sudden mad desire caused him to lean in as if to kiss her, but she stiffened and backed away. Abruptly she turned and left.

"Princess, wait," he called. "I'm sorry, it was a mistake!"

She ignored him and continued walking.

⇒◆⇐

Waking up with sand in your nose, mouth and eyes is never a pleasant experience. Waking up and finding that you are still alive, however, makes the sand seem insignificant. Jason was violently brought to consciousness with a sneeze and severe coughing. He sat up and rubbed his eyes between several more sneezes. His mouth was dry and his lips cracked and salty.

Looking around in confusion he saw he was on a beach, behind him were only a few boulders and rocks where a gull was perched and ahead was a large lagoon, which joined the ocean further out. His brow creased as he tried to remember how he got there. He was on a ship and something happened – that much he could remember. But why was he on a ship? He had to find something,

something important for someone – Bastian! Memories started flooding back and he remembered the pirate attack and being thrown overboard. Just the memory of almost drowning made his chest tighten. But how did he wash up on this island? He was tied up! Someone must have freed him, but who and how?

He tried to stand up, but his legs were so weak and shaky that he collapsed back onto the warm sand. In this state he was too weak to do anything. How would he find food and water? With great effort he started to lift himself again, slowly so that he did not fall over again. He made his way to the boulders and the gull took off. Beyond the boulders was a vast tropical jungle that stretched endlessly. He would get hopelessly lost in there! He slid down and watched the waters gently lap the sand with a sigh.

Jason must have dozed off because he suddenly found himself lying down and something cold and wet was on his arm. He jerked upright and scrambled away quickly. A young woman, dripping wet, with long dark hair and slightly pointed ears was smiling at him. But his focus was not on her face, but on the tail sprouting from her waist ending in two fins.

"Y-you're a mermaid!" he finally managed to croak. The woman giggled and nodded.

"Very observant of you."

He still could not tear his gaze from the tail, it was so – *bizarre*! But unlike pictures or descriptions he had seen, the tail was not covered in fish scales but smooth skin like those other fish things they saw earlier on the voyage. What did Roan call them again? Dolphins?

"Did you save me?" he asked, his voice was hoarse and it hurt his throat when he spoke.

"I did."

"How?"

She rolled her eyes and moved a little closer to him. "Simple, I brought you onto the beach and cut the ropes off."

"You *carried* me?"

"Things, or at least humans, are much lighter in the water than on land."

"Oh." He did not ask any further questions, though the mermaid was watching him expectantly.

"My name's Iliana," she said. "What's yours?"

"Jason."

"How did you get in the water in the first place?"

"I was thrown into the water by pirates, they've captured my friends and I have no way of finding them now."

"Oh, you poor thing!" she cooed and the next thing he knew he was folded in a very tight, very wet embrace. As politely as possible, he wriggled out of her arms and scooted a little further away, but she just scooted closer.

"You might not know a way for me to find the pirates' ship do you?" he asked and moved a few more centimetres away.

She paused in her advance and after a second of thought she said, "My father might help, but he's very temperamental."

"Er, where is your father?" he eyed her tail uncertainly.

"Underwater of course!" she giggled. "I'll take you now if you want."

"Er, humans can't breathe underwater," he said quickly.

Iliana rolled her eyes again, "I know that, I'm not stupid. Wait here, I'll be right back." She slid down to the water and swam away. Jason stared after her wondering what she was doing.

Iliana's return was unexpected; she shot out of the water and landed on top of Jason. He jumped and tried to squirm out from under her, but she pushed him back down.

"Sit still," she ordered. He obeyed and watched as she put what looked like a slimy green collar around his neck. He tried not to recoil, but the thing was cold and covered in thick mucus. It was a very unpleasant sensation. The collar hung loosely around his neck, but gradually got smaller until it fit snugly around his throat. He reached up and tugged at it and found that it loosened itself easily. Assured by this he allowed it to tighten again and looked expectantly at Iliana. "Now you can breathe underwater."

She slid off him and into the water and he followed, feeling a little stupid. Should he just walk in or dive? She floated where it was deeper, waiting for him. With a coy smile she said, "It would be easier for you to swim without those clothes."

He blushed furiously and avoided her gaze as he walked into the warm waters. When he was deep enough he kicked away and experimentally ducked his head beneath the surface. Instinctively his throat tightened, but he dared it and took a deep breath. He expected water to wash down his throat and fill his airways, but to his surprise moist, salty air came through.

"What magic is this?" he asked and he was pleased that he could talk too.

Iliana laughed. "It's not magic. It's just crafted by merpeople."

Despite her assurance, Jason found it hard to believe that it was not magic. No human could ever create something like that. But this was no longer the world of humans, after all.

Iliana led him out to the open ocean and then took him straight down. They swam through coral cities inhabited by dozens of colourful little fish, past seaweed forests and around anemones. There was a whole other world down here! A lone shark swam past high above them, but did not even throw them a glance and a school of dolphins greeted them as they raced by.

Jason's eyes widened as they entered an underwater valley because at the centre was a vast and brightly coloured city that seemed to glow with its own light. Hundreds of merpeople swam in and out of buildings and through the streets. There were even patches outside the city tended to by farmers. It was straight out of all of the fairy tales that Jason had ever heard about.

They received many curious glances when they entered the city. Like Iliana, all the merpeople's tails were covered in skin, not scales, but they all had different patterns and colours. Their hair was equally bizarre, ranging from colours like blue to purple to green. Some had a faint bluish tinge in their skin. A young merman with navy blue hair approached them.

"What is this Iliana?" He came to a halt in front of them, floating with his arms folded across his chest.

"It's a human, what does it look like?" Iliana snapped.

The merman's cheeks flushed blue as he blushed, but his frown only deepened. "I know it's a human. What's it doing here?"

"I saved him," Iliana replied loftily and started to pull Jason along, but the merman blocked their way.

"Father won't be happy about it," he said.

"For your information, Kage," she said loudly, "I'm taking him to Dad."

The merman's eyes widened slightly in surprise and he raised his brows.

Iliana smiled triumphantly, pushed him aside and said, "Now if you'll excuse us, we have an appointment."

"I'd love to see the look on his face when he sees the human!" Kage jeered after her.

Iliana rolled her eyes and gently pulled Jason along.

"Excuse my idiotic brother," she said. "He's just trying to find a way to suck up to Dad."

"That's your brother?" Jason glanced over his shoulder.

"Unfortunately," she sighed.

"Why does he want to impress your father?"

"He accidentally released the sea monster from its cage. It went on a rampage, but luckily no one was hurt too badly. Dad had been angry at him ever since."

"That's a little harsh. Kage is his son after all."

"Yes, but when you're king you are held responsible for, well, everything."

"Your father's the king?" Jason spluttered. What was it with him meeting the whole world's royalty? He soon noticed that they were swimming straight for the largest building in the city, obviously the palace.

At every entrance two sentries armed with vicious spears were posted. Their armour was skilfully made to look like fish scales and their helmets like vicious shark heads. The main entrance was a grand double door the colour of amethyst which opened seemingly on its own. Jason's neck started hurting from trying to look at everything. Every surface; be it ceiling, wall or floor, was decorated with ocean-themed patterns. Inside the palace were several more merpeople and other creatures that were just as unique to Jason.

On their way to the throne room, everyone they passed bowed their heads to Iliana and greeted her. She impatiently returned the greetings and Jason was a little shocked by her rudeness. When he looked back over his shoulder, the people seemed unbothered. This must be a usual mood for her.

When they entered the throne room Jason's eyes threatened

to pop out. The throne was a large natural structure carved out of a strange stone. It was porous like coral, but it shimmered. The glittery structure appeared to have grown from the ceiling down until it met the ground. A small alcove for sitting in was carved out and seated in it was a magnificent merman with bronze skin and flowing blue hair and beard. To Jason's disappointment there was no trident in sight, but the king did wear a crown.

The king's eyes were dark grey, almost black, so when he fixed his gaze on Jason, the teen could not help but shrink away. With a voice like a stormy sea, the merking asked, "Daughter, what have you brought to my hall?"

"I saved him, Dad. He was thrown in the water by pirates."

A strange rumbling sound echoed in the king's chest. "Pirates," he growled, "they are the eternal thorn in my side. Why have you brought him here?"

"His friends were taken prisoner and he wants to find them."

"Out of the question!" the king exploded. "Madness! I will not allow it!"

The outbreak was so sudden that Jason nearly had a heart attack.

"But, Dad!"

"No, my decision is final. Why should we risk our lives to help this human?"

"Dad—"

"Silence! Leave me, I must rest."

With nearly the same stormy force as her father Iliana grabbed Jason's wrist and dragged him away.

"What now?" he asked once they were out of the king's earshot.

"I don't know," she replied abruptly. "I'll try again when he's in a better mood."

Jason chose not to say anything further. He did wonder where they were going though. Wherever it was, Iliana was swimming with a mission. At the outskirts of the city, Iiana pulled him toward a cave. Claustrophobia threatened to overtake him as they entered the dark hole. It was literally only a metre and a half from the entrance to the back of the cave. Why did Iliana bring him here? A nasty suspicion that she had just lured him there to flirt in private formed in his mind and he opened his mouth to confront her when she began pulling him upward. Following the direction with his gaze he saw that the cave continued as a tunnel straight upward as far as he could see.

"Where does this go?" he asked, but she was already swimming upward ahead of him. He followed her along the tunnel when they unexpectedly broke free of the water's surface into another small cave. He crawled onto the sandy bank and gazed at the rough ceiling. The ripples from the water reflected bluish patterns on the walls and ceiling.

"You can stay here," Iliana said from where she was floating in the water. "It's not comfortable, but you can't exactly stay underwater for too long. I'll bring you some food." She dived and disappeared down the tunnel leaving him wet and shivering on the small sandy bank.

Some while later a dark figure started to emerge from the tunnel. But instead of Iliana, Kage's head broke free of the surface. The intensity of his glare was enough to make Jason's skin crawl.

"Why are you here, human?" Kage demanded.

"Well Iliana said I can't stay underwater so she brought me to this cave—"

"I meant what are you doing *here*?" Kage exploded. "What are you doing here in *my* kingdom?"

"Er—"

"You should leave."

"Trust me I really wish I could."

Another dark shape emerged from below and Iliana appeared.

"What are you doing here?" she hissed at her brother.

"This is so unfair!" he cried out. "When you deliberately disobey a law, Dad does nothing! But when I accidentally release a stupid giant fish I get punished for life."

"At least when I broke a law it didn't destroy the city," she smiled smugly.

His cheeks blushed blue and he dove huffily beneath the surface. Iliana eased herself out of the water and settled beside Jason, placing a basket woven from sea grass on his lap. Peeking inside his stomach did a somersault as he saw it was a raw, skinned fish. Placing the basket to one side, he drew his legs up.

"What exactly happened with your brother?"

Iliana sighed and started inspecting the skin of her tail. "There is a fearsome monster called the firend, it's like a shark crossed with a sea serpent and an octopus. It terrorised our flocks and the outer reaches of the city until one day my father and a dozen brave warriors set out to catch it. They put it away in a cage under heavy lock and guard. But my brother, the idiot that he is, accidentally released it when he tried showing off to his friends. It destroyed a whole lot of buildings and injured a few people, but luckily no one got killed. Our father still hasn't forgiven him for it."

"That's horrible,"

She shrugged. "He deserves it."

"But he's your brother, isn't he?"

"So?"

He fell silent, not knowing what to say.

"Well, goodbye," Iliana said suddenly and slipped away into the water.

With a sigh of his own Jason opened the basket and looked at the pink fish. It looked very unappetizing; the dead bulging eyes seemed to stare at him.

"Are you angry at me too?" he asked and rested his chin in his hand.

Chapter 12:
Bloody Big Fish

Darryn was leaning against the railing of the ship, staring at the gentle waves caressing her hull. A heavy sigh escape through his nose and his heart sank further. Jason's absence was felt deeply. He may not have been very talkative, but in his own quiet way he had left an impression. The last horrible image Darryn had of Jason played over and over in his mind, haunting his every waking moment, even his dreams. Was this how Jason felt about his brother? Did he have the aching hole in his chest that refused to go away?

A pair of heavy feet stomped across the deck and halted alongside Darryn. He did not bother to look up and just continued gazing at the grey waters.

"Good morning, young master," the captain's voice greeted. But Darryn gave no answer. The seasoned seafarer softened and placed a hand gently on the boy's shoulder. "I am deeply sorry for the loss of your friend. He was—unique. If there was anything I could do I would, but bringing back the dead would be folly."

"Thank you Captain, I appreciate it," Darryn said and managed a small smile.

"Your sister," the captain said, "How's she taking it all?"

"I don't really know, Captain," Darryn sighed again. "I just don't know."

"Maybe you should see to her instead of wallowing in your own misery, eh?"

Darryn straightened up and glanced to the ship's prow where Rose's solitary figure stood. His eyes mirrored the grief he felt, changing them to a dark grey-blue. How was Rose handling the loss? She had spent some time with Jason when they were lost in the desert, but it was hard to decipher her emotions. Even Darryn, who had spent his entire life with her, could not always guess what was on her mind or in her heart. Slowly, he crossed the short distance and stood beside her.

"Hello," he greeted softly.

Rose continued to stare into the distance. Her eyes were hard and betrayed nothing that lurked beneath the surface. Her whole face was an expressionless mask, as always. Darryn felt pity well up unexpectedly. What must it be like to constantly hide your true feelings: never to be able to laugh or cry or even shout in anger? He knew this was her way of protecting herself against the world, against the hurt and the pain.

"Are you all right?" he continued.

She breathed in deeply, almost sighing. Carefully, gently, he reached out, something he had not done in a long time, and touched her hand. His fingers closed around hers and he squeezed them softly.

"Everything will be all right," he murmured.

"But he's gone," she spoke, her voice steady and calm.

His throat tightened and he tried to swallow around the lump that has risen. Choking slightly around the words, he said, "I know."

She spoke again, "He was," and she hesitated, "my friend."

Darryn looked up at her and saw a small weakening in her defences. In her eyes something had softened.

Jason tried in vain to examine himself from head to toe with a mirror the size of a clam shell. Iliana had brought him a shirt of glittering fish scales which just fit him. She tried to stay and watch him try it on, but he sent her off with a few carefully chosen words. The reason for the new attire was that Iliana reasoned her father was more likely to approve of him if he looked more presentable. They were going to find out later when Iliana took him to see the king again.

Iliana's head broke free of the surface and she bobbed there as he finished the last few adjustments to his attire. When he turned around she beamed at him.

"You look absolutely dashing," she said.

Blushing faintly, he jumped into the water and followed her back to the grandiose palace. As they passed the sentries again a thought occurred to him, how did the merpeople forge weapons underwater? Instead of taking him to the throne room like the previous day (or whatever it was since he could not tell day from night so deep underwater) Iliana led him to a smaller private room where the king was examining what appeared to be a large yellow fish. Ignoring the absurdity of it, Jason halted at a respectful distance and bowed as best as he could in the water. The king glanced up lazily and his brows met in scorn.

"Daughter, why is the human before me again?"

Iliana opened her mouth to reply, but was interrupted as Kage raced past her and floated in front their father's chair.

"It's unfair!" he shouted. The king glared at him.

"Is shouting necessary, Son?"

"But it's not fair! She disobeys a rule and she gets help, but I have an accident and I'm treated like slime."

The king stared long and hard at Kage, so long in fact that he started to squirm under the gaze.

"Very well, if you feel so strongly about this Son, then I have a solution," the king said. Kage grinned eagerly and stuck his tongue out at his sister who returned the gesture. "The human shall accompany you when you go out to recapture the beast."

Both Kage and Jason exclaimed, "WHAT?" Kage's expression was one of disbelief and anger, and Jason's one of utter terror.

"No more!" the king bellowed, causing a slight tremble in the palace. "This is my final word. Do not return unless you have the firend bound by chains or dead."

With murder all over his face, Kage turned around and he swam toward Jason. He brought his face up close and hissed, "This is your fault, human."

And this is how Jason found himself, not so many hours later, on the back of a giant creature called a seahorse, armed with a short sword made from some blue metal or stone and a large net woven from a similar substance. Completely dressed in battle armour and armed with a spear and net, Kage looked like one of the ocean gods in Jason's storybooks. He looked like a pathetic imposter, or so he thought of himself.

They were far away from the city and were travelling ever deeper into a thick, tangled forest of ocean plants. The seahorse was nothing like Blue, and frankly Jason preferred the pony. He kept slipping off the bizarre creature and it made unnerving jerking movements with its body as it moved through the water. Ahead, Kage parted the plants with his spear while keeping a wary eye out. Kage's face was covered by his helmet, so Jason had no idea if he felt as terrified as he did.

When the forest suddenly ended, Jason's heart lurched. Not too far ahead was a cave, a steady stream of bubbles shooting forth occasionally betrayed its resident. For a long while both boy and merman were frozen as they fully registered the danger ahead. Jason felt familiarity crash upon him. He had the same sort of feeling when he and Rose went to face the dragon. But he also had a feeling that this time they would not have the luck of encountering a semi-friendly creature who just craved freedom.

"All right," Kage breathed. His voice contained a slight tremor and the hand clutching his spear was shaking. "I'll sneak in while you wait outside."

"But—" Jason started to protest.

"No, human!" Kage snapped, then more shakily, "I have to do this. Wait outside and if something—" His voice broke on the word but he continued nonetheless, "—if something happens to me, please—please tell my father that I'm sorry and I tried my best."

Before Jason could protest further the merman dismounted and sped toward the cave. For a moment, Jason waited undecidedly on the seahorse's back. Should he obey Kage or plunge headlong into danger? He dismounted the seahorse, knowing with a groan what his decision would be.

Kage peered into the cave with his heart hammering in his throat. His limbs were trembling even more now that he was completely alone. The cave was dark, but there was enough light to see his foe at the back of the cave, lying on the ocean bed while bubbles streamed from the gills situated on either side of its head. Razor teeth that could easily bite through his middle protruded from it maw at all angles. But the black, merciless eyes were shut in slumber. Tightening his grip on the spear shaft, Kage silently drifted inside. He slowly reached over his shoulder and retrieved the net secured there. As he got ever closer to the creature he readied the net to be thrown. So far everything was going smoothly. When he got into the perfect position to throw the net he started swinging it above his head. The design of the weapon enabled it to cut easily and soundlessly through the water without meeting any resistance.

But then its eyes opened.

Kage's limbs went limp and his blood ran cold. He was utterly stricken by terror. With predatory confidence, the firend slowly rose from its bed and approached its stricken victim. It moved its body hypnotically from side to side, like a shark. Suddenly it lunged, jaws opened wide. Kage lunged out with the spear and jabbed the firend in between its eyes. The beast recoiled and Kage threw his net, but it got stuck against the firend's back so only its head was caught in the net. It struggled against the annoyance, causing part of the net that Kage still had in his hands to become tangled around his wrists. The unfortunate merman was pulled along with it in its struggle. It rolled over and over, only managing to tangle itself further and fastening poor Kage to its back. As Kage desperately tried to free himself, the creature struggled ever more violently. It started bashing itself against the walls of the cave, severely jostling Kage as it did.

Amidst all the chaos Kage got a glimpse of a small figure at the cave entrance and he felt a mixture of relief and anger. How dare the human disobey him! But he secretly hoped that the human would somehow help him.

Just then, the firend smashed Kage into the wall, causing him to lose consciousness.

Jason watched the spectacle in alarm. The first thought that popped into his head was, *that's a bloody big fish!* What on earth was he to do? Then strangely he felt irritated. Why was it that the capable warriors constantly left everything to him, an inexperienced healer's apprentice? Strangely, the irritation boosted his courage and he ventured into the cave almost without thought. He saw Kage slumped on the terrifying creature's back, in great danger of being killed by its wild thrashings. He had to do something fast. Using the net would be out of the question because he might strangle Kage. Glancing about he searched for anything that might provide a solution.

A blue glint caught his eye and he swam over to it, discovering it to be Kage's spear. He would still have to get uncomfortably close to the creature to use it properly. He had little faith in his aim as he was completely untrained in wielding a spear. There was always the danger that he might hit Kage. As he thought, he watched the firend get ever closer to the cave mouth and an idea occurred to him. But he had to move fast.

He raced for the exit and tied one part of his large net to a protruding rock and stuck the other end into the ocean floor with his sword. With the net nearly spanned across the entire cave mouth, he slipped through the small remaining gap and stuck the spear into the floor at an angle with the help of some rocks.

The firend crashed into the other net, losing some of its momentum, and getting its fins tangled, it skidded across the floor into the spear. It pierced its own skin and flesh as it thrashed about, and with a few more terrible movements it became still. After making completely sure the monster was dead, Jason hurried to free Kage, who miraculously did not suffer any further harm from his daring idea.

After he had freed Kage, Jason stood—or floated—back to examine the scene. How was he supposed to return an unconscious prince and dead creature back to the city? He glanced back at the seahorses and a smile spread across his face.

Kage woke with a yell, but he blushed a brilliant blue when he saw where he was. Jason grinned at him from the other seahorse's back. Behind them, pulled along by the seahorses in the nets, was the enormous dead firend.

"Thank you, human," Kage said quietly, avoiding his gaze.

"Don't worry about it. Oh, and let me do the talking when we see your father."

Kage frowned quizzically, but nodded his agreement. "Very well, human."

"And my name is Jason."

"Jason," Kage repeated.

There was a great uproar when they swam into the city with the firend in tow. Merpeople crowded round from everywhere, pointing and shouting and talking excitedly. Some cheered Kage's name, while others played instruments. But for some reason Kage still looked unhappy. When they entered the king's throne room Jason thoroughly enjoyed the ruler's expression of surprise when he saw the firend. Glancing from firend to his son a few times he finally stuttered,

"How?"

Jason came to Kage's rescue. "Your Majesty," he said with a flourishing bow. "Your son has singlehandedly and valiantly slain the beast while I was helplessly caught against its back with my own net, knocked unconscious. He has saved my life and I am in debt." Jason bowed now to Kage, who looked properly bewildered.

"No, I—" he started to protest, but the glance Jason shot him made him fall silent.

The king's mouth broadened into a wide smile and he rushed forward, enveloping his son in a tight embrace. The gesture was so unexpected that a sob escaped Kage's lips.

"I am proud of you my son," the king wept. "You are a hero!"

Kage's eyes asked the question that burned on his tongue across his father's shoulder at Jason. Jason just smiled at him and bowed again.

An hour later, Kage confronted Jason in his little cave where he was passionately describing Kage's heroic battle with the monster to Iliana. Kage gave them a small smile as he slipped onto the shore.

"Iliana, my I have a quick moment with Jason in private?"

She pulled a face at him, but Jason quickly intervened. "Just for a few minutes, I promise," he said to her. Her expression softened a little and flashing him a wide smile she disappeared into the water. Some awkward silence followed.

"Listen, er, thank you," Kage said hesitantly. "Thank you for what you did for me with my father and everything."

"You're welcome," Jason said. He was smiling, but Kage's expression was still serious.

"But why did you lie to everyone about what really happened?"

"Because you needed this more than I did. I'm not interested in taking the glory that should rightfully be yours."

"Thank you. But what can I do for you in return?"

"Is there some way you can help me find a particular pirate ship?"

Though the ship was heading in a generally southern direction it felt as if she was just drifting aimlessly about. There just was no fire or spirit behind the mission any more. Darryn spent a lot of time alone, becoming more withdrawn and distant like Rose. Outwardly she appeared her normal self, but who knew what was going on behind that pretty mask?

The captain stood at the helm, surveying everything with a practised eye. His heart ached for the prince and the princess for he had children of his own, Roan being the eldest. They needed something to distract their thoughts, to get their mind off things.

"Er, Captain?" someone shouted uncertainly. He glanced in the speaker's direction. It was a sailor leaning over the railings, ropes coiled across one shoulder. He approached the man and followed his gaze.

"Yes, Mr Octavian?"

"There's something down there Captain, something big."

His first instinct was to dispel the man's sighting to a trick of the light, but thought better of it. After peering for a long time he too imagined seeing dark shadows, not too near the surface, but not too deep. The waters this far from Tiethe were not as clear as the beautiful blue waters they left weeks ago. It looked like the distraction he asked for came too soon.

"Your Highness, lend me your young eyes for a moment," the captain called.

Darryn walked over like a man in a daze. After being briefly informed on what he was looking for, he peered over the edge. After some time a slight crease formed on his brow, which deepened further. Suddenly the worried look disappeared as his brows pulled back in disbelief, his blue eyes wide.

"Rose," he called. "Rose, come here quickly!"

The captain and the sailor hurriedly peered over the railings again and the sailor cursed. Bobbing up and down in the waves was Jason's head, beaming up at them.

Rose arrived and peered over the edge, her eyes widened incredulously and her mouth opened slightly.

The captain reacted first. He called for men to throw lifelines in and they pulled the dripping boy on board. At first, he was surrounded on all sides by curious men prodding and checking him to see if he was all right and *real*. When the satisfied men stood back, Darryn and Rose stared as if seeing a ghost. Jason spread his arms out and grinned.

"I'm back!"

Darryn's expression turned into a broad smile as he said, "You little—!" and he embraced his friend as a brother. "Where have you been? We thought you were dead!"

Jason met Rose's gaze and gave her a small smile. She smiled back, a proper smile for the first time.

"It's a long story. I—" Jason stopped as he seemed to remember something and he rushed to the side of the ship, leaning over. Darryn and Rose hurried to join him, trying to see what he was looking for. All Darryn saw was a tail, not unlike a dolphin's, disappearing beneath the waters. Glancing at Jason, he only saw a sad smile on his friend's face as he stared at the spot where the thing disappeared.

Sometime later, after Jason had changed into dry clothes and been given some food, he recounted his adventure underwater. His friends and some of the crew listened eagerly, roaring with laughter when he described how he was "knocked unconscious" by the firend and caught against its back with his own net. He had kept his and Kage's secret.

With tears in his eyes and choking with laughter, Darryn cried out, "I can imagine you strapped like an idiot to a sea monster's back!" And they fell into another bout of hysterics.

"So then the prince said that because I sort of helped him kill the creature, he would help me find the pirate ship. We set out this morning, although it's so hard to tell the time when you're deep underwater. We took the seahorses and by means I don't really understand, we found the ship, and, well, here I am. But what happened while I was gone? I expected you to be bound in chains needing to be rescued from the pirates."

Darryn very briefly informed him on what happened—only vaguely recounting the explosion—and when he finished Jason was silent for some while in thought.

"How far are we from the Blacks?" Jason asked.

"The captain said as far as I remember that we should see the first signs of it in two or three days, depending on the wind."

Jason nodded and stared southward where he might, or might not find his only hope of saving Bastian.

Chapter 13:
The Blacks

The following day was mild in its weather and a favouring wind sent them steadily toward their destination. It was one of those types of days where you just could not help but feel lazy and unwilling to move. Captain James Swift did not trust it. Not when they were so close to the most dangerous waters known to him.

"Captain!" a sailor barked.

Reacting on the call he turned around. "Yes?"

"Something be approaching from the east, Sir!"

Immediately on the alert, the captain checked his spyglass for any signs of danger. The man spoke the truth. A ship was steadily sailing in their direction from the east. If it was another pirate ship, they might not be as lucky as they were before. Maybe if they flew their ship's black flag they would be left alone.

"Captain?"

"Fly the colours," the captain ordered.

The lazy atmosphere shattered as sailors jumped to attention on high alert to the possible danger. The tension hung in the air like a bowstring. It took some time for the other ship to come reasonably close. It was moving very slowly for some unknown reason. Through his spyglass, the captain saw that the ships sails hung in limp tatters from the mast, the deck devoid of life. The sight of an unmanned ship sailing on its own made the captain's skin crawl. Steadily the ship continued on its ghostly journey until it was abreast of their ship. Everyone aboard the ship watched the other uneasily, shifting where they stood from foot to foot.

Jason felt the hairs on the back of his neck rise. He could almost hear the eerie creaking of the riggings on the other ship. The torn sails flapped uselessly in the wind. A sudden cry caused him to almost leap from his skin. He glared at the captain, thinking it was stupid to taunt or tempt whatever was driving that ship onward.

"Ahoy!" the captain called again.

Something slammed, possibly a cabin door on loose hinges, on the other ship. Then in the stillness a rhythmical *thump, thump* could be heard crossing the deck. Jason swallowed and gripped the railing tightly. *Thump, thump, thump, thump.* The steps continued until a figure appeared at the shattered railings. A chill ran up Jason's spine, the sailors cursed collectively under their breaths. But Captain James stood his ground.

"Who is the captain of this vessel? I wish to speak with him."

The figure opposite was dressed in rags which once must have been very grand clothes. His dark grey hair was long and tangled as well as his beard, but his posture was tall and proud. His mouth opened and laughter boomed forth, long and loud. It caused more unease with the crew.

"I am the captain," the man called after he calmed down. His voice was deep and gravelly.

"Where is your crew?" Captain James called.

"Gone. They jumped overboard from madness."

Jason and Darryn exchanged glances. What could drive a man to such desperation?

"What madness caused this?"

"Sirens, a fortnight's journey eastward."

Jason did not know what sirens were, but by the sailors' reaction he judged that they were something bad.

"How did you come to survive?"

Here the man laughed again. "I got trapped when my cabin door locked itself on me. Can't really remember much after that."

"What is your name, Captain?"

The man straightened up smartly, "Captain Robert Jones, at your service!"

"Would you like to come aboard our ship Captain Jones? Forgive its appearance, but we were captured by pirates and we took their ship."

"You must tell me the tale!" Captain Jones called.

After they brought him aboard and salvaged what little they could from Jones' ship, the poor man was taken to a cabin where he could get dressed and cleaned up. When he emerged, his hair was cut neatly and his beard trimmed. He was wearing one of the captain's navy blue coats.

"So tell me, Captain," Jones said, walking with his hands clasped firmly behind his back. "Where are you and your merry crew headed?"

"I will explain thoroughly later, but for now all you need to know is that we are on a course for the Blacks."

"The Blacks?" Jones paused, his brows lifted. Then he laughed that strange laugh of his and he rubbed his hands together. "Excellent! This is a venture worthy of history books."

"There is a large chance that we will not make it through, Jones."

"Yes, but isn't that what makes it so terrific?"

"Hmm," the captain replied. "But I will be grateful if you aid us through. No doubt, your experience will be useful."

Jones puffed his chest out slightly. "Yes, I have been through many dangers, the most of which I have daringly escaped from on my own. Which reminds me, I must tell you of the time when I was stranded on the island of women cannibals—" Jones started recounting with the unfortunate captain in tow.

Near the end of the day a strong wind picked up, speeding the ship onward. Jason was both heartened and terrified. He had heard the sailors speak and what they murmured of the Blacks was grim.

"Do you think," Jason asked of Darryn. "That I'm just sending us all to our death?"

Darryn gripped his friend's shoulder with a smile and said, "Not even you are that powerful, Jason. Everyone on this voyage is here because he volunteered to be."

"But still,"

"Don't worry, anything is possible. Why you came back from the dead, didn't you?" Darryn chuckled.

The first sign of bad weather could be seen on the horizon the following day. A never-ending mass of dark and ominous clouds stretched across the distant sky. Lightning flashed constantly, illuminating that dark sky for brief moments. But the wind held and surged them ever on. The waves steadily became larger and rougher, but not enough for it to be too noticeable. Everyone was tense and nervous, snapping at the smallest provocation. Many angry words were exchanged and violent outbreaks threatened to occur. The greatest danger, however, was that the sailors would completely lose their nerve and commit mutiny.

Jason stood at the prow of the ship, his shirt billowing in the increasing wind. He said a silent prayer and hoped that God would as merciful to him as He had been throughout his adventure. They had come so far now, through so many things. It could not end now, not here.

Rose unexpectedly spoke behind him. "Nervous?"

"Well—" Jason grimaced. "Are you?"

She shrugged, her eyes roving the horizon. "Not really."

"Is there anything you are afraid of?" he asked.

"Just one," she replied evasively. Then she said, "You have faced shadow beasts, a dragon, a sea monster and a lot more, and yet you are afraid of a storm?"

He nodded. "I cannot fight a storm."

"No, but you can survive."

They passed into the Blacks in utter silence. A black wall of storm clouds was before them, stretching as far as the eye could see. Thunder rumbled nonstop from within. Every man was at his post, threatened with execution should he leave it unless by order. They all watched with wide eyes as the prow plunged into the darkness, disappearing from their sight as the Blacks slowly devoured its prey.

"Steady men!" Jones bellowed, his sword drawn and pointing at the Blacks. His eyes sparkled madly as the ship continued to disappear.

Jason recoiled as he passed through the dark cloud, but nothing happened to him. Inside it was pitch-black except for the occasional lightning flash. There was an eerie silence all around but for the creaking of the ship. The waves were deceivingly calm, licking at the ship's hull. No one dared to break the silence, no one but Jones, that is.

"Don't be fooled men! She's only tricking you—the storm is coming. I can smell it!"

Jason felt the back of his head prickle and slowly he turned around, not really wanting to see what horror waited. His mouth opened in a silent yell and his eyes were as wide as dinner plates. Rising metres above the ship was a gargantuan wave. Dark foam frothed at its zenith as it curved, ready to pounce upon them. Darryn saw Jason's face and when he turned around he shouted at the top of his lungs,

"GET READY!"

The wave crashed upon the ship's deck, drenching them all. Thunder boomed. Rain poured down upon them as the ship rose and fell at crazy angles. All the while, Jones was clutching at the railings of the ship, laughing like a maniac as the ship pitched and fell.

"Furl the sails!" the captain bellowed, but as the men started to climb lightning flashed and struck the top of the foremast with a deafening crack. The mast splintered and fell to the deck below, narrowly missing the crew. "Belay that!" the captain roared. "Leave 'em!"

Three men were wrestling with the tiller, struggling to keep them on their course. Jason was dashing around carrying out orders or assisting others. He slipped on the wet deck and fell heavily.

"Master Davies!" the captain roared. "Secure the lifelines!"

"Aye, Captain!" Mr Davies ran to the stump that remained of the foremast where everyone's lifelines were tied. He checked every knot to see if they were still secure. Jason helped him while rain beat at them, running down their shirt collars and soaking them to the bone.

Another tremendous explosion caused them to look up. Nothing appeared to have been hit as they squinted through the torrents. Suddenly, a giant bird-like creature swooped down and everyone ducked out of its reach. Jason actually heard its plumage crackle as it narrowly missed his head. The flying thing circled the ship high above before diving again. Its body appeared like black smoke with millions of tiny lightning bolts running along it, writhing and sparking like tiny fireworks.

"What are these things?" Jason cried out.

"They're thunderbirds," Jones yelled calmly. "They're born in only the roughest of storms."

Three more explosions gave birth to three more thunderbirds, and they continued to antagonise the crew while they wrestled with the storm. Another tsunami-size wave crashed down upon them and for a few terrorising moments, the ship was submerged before she faithfully broke free of the surface again. Jason's laughter died on his lips as the ship was yet again plunged into the freezing water. When she re-emerged, he was spluttering and coughing on the deck. When he recovered, Jason glanced around through his wet tresses to see if anyone needed help, but they were all too preoccupied with surviving to notice him.

Then the wind changed direction.

The entire ship lurched to one side as it was buffeted. Stinging fat drops now blew in from the side and the ship was being taken into the wrong direction. The men at the tiller had increased to six, but even that was not enough to get the ship back on course.

"We have to furl the sails!" Jason called out, but no one heard. He looked about desperately and realised with a sinking heart that he had to do it. Taking a deep breath, he started to climb along the rigging of the main mast, rain battering down upon his upturned face. He had to shut his eyes to protect them, so he was going mainly on feeling. Once when a particularly violent wave crashed against the ship, he lost his footing but grabbed on with one hand. For a few terrifying moments he hung there, staring at the deck meters below. If he fell from that height, with or without the life-line, they would have to scrape his remains from the planks below.

Gritting his teeth, he pulled himself back up and continued the climb. His hair was plastered to his brow and face while streams of water poured down his back and the front of his shirt. This high up the mast swayed dangerously in the storm, he could easily be thrown off if he was not careful enough. When he reached the first boom he crawled onto it, holding onto the mast for support and balance. With one hand clinging to the mast he inched outward, the other hand stretched out. He shuffled slowly across the slippery surface until he could stretch no further. He tried to lean outward, but even that was not enough. Slowly he released his grip on the mast and inched further outward with outstretched arms. He wobbled and swayed, but continued grimly.

Far below, Darryn had realised Jason's absence. He looked everywhere for his friend, fearing that he had lost him to the ocean again, but then he looked up and saw Jason battling with the sails. He cursed loudly, but his words were caught in the wind.

Jason's shirt billowed wildly around him as he tried to keep his grip on the ropes. They lashed about like wet snakes and were hard to hold on to. Losing his balance, Jason's heart lurched as he fell. What would it be like to die? Would it hurt? But a hand unexpectedly gripped his wrist. It hurt terribly, but he almost cried with relief. He was blinded by the rain and could not see his saviour until he was back safely on the boom.

"Are you barking mad?" Darryn cried out, but he was grinning broadly with relief. Jason laughed as he gripped his friend's shoulder. Together they managed to furl all the main mast's sails without further incident. When their feet were safely and firmly planted back on deck, it was obvious that the ship was more under their control. But they were still in the storm.

There were now six thunderbirds crackling above their heads, but they had stopped attacking for some reason. Jones waved his sword at them, hopping from one foot to the other and he roared, "Yar, you cowards! Come at me!"

"Why have they stopped?" Jason called over the storm, but Darryn did not hear, he was concentrating on the birds.

An exceptionally violent crack of lightning threw them all off their feet. Jason shakily stood back up and searched about. Everything seemed to go quiet but for an odd sound that echoed in the stillness. The thunderbirds screeched excitedly and Jones muttered something, but no one cared enough to hear.

The sound nagged at Jason's memory, but he could not remember where he had heard it before. It sounded—it sounded like the flapping of—giant wings. His memory recalled the sound from when he had ridden on Gamon's back.

"Here comes mama," Darryn said grimly and drew his sword.

A thunderbird easily half the ship's size descended from the stormy heavens and hovered with her offspring for a few moments before diving. Jones charged at her with a bloodthirsty cry, but Jason tackled him before he could foolishly stick his weapon into her body. He had tackled the man hard enough to knock him momentarily unconscious.

"What should we do?" Jason yelled.

"I don't know," Darryn replied, his long hair whipping into his face. He irritably held them out of his eyes with one hand while the other was ready with his sword.

Jason realised with an icy feeling that he had forgotten about

Rose and immediately he searched about for her. He found her with her hair blowing wildly around her as she followed the mother thunderbird with her gaze.

"Rose, no!" he yelled, but she could not hear him.

As the mother gained enough altitude she turned and swooped down again. Rose started running and so did Jason. He ran as fast as he could to stop her from what he knew she wanted to do. But he slipped in a puddle of water and slammed into the deck. He watched in horror as Rose gained distance between her and the bird. He saw her raise her sword and he looked away, shutting his eyes tight. All he heard was a terrible cry from the bird, which was like thunder but more high-pitched. Daring to look, he glanced up and saw the bird stagger about with Rose's blade in her breast, lightning crackling around the blade and hilt. But where was Rose? To his relief he saw her not too far away, watching the bird. How is she still alive? With a final cry, the bird exploded in a flash of blinding white light accompanied by the loudest boom of thunder he had ever heard. When he opened his eyes again Rose was picking her sword up from where it lay on the deck, no sign of the thunderbird remained.

"What happened?" he asked her when she approached him.

"I threw my sword at her."

He felt terribly stupid now, but did not have long to feel embarrassed as the storm seemed to reach its climax. The rain was replaced by enormous hailstones that not only bruised, but bit viciously into the skin. The other birds left with the arrival of the hail, but after only a few minutes the sailors realised that they preferred the birds over the icy stones pelting them. Jones was in danger of being killed where he lay still unconscious. Jason less than graciously dragged him below deck where he was out of the way.

Nearly all of the waves were now larger than the ship. If they remained in the Blacks any longer, the crew would not survive, never mind the ship. Captain James yelled orders non-stop to keep the ship afloat and Jason was certain if not for him they might have perished a lot sooner. Roan proved quite capable of a lot himself, earning some grudging respect from Jason. At least he seemed to be leaving Rose alone now.

The mother of all waves started to form, rising metres above the ship's main mast. They needed a miracle to survive this growing monstrosity. Jason felt with certainty that this was the end. He had come very close to dying several times throughout his journey, but every time he had friends to help him through it. Now, no one could help him. He had doomed them all.

Suddenly they passed through a thick wall of cloud, the hail stopped and the wave was gone. They had survived the Blacks and had reached its heart where the waters were as still as a garden pond and the sky the clearest, cloudless blue. Jason's heart swelled with gratitude and he drank in the warmth of the sun on his cold, wet limbs. Everyone was rendered speechless as they just stared at their surroundings. They were alive! They made it!

Slowly and softly their quiet murmurings swelled to cheers of triumph. Men shook hands and grasped shoulders or wept openly. They would live to see another day! Tears streamed down the captain's face as he prayed to the sky, eyes closed and lips moving silently.

Jason grinned at his friends and even Rose smiled back. Nothing would dampen their spirits, at least for now.

The captain gave his crew the rest of the day off and they all gratefully retired to their bunks and slept. Jones woke some time later, completely disorientated and convinced that he had singlehandedly steered them to safety.

Jason rested contently against the ship's railings, too excited to sleep. His journey was nearly complete. Once or twice, he did wonder how they would get back, but he quickly pushed that thought away. They would deal with that later.

The ship was caught in a gentle current that led them further toward the centre of the heart. In the sunlight, it was obvious that she was in desperate need of repair. She seemed to be held together by mercy alone. But no one seemed to care; they were all filled with a strange calm that could not be broken.

When the black cloud walls were completely out of sight something else loomed above high up in the sky. Except for the three friends and the captain, everyone was else fast asleep, dreaming sweet untroubled dreams. Jason spotted the thing first and gazed dreamily at it. Later his friends joined him.

"What do you suppose that is?' he asked softly.

"A bird?" Darryn suggested and rested his chin in his hand.

"No, too big."

The current gradually picked up in speed, but not at an alarming rate so the object got closer and closer by the league. Jason gasped loudly, the volume increased by the drowsy silence.

"I—it's the island," he said incredulously.

Darryn nodded dumbly.

"How on earth are we supposed to reach *that*?" he cried out.

"Calm down lad, get some rest. We'll think of something tomorrow," the captain said and retired to his cabin.

"He's right, Jason, come on," Darryn said.

The gentle happiness descended upon Jason again and he floated down to his bunk where he promptly fell asleep.

Chapter 14:
The Island

Waking up was a completely disorientating experience. Instead of waking up in their bunks on the ship the sailors opened their eyes to a blue sky above with soft grass beneath them. They sat up grumbling and muttering among each other, wondering where they were and how they got there.

Jason momentarily thought he was back at home waking up in one of the nearby fields, but after he looked around he only felt confused. Standing up, he walked over to Darryn, who was surveying his surroundings.

"Where are we?" he asked.

Darryn turned and with a funny look on his face said, "I have a suspicion that we are *on* the island."

"But the island was kilometres above us!"

Darryn shrugged. "Then I don't know," he paused. "Unless we only dreamed we passed through the Blacks and are actually dead and we're in heaven."

Jason opened his mouth to say something, but thought better of it. He just shook his head and walked toward the island's edge. Inching forward, he peered down and his head starting spinning from the dizzying height. Far below, the ship was a mere smudge on a large blue canvas. He stumbled backward away from the edge, trying to control his insides that suddenly felt upside down. When he turned around he nearly collided with an elderly man with short, cropped grey hair and a neat beard speckled with black.

Jason's eyes widened in alarm and he took a step backward as the stranger glared at him from under heavy brows. His eyes were a dark stormy-grey and they had a hawk-like quality in the way they stared. Clothed in a blue-grey robe-like garb he looked like some ancient scholar that had walked straight of the page of one of Jason's storybooks. All the others also noticed the man who apparently had appeared out of nowhere and whispered uneasily to each other. The strange man examined each and every person carefully and with great intensity, although Jason thought that his gaze stayed longer on him and his two friends than the others.

His voice was deep and echoed with age and wisdom when he finally spoke. "Welcome, weary travellers to the Isle of Dreams."

"The what?"

"What did he say?" sailors murmured.

Jason took a deep breath and ventured to ask, "Sir, are you the Dream Keeper?"

The man fixed his gaze upon him, but he remained firm though his limbs trembled.

"I am, and who is it that seeks me?"

"Jason Thorn, Sir," Jason said.

"Did you bring us onto this island?" Darryn called.

The Dream Keeper turned and faced him as if he was a naughty little boy who had been caught in doing something wrong. Darryn's smile faltered and he seemed to shrink under the Dream Keeper's stare.

"No," he replied. "The only way to get to the Isle of Dreams is to fall asleep."

"So, we're actually still asleep? This is a dream?" a sailor asked.

"No, you are awake."

"What magic is this," someone else cried out.

Jason's heart sank, was this the person who was to help him? This stern, unsmiling figure?

The Dream Keeper spoke again, a little more commanding in his tone now. "The three who sought me must step forward now."

Darryn looked uncertainly at Rose and then at Jason before stepping forward and saying, "I am one of them, Sir. Darryn Conall."

Jason also stepped forward and then Rose. The three stood before the Dream Keeper and he examined each of them before speaking again.

"You have come far for ones so young. You have great courage and—" now he was looking at Jason. "Great hearts. Because of this, I will allow you into my palace. Inside there is a room full of treasures among which there is a tree—"

The Wish Tree, Jason thought, remembering what he had read in Setar.

"This tree grants any wish at all, but only one to each person. The wish comes at a price though; the price of blood must be paid. Only a small drop is needed."

Jason released a sigh of relief, it sounded simple enough.

"But," the Dream Keeper said, bursting his happy bubble. "I must also tell you. Before you reach the treasure room you must pass through two levels first: Dream and Memory. I must warn you, you are entering the world of your dreams while fully awake. The dangers are innumerable. Always remember that, for it could save your life. And you must not eat any of the food or drink once you enter the palace. The consequences could be disastrous, if not fatal."

Jason exchanged an anxious glance with Darryn.

"Once you have passed through Dream, you must go through Memory. My warning here is: do not tarry, do not falter. If you leave the path you may get lost in your past forever. Do not look back, only forward until you reach the door to the Treasure Room. If you are fortunate, this is where your paths will meet again."

"Anything else?" Darryn asked.

"Yes," the Dream Keeper replied, the word dropping like a heavy weight. "Know that when you enter the palace, you enter it alone. You will face danger and you will face temptation. Now it is for you to decide if you wish to proceed."

After a few moments of consideration, Jason said, "I'll go." Then he turned to Darryn and Rose and said, "You don't have to take the risk, but I must go. Thank you for everything."

"No," Darryn said. "I'm going. Rose?"

She nodded firmly.

"Very well, if this is your decision then you may proceed. Good luck, and may you find what you seek," the Dream Keeper said. He then faced the large empty stretch of grass that continued on to the edges of the island.

A deep rumbling echoed through the earth along with a tremor that shook the ground beneath their feet. In front of their eyes a great building that seemed to be entirely made of crystal and other precious stones rose from the island, its towers glittering in the bright sun. The grassy ground tumbled from its walls as the structure grew ever taller. With a final shudder, it came to a halt.

Exchanging a last few glances with his friends, Jason took the first step. The door opened by itself when he stood a metre from it.

Beyond, there was only a blinding white light. Clenching his fists and squaring his shoulders, Jason stepped through. Rose walked calmly forward next, closely followed by Darryn. There was no turning back now.

Chapter 15:
Jason's Dream

After he had passed through the white light, Jason found himself in a dimly lit circular room. He blinked a little to get used to the sudden change in surroundings before properly examining it. Every available portion of wall was covered in clocks: old wooden ones, absurd ones with uncountable hands, metallic ones, cuckoo clocks and more. None of them showed the same time and some of them even had more time than others. Every now and then one would chime or boom or sing. When he had gone around the room twice, he found that there was no door. Glancing upward he saw that the room continued seemingly without end into darkness.

A droplet fell and landed on his brow. Frowning, he wiped it off and looked up again. Another droplet fell, landing on his nose this time. It couldn't be raining, could it? Not inside? Well, it was his "dream" after all, so why not?

Just as Jason wondered how to go up, he heard an odd sound. *Tik-a-tik-a-tik-a* – Descending into view was an odd platform construction with a propeller underneath it. It stopped in front of him at knee height and hovered there. Could he trust this strange thing? Hesitantly, he placed one foot upon it. It rocked a little under the pressure, but not too severely so he stepped on with his other foot. He wobbled a little, but once he regained his balance the thing slowly began to rise.

What seemed like ages passed as he rode the platform upward. The room or tower seemed to have no end. But finally the darkness receded somewhat as he passed through a hole in the ceiling and emerged into a wide, dark space filled with twinkling lights. The hole closed underneath him and the platform unexpectedly threw him off before it whizzed away. He stood up indignantly and dusted himself off. Dozens of little silver things suddenly raced by in the air and he stared curiously after them. Another large group came from another direction and he had just enough time to see that they were fish. Hearing a high-pitched whine, he looked up and his jaw dropped as a whale floated or flew overhead. What strange things go on in his head? An enormous turtle lazily drifted past close to his head and he decided to follow it.

As he walked around, Jason saw all sorts of strange aquatic creatures swimming the air and he wondered about the little glowing lights. They looked like stars in a velvety night sky, but when he ventured to touch them they darted away.

The floor opened up beneath his feet suddenly and he fell, landing with a hiccup on a stone surface. When he recovered, Jason saw that he was on a broken bridge, floating in a surreal blue space. Stone objects that looked like they could have been part of a castle once floated about, rotating in the air and bumping into each other. A long distance away there was a floating rock with the castle's ruins. The bridge must have spanned the great void once.

For a brief moment Jason wanted to leap from the bridge and fly to the other side, like in his dreams, but the Dream Keeper's warning echoed in his head and he thought better of it. Hopping from floating piece to piece to get to the other side, however, did not seem any better. Focussing on Bastian to gather his courage, he took a running start before leaping into space. For a few terror-izing moments he was falling before he crashed into a chunk of wall that floated on its back. The momentum of his jump sent it spinning forward, sending other pieces that came in the way flying in all directions. When it slowed down, he waited for the world to stop spinning before he leaped from his perch to another. Once or twice he nearly slipped and fell into the never-ending void below, but eventually he made it safely to the other side, bruised, battered and drenched in sweat.

Venturing into the ruins his heart leaped when he saw a soli-tary doorway standing without any support. Was this the entrance to the next level? Turning the handle, he smiled in relief as it opened into bright light.

Chapter 16:
Darryn's Dream

Darryn emerged onto a wasteland. Nothing but white sand stretched as far as he could see. He admittedly felt disappointed. Was this what he dreamed about? With a sigh, he started walking. The sky overhead was an odd pale blue, almost white like the sand. Very soon the heat became unbearable and his throat was aching from lack of water. He was desperate, he needed to find something to drink or he would die. He had completely forgotten the Dream Keeper's warning.

When he was on the verge of collapsing Darryn spotted the most beautiful thing: a wide, lush green hill rose from the dead, white ocean of sand. Heartened by the sight, he stumbled toward it and started climbing. On top of it was a shallow marble pool with four pillars around it. Happily, he collapsed by the pool and was about to plunge his head into the water when he caught movement at the edge of his vision.

Looking up his eyes almost popped out. An unbelievably beautiful woman with long black hair and bronze-like skin in a white flowing sleeveless dress was walking up the hill, carrying an urn on one shoulder. She smiled at him and knelt by the pool to fill her urn. Darryn's insides began to melt and he completely forgot his thirst. He was too absorbed by her beauty. When she was done she walked back down the hill, beckoning to him to follow. Entranced, he obediently trotted after her like an eager puppy.

On the other side of the hill was a prosperous green valley overgrowing with fruit trees and flowers. The woman led him to a sort of pavilion with comfortable cushions strewn about and low tables laden with bowls of fruit. Remembering his thirst and now feeling famished, his mouth watered at the sight of all the food. The woman indicated – with a smile that caused shivers of pleasure down his spine – for him to sit down. He collapsed onto the cushions and sighed with contentment as he watched her pour the urn's water into a wide basin. Then she sat down with him, resting his head in her lap. He closed his eyes as she started to comb her fingers through his hair. Her perfume was strong and exotic and it clouded his senses.

Gently, the woman removed his head from her lap and she fetched a bowl of fruit, which she placed in his lap with a coy smile and then walked away. With an idiotic grin on his face Darryn watched her go, absently reaching into the bowl and taking a grape. He popped it into his mouth and bit down, releasing the heavenly juice. It was only after he swallowed it that he realised his grave mistake. Jumping to his feet he stared in horror at the bowl of fruit, his heart sinking deep into his shoes as he realised that he had fallen into temptation and was now to pay for it.

The first after-effects of the food started mere moments later. The skin between his shoulder blades started itching madly. He desperately tried to reach back and scratch, but he had difficulty reaching. A crippling pain shot through his spine and with a cry he collapsed. The pain increased and spread to his back muscles and then to the rest of his body and into his very bones. Veins bulged out in his neck and face. His mouth opened wide in a silent scream as he endured the torture. The pain disappeared for a brief moment and he collapsed gasping, before it returned with renewed fury. He writhed about on the ground, groaning and moaning, wishing he could just get his sword out and kill himself, but the pain was too much. Crouched on his hands and knees with sweat rolling down his body, he tried to keep himself from trembling. His breath came in desperate gasps, whistling through his gritted teeth. It felt as if the pain had been going on for an eternity. He could not see anything; his vision was obscured by darkness. A new sensation started and spread to his skin. It felt as if something was trying to burst through. A cry escaped his lips, spittle forming at the corners of his mouth. Then slowly, painfully slowly, something started breaking through the skin and continued growing until it was straining against the material of his shirt. The fabric did not last long before the thing burst through and continued to grow. By now, Darryn was reduced to a shivering heap on the ground, sobbing and gasping for it to stop.

Moments later, the pain was suddenly gone. He waited, expecting it to return any moment. Slowly he stretched out his cramped muscles, and he became aware of something unusual. It was the strangest feeling, but he could feel two extra limb-like growths on his back. Standing up he was surprised by the weight. Experimentally he moved the new limbs and he craned his neck to see. Darryn almost yelped in fright as he saw an enormous wing covered in dark brown feathers the same colour of his hair. Glancing over his other shoulder, he saw another wing. Stretching them out, he was amazed at their enormous size. Flapping them slightly he could feel the wind through the feathers and it was an exhilarating sensation.

Darryn burst out laughing from relief and excitement. Then he ran, pushed off from the ground and flew. Somehow his body knew what to do and he was off. Scanning the ground, he spotted a door and swooped down, crashing slightly as he misjudged the landing. Dusting himself off, he passed through to the next level.

Chapter 17:
Rose's Dream

The moment Rose had passed through the door she drew her sword and clutched it readily. She was in a familiar place, the castle garden back home. It was exactly the same as the real one, yet at the same time completely different. For one thing, there was not the usual bustle of gardeners or guards on the walls.

A sudden sharp sound pierced the air and she froze, poised to strike. Listening hard, she heard the shrill sound of a child's laughter. Relaxing somewhat she followed the sound around the corner. Her breath caught in her throat and her sword dropped from her hand, landing with a dull thud on the grass.

A little boy of five with a thick mop of dark curls was running around, giggling excitedly as a man and a woman chased him. The man was not very tall or handsome, but he was laughing along with the boy. His face was unshaved and his hair short and neat. The woman, however, was tall and beautiful, with long, thick dark-brown curls and dark-blue eyes. She was smiling and laughing along with the other two until she noticed Rose. She stopped and smiled at her. Rose only stared wide-eyed, her hands trembling. The man had finally caught the boy and was perching him on his shoulders. They too spotted her and beckoned for her to join them.

"Come on, Rosy!" the boy shouted.

Taking a shuddery breath, Rose took a step forward, her eyes fixed on the woman. She walked until she stood close enough to touch. Her voice was shaking badly as she whispered, "Mother?"

Chapter 18:
Memory and Decision

Jason thought for a while that he was still caught in the white light in the doorway, but noticed that the whiteness was softer, not as intense. Looking down he could vaguely make out a narrow footpath. Squinting, he tried to peer through the mistiness around him and took his first step.

A scene started to take on a shadowy form not too far to his right. When he looked harder, the scene became more vivid and he saw it was his parents' room, but it was a little different. His mother was lying in bed, with two other women standing by her side. There was no sound, so Jason struggled to comprehend what was going on. Then he realised that she was giving birth! He watched feeling intrigued, disturbed and somewhat embarrassed all at the same time. But the image was still a little hazy. Lifting one foot to take a step closer a warning bell went off in his head and with a chill he realised what he had almost done. Immediately, he averted his gaze and hurried onward.

Many images taunted him at the edges of his vision and sometimes he would pause to watch. Some memories he had forgotten, others were very dear. They played out before him in third person. It was surreal. But every time he looked, the temptation to leave the path became stronger. Jason became frightened and started running, looking down so that the images could not taunt him, but then sounds drifted toward him. Happy memories that made him smile and sad memories that made him cry all over again were all there to tempt him from his path. Part of him wanted to just walk into one of the wonderful memories and forget everything. There, Bastian was still alive and well and the whole family was together and happy. It was with great relief that Jason finally reached the door and walked through. But this time, he did not walk into light, but into darkness instead.

———❖———

Darryn flew over the mist, ignoring the images below. They were not memories he wanted to see or remember so he moved swiftly, making sure that he was directly above the path at all times.

———❖———

Jason thought the treasure room was like a dim wasteland with no end: mountains, hills and small piles of gold, jewels, precious stones and other treasures stood everywhere. In the ceiling, there were small holes that let in tiny slits of light, glinting dully of the treasure's surfaces. Jason climbed the nearest hill, slipping slightly as the coins slid down beneath his feet. When he reached the top, he tried to establish his surroundings, but it was hopeless. Everything looked exactly the same, treasure mounds stretched on into oblivion in all directions.

Sliding down the other side he walked through the maze, looking for anything that might give him a remote hint as to where the tree was. A spark of excitement threatened to erupt, he was so very close. He had come so very far and he only had a few more steps to go. While he walked, he admired the many beautiful things that lay about. Ornate weapons, both foreign and familiar glittered with jewels and gold were scattered about like leaves in an autumn forest, while statues loomed like bare trees in that dying forest. Coins and gems clinked under his boots or when they rolled down the various hills and mounds.

Jason noticed a slight brightening in the light after several minutes and increased his pace, climbing another hill to get an idea of his surroundings. He saw the source of the light and his heart leaped. He jumped down the hill and ran toward the pool of white light emanating from a curious tree. It stood in the centre of a large square of marble tiles surrounded by a circle of seven pillars. The tree leaned at an odd angle, its roots and branches twisted like a fairy-tale tree. A light pulsated from deep within it, spreading outward in a circle before failing against the gloom. The bark of the tree was dark, whereas the leaves were the purest silver.

The price of blood must be paid.

Jason was about to search for knife to cut himself when he heard footsteps coming from the opposite direction. He froze and listened harder. The steps were very quiet, as if someone was sneaking up on him. The person stepped out of the gloom into the light and Jason felt his whole world go upside down.

It was Bastian. He looked exactly the same as when Jason had last seen him. His messy hair, the crumpled outfit, even his carefree smile was the same. Jason took a few steps backward, shaking his head.

"No, it can't be!"

"Hello, Jason," Bastian waved, his tone brimming with amusement.

"H-how did you get here?"

"Does it matter? You can forget about everything now, come home with me."

"You're cured!"

"Yes. Dad found something. But forget about all that and come home. Everyone's been terribly worried since you left."

Jason felt like he was kicked in the stomach, the last thing he wanted was to worry them even more.

"We've missed you, Jason. Come home."

Jason badly wanted to believe him. He so wished that he could just go home. But something in the back of his mind nagged him, warned him, but he could not figure out what.

"How did you know I would be here?" he narrowed his eyes suspiciously.

"Jason, I'm your brother. Why don't you trust me?" he asked, looking hurt by Jason's words.

Jason faltered, nothing made sense anymore. What was he doing there?

"That's it," Bastian said soothingly. "Come home. Mum and Dad will be so happy to see you. Wouldn't it be nice to sleep in your own bed again?"

He nodded slowly, his body relaxed and he took a step toward Bastian.

"Come on, brother, everything will be just fine. Don't worry."

Bastian smiled and held out his hand, invitingly. Jason reached out, a content look on his face. It was all over! No more struggling, no more hurting. Suddenly something very large flew close by his head, crashing into Bastian. Jason froze, blinked and shook his head before he could properly register what his eyes were seeing. Darryn was wrestling with Bastian, two enormous wings sprouting from his back, while Bastian was rapidly dissolving onto thick black smoke.

"You have wings!" he managed to utter.

"Yeah," Darryn said through gritted teeth. "So I've noticed!"

The imposter managed to kick Darryn and as he stood up, his body completely dissolved into smoke before it took on a new shape. A humanoid figure with charcoal-coloured skin, hair like smoke and deep green eyes stood before them, grimacing.

"Shifter," Jason whispered and Darryn drew his sword.

The Shifter chuckled, a deep sinister sound. "Very good, Jason! I suppose I should thank you, for if not for you I would never have found this island."

"I don't understand?" Jason said.

"Don't listen to him, Jason!" Darryn said, but he was not looking at them. He was focusing on the five other Shifters emerging from the shadows.

"In return for your services, I will tell you," the Shifter said smoothly. "We needed someone special to find the Dream Keeper for us and we came across you. Not exactly exceptional are you? But what *is* special about you are the lengths you are willing to go to for your brother. We have tried many people, but none have succeeded like you have. Truly remarkable!" The Shifter clapped his hands mockingly.

"I still don't understand," Jason squeaked, retreating ever further away while the Shifter continued to approach, his comrades closing in on him and Darryn.

The Shifter sighed, "The snake that bit your brother was a Shifter, boy," then he dissolved into smoke and transformed into the creepy man who told Jason about the Dream Keeper back home. Jason retreated a few steps faster.

"Yes, Jason, it was I who suggested that you find the Dream

Keeper. I only had to plant a tiny little seed. Our brother was very clear that only a human could find him and congratulations! You are the first."

"If you wanted me to find the island, why'd you try to kill me?"

"Yes," the Shifter mused. "The hound was an unfortunate mistake on our behalf. He followed us, you see, from the Other Side."

"And the goblins?"

The Shifter chuckled. "An amusing coincidence. We have nothing to do with them."

"Why didn't you just kidnap him and save yourself all the trouble?" Darryn asked.

The Shifter sighed irritably and replied as if he was speaking to a dim-witted person. "Because – my idiotic friend – the outcome would have been wholly different. My brother was very precise in his instructions."

"Now to make my wish—but oh I need blood—" he smiled unpleasantly.

Rose suddenly appeared in the light, breaking through the Shifter's circle. The Shifters momentarily drew back, hissing as they did. Jason stared at her in surprise and noticed that her eyes were rimmed red, as if she had been crying.

"Run, Jason!" Darryn bellowed and attacked the nearest Shifter. Rose also had her sword drawn and jumped into the battle.

Jason had just enough time to stumble backward when the first Shifter slashed at him with its vicious claws. They cut through his left upper arm and he cried out, clutching the wound. Three deep gashes gaped in his arm, burning with an indescribable intensity. Following Darryn's order, he turned tail and disappeared amidst the treasure hills clutching his bleeding arm, with the Shifter's laughter echoing after him.

"I'm disappointed in you, Jason! Running away like a coward while you leave your friends behind?"

Jason dove behind a statue, breathing very quickly from fear and shock. He was still clutching his arm which throbbed and spilled blood through his fingers onto the floor. He had never bled so much before in his life! When he calmed down somewhat, he crawled from behind the statue toward the next cover while the Shifters' taunts rang through the air. He felt horrible about leaving Darryn and Rose behind, but what else could he do? He had no weapon. Even if he had one, he could not use it properly. He ran as far from the tree as he could, occasionally looking over his shoulder to see if he was being followed.

It was while he was glancing back that his left foot got caught against something and he slammed to the ground, grazing his chin, knees and palms. Pain shot through his left ankle; it was sprained again. Shakily rising, he looked up and almost yelped in fright. He was staring straight into the regal face of a stone lion, its maw open in roar. It was lying down, forepaws outstretched. It was over one of these that Jason had tripped. He backed away a little and a sound came from the lion that caused goose bumps along his arms. It was the sound of metal scraping across stone.

Jason peered into the lion's mouth where he thought the sound was coming from, and indeed something seemed to be emerging from the blackness. Slowly, but gradually, a sword hilt became visible, followed by the skilfully crafted blade. When the sword protruded halfway from the lion's mouth, it stopped. Jason admired the weapon; it was very beautifully made and decorated with a celestial theme. He drew the sword out, impressed by the weight and feel of it in his hand.

Something about holding the unusual weapon emboldened him and he felt his fears melt away, replaced by courage. Suddenly a voice in his mind said, "*Use now this gift to do what is right.*"

He stood tall with new purpose and limped as fast as he could back to his friends.

On arrival, he saw that only three Shifters remained: the one who pretended to be Bastian, and two of his friends. Rose was furiously battling with a cat-like female, while Darryn battled it out in the air with the other. The first Shifter was standing by the tree, one bloodied hand (or claw) pressed to the tree's bark, his face upturned and eyes closed as he made his wish. Aghast, Jason watched light shoot through the tree into every branch and every leaf until the entire thing was glowing white.

"Now you are free, brother!" the Shifter whispered.

Whoever the Shifter's brother was, Jason was certain that it would be bad if the wish came true. He had to do something. He was faced with an agonizing decision of having to choose between Bastian and stopping the Shifter's wish. It felt like several moments before he made his decision.

Closing his eyes Jason gripped the hilt of the sword even tighter and in his mind he whispered, "Forgive me, brother."

Jason stormed from the shadows and plunged the sword's blade as deep as he could into the heart of the tree. The Shifter screeched and turned on him.

"You stupid boy!"

But Jason did not let go of the blade. There was no explosion, no flash of light, the tree's light just died out and a silvery white liquid poured from the wound onto Jason's hands and spread across the floor. The Shifter raised one claw to strike Jason down, but Rose intervened. She sliced at him and he jumped aside with a hiss, but not before she could plunge the blade into his heart. He and the other Shifters disappeared into black smoke.

Jason fell to his knees, staring at the increasing pool of the tree's blood. His own blood dripped down, red mixing with silver. His expression had gone blank.

Gone. Just like that, his last chance was gone. And the worst part was that he destroyed it. A haze obscured his view as tears spilled down his cheeks, creating trails through the dust. Giving the sword a heartless tug, it pulled free and his arms dropped. The sword clanged against the stone and spattered silver blood on his clothes.

Darryn and Rose stood a little way behind him. They had no words that could comfort their friend. They almost felt his sorrow as deeply as he did, for it was this quest that had brought them together and brought them close. Together they had overcome so many obstacles and faced so many dangers.

When they heard the footsteps approach they turned around with raised swords, only to lower them again when they saw that it was an ancient creature, completely covered in silver-blue-grey fur with a goat-like face and three fingers on each hand. Its eyes were a deep, watery-brown that seemed to contain unending knowledge, kindness and warmth. It stood at least a head shorter than both of them, though it must have been a magnificent being in its time. There were two stumps on its head that must once have been horns, broken away by the ages.

The creature walked slowly past them, acknowledging each in turn with a bow of its wizened head. Its soft paws splashed quietly through the tree's blood until it stood at Jason's right shoulder. The boy looked up, grief clearly etched on his face. The creature smiled at him and placed a three-fingered hand on his shoulder.

For the first time the creature spoke, its voice was like the gentle lapping of waves on the shore or like a breeze blowing through a forest. "Come, you have done well."

Jason got to his feet and hobbled after the creature as it walked into the opposite direction of the room's entrance. He still clutched the sword in his right hand, but did not notice. Darryn and Rose followed them, leaving the dead tree behind. They walked until they arrived at a large empty space where no treasure mounds rested.

"This space is reserved for the mounds yet to come," the creature said. "Do you know what all these treasures are?"

Darryn and Rose shook their heads; Jason just stared ahead.

"They are dreams, each and every one. The most treasured dreams of every single person that ever was and is."

"What about the tree?" Darryn asked.

The creature smiled and answered, "Later." Then it called out. "We are ready to leave!"

The palace slowly sank back into the ground around them, gold and jewels tumbling down huge rifts that had opened. Then the palace was gone, leaving no gaping hole or any sign that it had ever existed. Ahead there was a small cottage, homely and welcoming. The creature took them inside and they found themselves standing in a small living room. It indicated for the twins to wait and took Jason through another door. After half an hour or so, it returned and beckoned for them to sit down. Darryn had some difficulty with his wings, but eventually found a position that was comfortable. From the kitchen, it brought each of them a simple wooden cup filled with clear liquid that looked like water yet smelled like spring.

"Drink," it said gently.

Darryn and Rose obeyed, swallowing the contents down until the cups were empty. It did not really taste like anything in particular, but it lightened their hearts and brought the colour back to their cheeks. Their weariness disappeared and they felt like they had just woken on the first day of summer.

The creature sat down opposite them and waited.

"Sir," Darryn asked politely. "Will he—will Jason be all right?"

"He's suffering from shock and has a few nasty bruises and scratches, but he should recover. What he needs is rest."

They sat in silent thought for a time before Darryn ventured another question. "Er, sir, I have two questions. First, why didn't I die when I ate some of the food in the palace like the Dream Keeper said?"

The creature chuckled, "The Dream Keeper is many things, and one of them is grim, but he was right to warn you. You got off lightly from what could have been a disaster."

Rose quickly interrupted before Darryn could ask his second question, "How will we return home, sir? Darryn can't exactly walk around half-naked with wings in the coldest country in Balisme?"

"Oh!" Darryn exclaimed. "I forgot to tell you. Watch," he stood up and for a few moments nothing seemed to happen. Then his wings started shrinking, or more correctly growing *backward* until there was nothing but two bumps on his back. "They're retractable!"

"Well, there is your answer!" the creature said. "You had another question?" he turned to Darryn.

"Oh, yeah, about the tree—"

"I apologise, but that is a tale for Jason's ears. Should he choose to tell you afterward, then he may."

"All right,"

"Anything else?"

"If you don't mind, sir, who are you?"

"Ah, here we come to a real question! My name is Priam. I am—how shall I put it, a type of guardian for heroes and you three have interested me greatly."

"What does a guardian do?"

"It is difficult to explain with all sorts of rules that I will not bore you with. Now I think it is time that you get some rest of your own. Tomorrow is another day!"

Darryn and Rose were each taken to their own room where they could clean up and change into new clean clothes set out for them. With the excitement of the day suddenly catching up they climbed into bed, exhausted to the bone and they dropped off the sleep. Unknown to them, the drinks Priam gave them was a type of draught that granted them deep dreamless slumber.

Late that night, a silent figure drifted through their rooms keeping a silent watch and leaving sweet dreams in its wake. Priam smiled from his window as he watched his old friend at work. Sandman was only one of the Dream Keeper's many names.

Chapter 19:
Home

Priam was drinking tea from a small cup while watching the sun rise. He did not turn around when he heard the cottage door open and close behind him, or respond to the footsteps approaching across the grass.

Jason was carrying the sword he brought with him from the treasure room. When he woke he cleaned it up and found Priam. Holding it out to the ancient creature he said, "I should probably give this back."

Priam turned and smiled at him. "You deserve it, after all you did."

Jason shrugged, unsmiling. "I don't want it. I don't want to be a hero."

With a sigh, Priam took the sword, inspecting it critically. After a while he said, "Tell me Jason, what makes a person a hero?"

"A hero is brave and always does the right thing."

"And you think you're not a hero?"

"I'm not brave, most of the time I was so afraid. Darryn and Rose are true heroes, I'm just a coward."

"I see," Priam nodded. "Now tell me, does doing brave things make someone a hero or does being a hero make you brave?"

Jason pondered the question before saying, "I guess it would be the first one, Sir."

Priam nodded slowly again and said, "Jason, everyone feels afraid at some time in their life, some more than others. But I will tell you a secret. It is what you do when you are afraid that determines whether or not you are brave. If you run away every time you must face your fears then you are a coward, but when you stand with your friends and for what you know is right, you are a hero. Even the bravest heroes feel afraid, but because they act against their fears they become great and memorable. You, Jason, are a true hero."

"But I failed," Jason said. "I didn't do anything. It was all for nothing."

"Do you call helping your friends, freeing a dragon, restoring a merprince's honour, facing Shifters and more *nothing*? You have done so much Jason, but you cannot see who and what you are! I have seen your heart and it is pure and good. Not very many can say that."

After another moment of silence Jason said, "I'm sorry for killing the Tree, now no one can make wishes anymore."

Suddenly Priam started chuckling. Jason frowned at him. "Jason," Priam said, "before you arrived on the island the Tree did not even exist."

Jason opened his mouth but shut it again.

"It's true," Priam said. "As I told your friends yesterday, everything in the Treasure Room is the most treasured dreams of all the living creatures in the world. Because you desired to find the Tree and it became your greatest dream and it naturally came into existence. Before you, it only existed in legend."

"Did the Shifters know?"

"I do not know, maybe."

"So there's no chance of it existing again?" Jason asked hopefully

"No, I'm sorry. Unfortunately that is one of the Dream Keeper's rules; no two dreams are alike."

"Who or what exactly is the Dream Keeper?"

"Like his name implies, he is the keeper of all dreams. He also has the power to create dreams and to destroy them. But like me, he is under Fate's command. "

Another thought occurred to Jason. "I don't think our ship will survive another journey through the Blacks, how will we get back home?"

"Leave that to us."Once more the Dream Keeper called up the palace and it rose to its majestic heights. Everyone was gathered before it, fidgeting nervously as they waited for Priam to speak.

"My dear friends," the old creature spoke in a voice surprisingly strong for one so ancient. "First of all, I will congratulate you on surviving the hard journey here. It takes a special type of man to take on such a journey willingly." Many of the sailors unconsciously puffed up their chests and grinned at each other. "Unfortunately," Priam continued. "The return journey will be more difficult because your ship is nearly destroyed and your provisions spent."

The company murmured among each other, now suddenly aware of their situation.

"Do not lose hope though!" Priam cried out. "We can provide you safe passage back to your respective homes, all we require is your trust."

The Dream Keeper took his place alongside Priam and said, "Your path lies through these doors," he gestured to the palace entrance through which Jason and his friends have passed through only a few days before. The sailors recalled how injured and battered they were when they came out, so naturally were more than reluctant to trust the man.

"The Keeper opens and closes the gate. Dreamer you must discover your Fate," Jason murmured quietly, yet everyone heard.

"Well put young man." The Dream Keeper bowed his head in his direction.

"Don't the doors lead into the palace?" Roan demanded.

"Did you not hear what he just said?" the Dream Keeper cried out irritably.

Priam replied in a kinder manner, "These are the Dream Keeper's doors, they will lead you wherever he so commands."

"So, it's going to take us home?" Roan asked again.

"Yes," the Dream Keeper replied impatiently.

Jason felt his shoulders sag. He wearied far easier since the ordeal inside the temple. Now more than ever he longed to be home, to forget his adventures and live a relatively normal life. He was even willing to face the inevitable that awaited him back home.

Priam suddenly turned his gaze upon Jason. His eyes were thoughtful and slightly expectant. Then he spoke very softly, yet the boy still heard him. "Are you ready to go home?"

Jason took a step forward and nodded, His back straightened as he strolled toward the palace entrance.

"Jason," Priam called softly. The boy paused and turned around. "Aren't you forgetting something?"

Darryn and Rose had followed him and stood a few metres away. Darryn was smiling sadly, his hands firmly clasped around his sword hilt, of which the point was stuck into the ground between his feet. His great wings protruded from behind each shoulder, the shirt he wore had two holes cut in the back through which the wings could grow and retract. Rose—ever expressionless—stood close beside him, her long hair whipping about in the wind. A smile sprang to Jason's face, but it was tainted with sadness.

"Well, goodbye," Darryn said awkwardly.

"Bye," Jason replied softly.

"Thanks for the adventure, brother," Darryn smiled.

They embraced briefly before Jason turned to Rose.

"Goodbye, Princess," he half bowed.

"Goodbye," she replied and the smallest of smiles came to her face.

Hesitantly she stepped closer and put her arms around him. For a moment he was too stunned to react, but then he hugged her back. A flood of thoughts, memories and emotions passed through him, then they stepped apart.

With a pang, Jason knew he would never see them again. With another wave in their direction and a glance at all the others, he turned once more to pass through the palace doors. He walked forward and they opened before him. With one last look over his shoulder he walked into the blinding white light. As he walked, his adventures rapidly played out before his eyes. He could hardly believe what he had been through.

The light started to fade and the smell of home filled his nostrils. He breathed in deeply and took the last step out of the light.

Jason stepped out onto the top of Nameless Hill while cold winds chilled him to the bone. The grass was dead and brittle beneath his feet while the naked skeletons of trees and bushes greeted him from everywhere. The winter was in full possession of Bristan, though the snow had not yet fallen. Freezing in the thin clothes he was given, he limped down toward Brim. There were very few people in the streets and they were all dressed in thick warm coats. They greeted Jason with surprise and curiosity, but were in too much of a hurry to get to their warm homes to enquire after his absence.

His steps became slower as he got closer to his own house. When he reached the garden gate he stopped. Blue stood next to the house and neighed when she saw him as if she had always been there.

He was finally home. The world around him was so exceptionally ordinary that he almost missed all the magic. Reaching out he opened the gate and walked down the small path. When he reached the door he paused, should he knock or just go in? It felt ridiculous not knowing how to enter his own house, but he has been away for so long. Raising his right fist he took a deep breath and knocked twice.

When the door opened and he looked up, he barely had enough time to register in surprise that it was Catherine who answered before she attacked him in a heartfelt embrace.

"Oh, Jason!" she sobbed. "Thank goodness you're all right! We were so worried!"

"Cathy?" he wriggled out of her arms. "What are you doing here?"

"When Mum mailed us that Bastian was very sick and you went missing, Michael and I came immediately!"

Jason tried to peer past her shoulder, but she embraced him again and did not want to let go.

"Cathy, who's at the door?" another voice called. Michael, her husband appeared and his eyes widened in surprise when he saw who she was hugging. Even though he hadn't seen Jason since he was thirteen, Michael recognised him immediately. "Jason?" He also ran forward and joined in the embrace.

"Where have you been you rascal?"

"Can I come in please?" Jason pleaded.

"Of course!" Catherine released her grip slightly, but still clung on to his hand. "You must be freezing, come in." She dragged him inside, fussing over him the whole way. On entering the kitchen, he gently pulled free from Catherine's grip and stepped forward.

"Mum?" he said softly.

The woman at the stove turned slowly, afraid that her mind was playing tricks on her. When she saw Jason her eyes widened and a hand flew to her mouth. Behind her hand she murmured something that sounded like his name. She raced toward him until close enough throw her arms around him.

"My boy," she cried, "You came back! You're safe!"

"Hi Mum," Jason also wept.

"Where have you been?" she asked, still not letting go.

"Everywhere Mum, everywhere," he whispered. With a sniff he pulled slightly away and asked, "Where's Dad?"

"In his surgery," Mum said, but she looked reluctant to let him go.

Jason quietly opened the surgery door and stepped inside. Dad's back was turned to him and he was packing things away in the medicine cabinet. His hair was longer than Jason remembered, but then again what did he look like himself?

"Knock, knock," he said and stepped in. Dad paused in his work, his head slightly cocked to the side.

"Jason?" he asked, but did not turn around.

"Dad!" he said and rushed across the small space. Dad turned around just as he reached him and he fell into his comforting arms like he did when he was a little boy. "I'm sorry Dad," he sobbed bitterly now, tears rolling freely down his face. "I'm so sorry!"

"We thought you were dead!" Dad exclaimed, wiping his eyes. "But you've returned, safe and sound, why you're practically a man! Look how you've grown, and your hair!" he chuckled through his tears.

Finally when Jason calmed down somewhat he asked, "Where's Caleb and—" but he just could not finish the sentence.

"In your room."

After embracing Dad again, Jason walked down the hallway toward his room. With every step his feet felt heavier and slower and his throat tightened. When he reached out for the doorknob he could hardly breathe. Quickly he turned the knob and stepped inside. Slowly he let his gaze wander across the room until it landed on the bed. Caleb was seated beside it, and sitting cross-legged in the middle, was Bastian.

"How?" Jason breathed, his eyes wide, but not as wide as his brothers'. They stared at him as if he was a ghost. Then they tackled him.

"You're alive! You're back! Where've you been?" they demanded while crushing the life out of him.

He pushed himself away, his eyes riveted on Bastian. It was obvious that his brother was completely healthy. He had the usual sparkle in his eye and the mischievous grin on his mouth. "Yes I'm alive, but how are you?" he asked. Was the Shifter telling the truth after all?

Bastian looked to Caleb who explained, "It was a miracle really, and it only happened a few days ago. He was literally about to die when—*whoosh*! He was magically cured!"

Jason felt his head spin and he collapsed onto Caleb's chair.

"Are you all right?" Caleb asked.

Jason stared in wide-eyed shock at the floor, and then slowly his mouth pulled into a smile and life returned to his hazel eyes. Looking up with new enthusiasm he said, "You won't believe what I've been through."

"You'll just have to tell us I suppose," Bastian grinned.

Together they went to the kitchen where everyone gathered around the table, with Jason at the head. Then he started to tell his story. Starting with Bastian being bitten, right through to where he arrived at the doorstep. Everyone listened with undivided attention, almost unbelieving. When Jason finally finished telling his adventure, the sun was setting.

They were all silent, absorbing the fantastic tale. Bastian spoke first, "You went through all that, all that danger, for me?"

Jason nodded.

"And you met a real prince and princess?" Catherine asked eagerly.

"Quite a few of them actually," Jason said.

"Just promise me one thing," Dad said,

"Yes?"

"Never go off like that without telling us, ever again!"

Jason smiled. "I promise."

The sun eventually set and it became evening. Jason was sitting alone in his room, on his bed. The rest were in the kitchen, preparing dinner and setting the dining table. He became aware of something in his right boot and removed it, turning it upside down against his hand. A single gold coin dropped into his palm to his surprise. It must have slipped into his boot from when he was sliding down the treasure mounds in the Palace of Dreams. He flipped it and watched it glint as it reflected the lamplight. Pulling his boot back on and putting a warmer shirt on, he went to the living room. Settling into one of the thick armchairs he stretched his legs out toward the fireplace. A faint tapping came from the window and he looked up.

An odd white bird was tapping at the window with its beak, but what really got Jason's attention was the satchel slung across its left wing. He opened the window and the bird hopped in. Jason opened the little satchel and found a note inside. When he unfolded the note, the bird flew out the window. He closed the window and sat back down, reading the note through twice. It was written in curly script and it read:

> *Dear Jason*
> *For making the right decision, I have given you a gift.*
> *I hope you appreciate it.*
> *Until we meet again.*
> *Priam*

Jason knew that Priam was involved in Bastian's recovery even before he received the note. But what troubled him was the phrase: *Until we meet again—*

After staring a while at the note he tossed it into the fire. Glancing back out the window he saw to his wonder that tiny white flakes drifted down from the sky. The first snow of winter was falling and he was home to enjoy it.